On the Come Up

On the Come Up

A NOVEL, BASED ON A TRUE STORY

Hannah Weyer

NAN A. TALESE 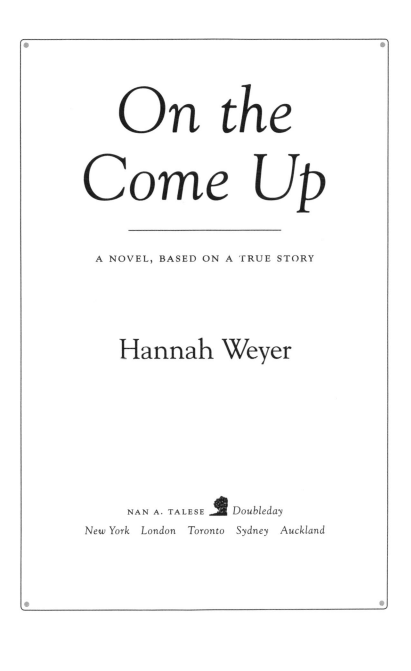 Doubleday

New York   London   Toronto   Sydney   Auckland

www.nanatalese.com

DOUBLEDAY is a registered trademark of Random House, Inc. Nan A. Talese and the colophon are trademarks of Random House, Inc.

Book design by Michael Collica
Map © Aaron Reiss
Jacket design by Emily Mahon
Front jacket photographs: girl © Monashee Frantz/OJO Images/Getty Images;
subway train © Cheryl Zibisky/Getty Images
Back jacket photograph: Rockaway Beach © Beth Perkins/Getty Images

Library of Congress Cataloging-in-Publication Data

Weyer, Hannah.
On the come up : a novel, based on a true story / Hannah Weyer. — First edition.
pages cm
1. African American girls—Fiction. 2. African American actresses—Fiction.
3. Teenage pregnancy—Fiction. I. Title.
PS3623.E96O5 2013
813'.6—dc23
2012047057

ISBN 978-0-385-53732-2

MANUFACTURED IN THE UNITED STATES OF AMERICA

1 3 5 7 9 10 8 6 4 2

First Edition

For Anna

and for Rio, Rose, and Chasity

On the Come Up

Family Tree

My mother's name is Blessed. That's not a traditional West Indies name but I guess her mother chose it 'cause she wasn't supposed to live. My mother had water on the brain, some kind a brain trouble when she was first born and they thought she was gonna die but she didn't.

When she was a little girl, seven years old, her mother left off and she got raised by her sisters. Then she met a guy and he left her a baby. His name was Jahar. After that my mother met my father and got pregnant with me when Jahar was like a year old . . . My father was a alcoholic. He killed that baby banging his head on the crib. This happened before I was born. Jahar's buried in Trinidad, may he rest in peace.

Yeah. But my father's still there. He's never been to America.

My mother came here, running away from him 'cause he was threatening to kill her and she believed it after he banged my brother's head. In Trinidad, it's what the man says that goes and the doctors believed my father when he said the baby fell. My mother cried and cried but couldn't do nothing.

That's what I know about my mother when she was coming to America and first had me. I was born in Brooklyn, not Trinidad. She worked as a health aide until she got sick and had to stop.

There's a bunch a different stories I was told about that little time period, like how I lived with this lady Pinky for a while, then with one a my aunts, then with some other friend a my mother's up in the Bronx. One a the stories that went around was that this person who supposed to watch me left me on a bench in Central Park and that's how I ended up in foster care. I don't remember that but maybe it's true. Blessed's story is that when she was sick, she paid some lady to take care of me but she took the money and ran. Left me in an apartment somewhere. I don't remember that either. All I know is I ended up in foster care with Grandma Mason. She wasn't my real grandma. She was one a those people took foster kids into they home. Five years stuck in a box, you try to get out, she there with her belt, twack twack twack she get you. Sit still. Don't move. You say what, you sass me? This a belt she sometimes peed on then let get stiff in the sun.

I was nine years old when Child Services placed me back with my mother again. I was eleven when she had her stroke. Those first two years together, those were good years. We had fun together, we'd do things. Go to church. Cook food, do laundry . . . little things people do. She'd be laughing with her chinky eyes . . . She's got these veiled, chinky eyes. I remember the day she got me, she was waiting at the agency with Mr. Clark. He was my caseworker. Blessed stood up and hugged me and Grandma Mason just looked like this California raisin next to my mother—small, black and wrinkled.

I don't know what happened to Grandma Mason. She was old so maybe she's dead by now, I don't know. All I know is Blessed got outta the shelter when I was nine and wasn't homeless no more. I don't know how she did it but they gave her an apartment. She got it through Section 8. We said good-bye to Grandma Mason, got on the subway and went all the way down, all the way out to Far Rockaway, Queens. Last stop on the A line. Very *last stop. 1430 Gateway Boulevard. Number 4R. That was the apartment.*

When we went inside I thought it looked so nice and clean. It was three rooms with a window in the kitchen. My mother showed me my room and she had her own room and I was like, oh, is this mine? This mine, for real?

Far Rockaway is a neighborhood located
in Queens County, New York

Class Code: U4
Elevation: 16 feet
Area: 4.3 square miles
Coordinates: 40°36'03" N 73°45'25" W
Population: 56,184

The neighborhood is named after the Rechaweygh Indians,
who once inhabited Long Island and in whose language the
name means "place of our people."

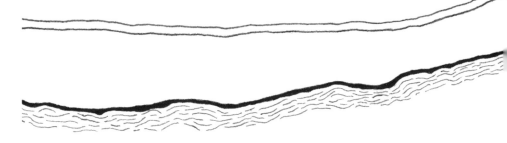

dolla, dolla bill, y'all

1

She took the peanut butter punch out of the freezer. The sticks poked up firm, dead center. They came out good. Sell those for a dollar. Sell 'em all, make twenty-four. Kool-Aid, that's another twelve at fifty cent. Sweet milk, make it seventy-five.

She did the math in her head while she wrapped the pops in foil and buried them, sticks up, in ice. Peanut butter punch on the left. Kool-Aid on the right. She left the freezer door open, feeling the cool air settle on her skin. It was hot. Not even nine o'clock in the morning and the sweat was beading there between her buds. She hoped Crystal remembered to make extra ice; they gonna need it today.

She closed up the cooler, put it in the cart, picture frames on top, checked the Polaroid. Eight pictures left. That's forty dollars more right there, they come out nice, people happy. If she hustled, she could get out before her mother woke and Miss Jessica came poking through the door. She slipped on her sandals, remembered the square of black cloth she used for a table, set that on top the camera, then stepped lightly, wheeling the cart to the door. But Blessed must've had her good eye open 'cause AnnMarie heard her call out, You ain't wearing the Cinderella?

It's too hot.

You make more you wear it.

AnnMarie shifted, her hand on the doorknob. Ma, it's hot.

What's that you got on. Come over here.

AnnMarie groaned but backed up and stood in the doorway of the bedroom. She knew the halter fit big but there was no way she was changing out of it. Crystal's cousin, Teisha, had let her borrow it. Teisha, who was eighteen and beautiful.

Where you think you're going in that?

Why?

You think you grown, AnnMarie, why d'you think.

The intercom buzzed—Miss Jessica, already.

Blessed swung her leg over the side of the bed and sat breathing for a moment in the darkness, her hair pressed flat inside the nylon cap.

Let her in, AnnMarie, and change out of that halter.

You want your wig?

You na hear what me say? Change outta that damn halter.

AnnMarie crossed to her bedroom and yanked open the drawer, sifting through her summertime tees. All of 'em ugly, plain and simple. Fuck that. Teisha's halter had mad dazzle. She knew how long it took her mother to get off the bed, inch across the floor with the walker, so she made a dash for it, grabbing the cart and slipping out the door.

In the hallway, Miss Jessica was stepping out the elevator, dabbing her neck with a napkin. She in there, AnnMarie said, moving past the home health aide, who stunk of clove and cinnamon. She said to go in.

Miss Jessica's forehead wrinkled. How about a smile, AnnMarie, a nice hello, then you know you'll be starting the day off right.

Hello Miss Jessica, how are you Miss Jessica, have a nice day, AnnMarie said, jabbing at the L button until the elevator door closed. She couldn't stand home health aides. Coming into the apartment, acting like they family. Feeding her mother pills, fluff a pillow or two, then sit down in front of the TV. Making calls on the telephone. One time she'd come home, found one a them asleep on her bed like Goldilocks, her mother don't say nothing.

She pictured herself in the Cinderella dress, the Polaroid camera strapped around her neck, walking right up to couples, *You wantcha picture, I take your picture.* Last summer the people giving her a extra dollar or two, saying how cute she was. But last summer was before the stroke and she'd been out there with Blessed who sat on the bench stringing beads into necklaces and it was okay then to play, the two of them together, mother and child.

She stepped off the elevator and into the lobby. You wanna buy a icy? I got peanut butter punch. I got grape Kool-Aid. Which one you want.

The security guard swiveled around in his chair, giving her the up and down.

Well, you a no-nonsense type, ain't you.

From behind, she'd thought it was Devon sitting there. Devon who was her fake uncle but this was some other fella, younger with a chip in his tooth. He looked like the boy Antwan's cousin. Maybe he was, maybe he wasn't. He was smiling at her now, so she dropped her hand from her hip and shifted, wishing for just a second she wasn't still wearing the halter with the words *Sexy Sweet* spelled out in glitter gold.

Come on then, mister, you want one?

What you charge?

A dolla.

Whoa, you a scrambler now, little shortie like you?

That how much they cost.

He tipped his head back and laughed. He said, Gimme one a them peanut butter punch.

She plucked the bill from his hand, then went out the door, stepping into a wave of heat that rolled up the sidewalk and smacked against her skin. Gawd *dang*. It caught her off guard and she stood for a moment in front of 1430, letting her eyes adjust to the white-hot glare, wishing she could dig into one of the icies herself. Wishing, for just a second, she could go back inside, curl up with a plate of scrambled eggs on toast, chill for a while longer in front of the window fan. But she had back-to-school to think about so she told her feet to move, dragging the cart behind, and went on up through Cripdaville. Around the corner on Mott Avenue, a few of them already standing in the shade the tree made, leaning against the rail, smoking. Sleepy eyes looking her way. She could feel her underwear bunching up in her crack and wanted to reach around and pull the elastic down but she didn't dare. She cut across the street quick and got inside Crystal's building where she could adjust herself.

Inside the vestibule AnnMarie buzzed, then waited, her eyes drifting to the street just as that hater Brittany came skating into view. Fat thighs jiggling, wearing some ugly neon-blue skates. Maybe she fall. I hope she fall.

Who's there? The voice came crackling through the intercom.

It's me, Grandma Kay. AnnMarie. Crystal come down?

Grandma Kay didn't answer.

Grandma Kay. It's Ann-Marie.

AnnMarie waited, then buzzed again, keeping an eye out, trying to glimpse where that girl gone to. But instead of Brittany she saw a group of older boys coming up the block. She pressed her face up to the glass, watching. What they doing over here. She knew them only by sight and from the fact they Bloods who hung out by Nameoke. She knew one of them was named Darius and boy was he fine. One time he looked at her passing on the street. At least she thought he did. Darius Greene. His hair in dreads, looking like a lion the way he moved—not caring two cents he passing through Cripdaville.

AnnMarie turned, put her finger to the buzzer and pressed

hard, leaning on it this time, the electric hum filling the vestibule. Come on now, Grandma Kay, AnnMarie thought, when the sudden *Pop Pop* of gunfire cut through the air, making her flinch and duck both at the same time. Shoot. What is going on. She edged to the door, trying to look out—it'd come from a distance, at least a block away but still . . . *Pop. Pop Pop.* She wondered what beef getting settled first thing in the morning.

Who's making that noise?! Take your finger off my bell.

AnnMarie pushed her mouth up to the intercom.

Grandma Kay, it's me, AnnMarie.

AnnMarie, what do you want.

Crystal come down?

Crystal's GONE child. Crystal's wit' her mother!

Oh.

She felt the air go out of her chest. Oh. That's the way with Crystal. Sometimes here, sometimes gone when her mother lift up to some other place. Last time was to a hotel by the airport.

Past few weeks they'd been in and out of Grandma Kay's apartment, riding bikes on the boardwalk, selling icies and splitting the profit. Best friends for life, they'd pinkie-swore it. Crystal was whip thin and small but it don't matter, someone say something, she be up in they face. *What you say? You say something, shut yo' mouth.* AnnMarie'd laugh and laugh. Up and down the stairs of 1440, running errands for Crystal's cousin Teisha and the older girls—female rappers they called themselves. Those girls slipping them sips of the St. Ides and laughing when it go down burning.

She thought to buzz again, ask when Crystal be back, but she didn't. She reached for the door handle, pressing her face up to the glass, and listened. A trickle of sweat slid down her back. Nothing. Nobody. She licked her tongue across her lip, then counted back from ten the way Blessed had taught her. She felt the latch click and she was out again, stepping into stillness. Bloods had disap-

peared, Crips gone from the rail. No one out now except the blue
and white crawling 'round the corner so she decided to cut back
down Gateway, take Beach 19 all the way to the boardwalk.

She dragged the cart along, eyes squinting against the brightness,
a little tune rolling around in her head. She didn't get far before
a sound made her swing around just as Brittany slammed into her
from behind, knocking her to the pavement.

Oh, 'xcuse me, Brittany said, laughing as she spun past on her
skates, disappearing along the path next to the vacant lot.

She felt the heat rush to her cheeks. She wanted to shout,
Bitch, get back here. I fight you now. Baboon-ass muthafucker.

But she didn't. Not without Crystal. She brushed the dirt and
pebbles from her palms, the pink gash on her knee pooling into
a strip of blood. She looked around, glanced up at the buildings,
all the black bars cutting lines across the open windows. Curtains
hanging limp. Not even a breeze to make them move. She picked
herself up, glad no one had seen, and kept going.

Fat bitch. Tail end of 7th grade, they'd followed her. Brittany
and a couple other haters. All the way home, talking shit, running
they mouths and AnnMarie'd been afraid but hid it behind a wall
of fuck-y'all silence, until one of them had shoved her, just like
that, pushed her from behind and she knew it's what they wanted
but she did it anyway—spun around and cracked the girl with the
flat of her hand. She saw the look of shock turn mean and ugly,
but it's what they'd wanted, all of them darting in then, fists and
blows, smacking and kicking. AnnMarie put up a fight but that
helpless feeling start to seep in and there was the one blow that
brought tears to her eyes and she heard them laughing. Laughing.
Jabbing and slapping. Then like a miracle she saw Brittany's head
snap back and there was Crystal gripping a fistful a Brittany's hair,

shouting *Get offa her, bitch, I fuck you up*, and Teisha, striding forward with a razor in hand, sent all the girls scattering.

AnnMarie's shirt had got ripped clear down the front, her ta-tas hanging out, even though they was just little nublets blowing in the wind. Teisha had covered her up but was laughing too, saying, Look how small you be. It was embarrassing. So dang embarrassing.

2

Icies!

Peanut butter punch! Grape icies. 50-cent icies.

What kind you want? Grape be 50. Peanut butter a dolla, you want the milk? I got condense milk for that extra sweetness.

No napkins. Sorry. You got to lick it fast, girl . . .

Lemme take your picture. You put it in this nice frame, give it to yo' girlfriend.

Lemme get the two a you together, come on now. Record the moment.

She'd set up near Beach 19, selling half the icies and two Polaroids, each in a frame, by the time Raymel showed up close to noon. It was hotter than a poker stick. She'd gone ahead and ate two icies herself, the Kool-Aid ones, then switched over to munching what was left of the ice. Her stomach growled with hunger. Maybe she'd get a hot dog. Spend a dollar, get a dog. Her hand went to her stomach. She liked how it felt, flat and not pudging over her shorts like it done last year when she was eleven.

Raymel was pedaling his bike slow, moving toward her up the boardwalk with Wallace and Jason. All of them riding one-handed, holding super soakers with the other. Raymel so ugly, his head dented in on one side but funny too—that boy could make her laugh. Just yesterday calling that muthafucker what was eyeballing her *twig leg. Twig leg muthafucker—his mama musta got fucked by a tree.* She'd laughed and laughed. He was Crystal's half brother. Different moms, same daddy.

Don't you fucking shoot me.

Come're AnnMarie, come're.

Don't get water on my stuff, you get the frames wet, you buy 'em.

That's some ugly shit right there.

AnnMarie shoved Jason who toppled from his bike, laughing.

Shut up. Now you got to buy one. You insult me like that.

Where Crystal at, Wallace said.

She with her mother. They left off to somewhere . . . AnnMarie paused, then said, I tell her you were asking though, Wallace.

And before she could blink, he'd pulled the trigger, sending a stream of water arcing through the air, smacking wet and cold against her skin. AnnMarie shrieked, laughing. He was nothing to look at but she knew why Crystal liked him. That boy opened his mouth to sing, his voice flowed like silk.

You been by to Teisha house, Raymel cut in.

Huh-uh.

They said they gonna cypher, I'ma bust a rhyme for you. Something new.

Word, I be there, AnnMarie said. But let me take y'alls picture. I give you a discount.

I ain't got no money for a damn picture.

Come on now. A dolla each, I know you got a dolla.

So the boys rolled up their bikes, Raymel, Wallace and Jason all in a row.

Nah, nah, scoot in, scoot in, make like a V.

Raymel leaning an elbow on his knee, his patent leather Reebok slanted against the pedal, throwing up Blood—*blat, blat, blat.*

Stop moving Raymel. Hold your hands still.

Looking at her with his funny-shaped head, Wallace and Jason holding their super soakers like Uzis. She start to laugh, dropping the camera from her eye they look so silly.

Take the damn picture.

She took the picture and when the shutter clicked, something clicked like joy inside, this feeling like she springing out.

They rolled around some. Raymel pedaling and she held on, one hand on his waistband, a finger touching skin. AnnMarie packed up her things and hid the cart beneath the stairs. Then they all went down to Beach 9, got into a water fight with the super soakers and water bottles and cups they dug out the trash.

They went down to the shore. Took their shoes off, went in with shorts and tanks on, jumping waves and throwing seaweed at each other. Laughing.

On their way back across the sand, they saw it. Just a dark bulky shape at first, they was so far away. Didn't look like bodies. But that's what it was, two people humping in the sand underneath the boardwalk. The man's body on top, pants down to his knees, his bare butt thrusting and clenching, their legs entwined, one of her breasts flopping and jiggling when he rose up and thrust.

Ooohhhh, what they doin'.

They fucking.

Oh, shit.

Laughing. Laughing.

Look at AnnMarie gaping.

I ain't gaping. Shut up, stupid.

But AnnMarie had to pull her eyes away. Never seen nobody doing it before, not like that, kids making out, sure, but nothing like this. A long, low moan floated toward them and AnnMarie couldn't help it. Her eyes flit back to the shadowy underside of the boardwalk just as the man clutched his shorts and rolled offa her, round breasts in full view, the small brown triangle glistening between her legs.

Four o'clock in the afternoon. It was hot. Even with the breeze coming off the sand. Pushing clouds high up there. Too hot to stand in the sun with no shade. No one wanted a picture. Icies melted to mush. The other boys had gone to the rec center. She'd wanted to go too but knew Blessed would ask how much she made, and expect a dollar or two. She turned and saw Raymel coming around again, pedaling slow up the boardwalk.

How'd you do?

She didn't need to pull the bills from her pocket. She'd been keeping track.

Thirty-seven dollas, she said.

He dropped his bike and crossed to where she stood. He said, we could buy some weed wit' that.

Huh-uh. This is for my back-to-school.

Why you need new clothes, you look good to me. *Sexy Sweet.*

Shut up, Raymel . . . She pushed him and he grabbed her hand, holding on to her fingers.

Stop buggin'. Let go my hand.

He held on though, lacing his fingers through hers, looking at her with that dopey smile, saying, Come on now, AnnMarie . . .

And she let him play until her palms start to sweat and he'd stepped into her, talking in her ear: I buy you some clothes. Go out to Five Town. They got all the stores you like out there.

She smiled into his shoulder and felt the smallest twinge, something move down there, making her chest pound. It felt good. But still she pushed him away, saying, Step back, Ray. It's too hot.

Raymel backed up, straddled the bike and sat there for a moment in the heat, both of them not speaking.

He'd told her he was fourteen but she knew he was older. Crystal had let it slip. Sixteen years old and embarrassed 'cause he was still in the 9th grade at Far Rock. She watched him push off, pedaling now in slow wide circles, rattling the planks.

Where you going, AnnMarie asked.

Raymel shrugged. Nowhere, away from you.

AnnMarie tsked, halfways smiling.

He'd told her once he thought she got talent. One time at Teisha's—the older girls bugging out a cypher. Rapping they rhymes in turn and she'd jumped in with a three-line hook she'd come up with on the spot. He looked at her later when they was alone and said, Damn, girl, you got some pipes. But in that moment, she hadn't cared about Raymel—the older girls were what mattered. Teisha, Niki, Sunshine. Called themselves the Night Shade. Female rappers, with they mad style and breezy take-charge attitude. Listening to them talk about clubs and open-mic night, mixtapes and producers, how they the only female rappers in Far Rock. How they gonna bust out. After she sang, Niki'd reached over and gave her daps.

They hadn't heard her sing at IS 53 June Talent. None of them had. Hitting every single note of "I Will Always Love You" by Whitney Houston, singing so beautiful, the whole auditorium had gone wild. Her choir teacher, Mr. Preston, had walked across the stage and hugged her, then turned her to face the crowd. First time she won a ribbon. First time she won anything.

She gazed out at the sand and the sea. Couldn't hear the surf. Man with his transistor listening to some ballgame. A girl shrieking, getting a bucket dunked on her head. Raymel riding farther down the boardwalk now, pulling his bike up alongside some fellas who'd come up the ramp and were settling in the shade of the gazebo. Who that. That him? Had his dreads pulled back now, shirt off, tucked into his back pocket. Yeah, it was him—the boy Darius Greene, giving Raymel daps. Dang, she didn't know they friends.

She suddenly felt dizzy, dots popping in front of her eyes. She leaned over the fountain and drank. First days living in Far Rock, Blessed had brought her down to the street to meet some kids. AnnMarie didn't know nobody. All of them in a loose cluster up the block, playing some game with a rope.

Make friends, Blessed had said but AnnMarie refused to leave her side so when the ice-cream truck pulled up, her mother drew the food stamps from her purse and started waving them around. She said, Who want ice cream. Who want ice cream? Miss Blessed buying you ice cream. All the kids crowded in then, calling, Me, Miss Blessed! Me. Me. Me. Thank you Miss Blessed! That yo' ma? Oh, my gawd. She the nicest ma in the world.

AnnMarie had looked up at her then, standing tall, with hair she kept natural, styled that day with a iron and eyes that stared straight, not dragging. Those chinky eyes. Veiled smiling eyes. *She the nicest ma in the world.*

All the kids sat on the rail, licking they rocket pops and rainbow sherberts and chocolate crunchies, AnnMarie right there with them, the ice cream melting across her knuckles, dripping onto her knee. Even still, she tried to make it last.

She took another drink from the fountain, then turned looking over at the gazebo. Someone over there had turned up the boom box. Method Man rapping. She watched Darius dip his head, keeping time with his fingers.

Hell, no. No way she startin' 8th grade without some Jordache. Guess. Diesel. The new Diesel jeans with the side stitch . . . Put the thirty-seven dollas with the hundred eighteen she got hidden in her drawer, that buy something. That get you something.

Plus she had days a summer. Days a summer still.

3

When AnnMarie walked in, Blessed was dozing on the couch, the fan blowing hot air around the room, Steve Harvey on the TV. She went straight for the fridge, pulled it open and found it empty except for the orangeade sitting there on the top shelf. Her stomach felt torn.

She knelt next to her mother, touched her leg. She knew Blessed didn't like being woke when she in one of her dozes.

Ma . . . she said softly.

Ma, I'm hungry.

Her mother didn't stir. AnnMarie wondered how long she'd been sleeping, what time Miss Jessica left off, the scent of clove and cinnamon still in the air. AnnMarie stood up, walked back into the kitchen, pulled open the fridge and stared. Mr. Chow's Chicken Stir-fry cost $5.49. $3.99 get you the lo mein noodles. A dollar get you rice with beef juice on top. She could feel the bills pressing through her pocket. She hesitated, then reached into the cupboard and pulled down a can of Chef Boyardee.

She dumped the ravioli in the pot, turned up the flame.

Halfway home Raymel had caught up to her, pushing his bike slow. We should go to my boy Darius' house, he said.

How you know him?

I know everybody.

Oh, you Mr. Popular now.

Raymel tsked, smiling. He got a studio set up in his room.

Word?

We could lay down some tracks. Throw in one a your hooks.

AnnMarie looked at him sideways. For real? You told him about me?

No, I'm just saying . . . We could lay down some tracks, see what come out.

AnnMarie glanced at him. Where he live at.

Over there by Nameoke.

He pushed the bike along, the two a them bumping shoulders, eyes on the ground.

He said, we put some work in, see what come out.

She ate standing at the counter, wiping up the sauce with a piece of bread. Steve Harvey going on about something. She tuned him out, drifting to Darius leaning back against the rail. His skin deep chocolate. A beedie to his lips. She let a picture roll out. His arm heavy on her shoulder, walking real slow, letting everybody see. She'd be wearing a halter, not this one, but another one she'd seen in Teisha's closet, soft like silk. And her breasts would be big. Big enough to push out the cloth . . .

AnnMarie turned off the TV. She stood for a moment in the stillness, listening to her mother breathe.

She ran all the way down to Beach 9. The sky was changing, pale blue folding into twilight. Yellow moon hanging low and fat over Far Rock train yard. On the boardwalk, kids were still roaming, hanging by the rail.

Yo, Wallace, where Raymel at?

They went by to Jason house.

Wha—? When he leave off?

Wallace shrugged and she stood for a moment, not knowing what to do.

What, he ditch you, AnnMarie? Wallace asked.

No, he didn't ditch me, what building Jason live at?

12-70.

She knew she couldn't go over there, not into Redfern after dark. She missed Crystal all of a sudden. Felt her heart banging in her chest, she didn't know why. Stop banging, she thought. Chill.

He come back, tell 'im I'ma be at Teisha's, she said, then turned and ran back the way she came.

She swung through the door of 1440 where Teisha lived, reached up and pressed the buzzer.

Who that?

AnnMarie.

She heard the click and she was in. She took the stairs slow, calming herself. Breathe, AnnMarie. These girls your friend. Don't matter Crystal's not here.

Hey y'all. What up—we cyphering?

No we ain't cyphering, Teisha snapped as AnnMarie stepped in.

Damn, Teish. Why you so nasty. This from Niki who was sitting with Sunshine at the kitchen table rolling and unrolling the sleeves of her red tee 'til they looked just right. Where you at today, AnnMarie, Niki said. We was here spittin'.

Raymel told me later.

Raymel stupid, Teisha yelled from the other room. Niki ignored her, picking up her story again—telling Sunshine how Nadette had chased her down the block, trying to run her over.

AnnMarie slid into a seat. She watched Niki pull the loose curls of her cinammon-colored afro back into a ponytail.

Shoulda seen her face, Niki said, shaking her head.

Sunshine just looked at her, rubbing cocoa butter on her elbow, the scent filling the air.

Teisha stuck her head into the kitchen. When we leave, I don't want no fighting in my house. Just tell the girl you sorry.

I ain't gonna be here, Niki said. I'm coming wit' y'all.

Sunshine tsked. You should *tell* the girl you sorry.

AnnMarie looked up at Teisha. Where y'all goin?

Open mic.

Oooh, where at? Can I come, can I come?

No you can't come. You *twelve*.

She followed Teisha to the bathroom. Leaned against the door and watched her put on her lashes. Sephora brand.

They got glitter on them?

Mm-hm.

AnnMarie's eyes drifted from the mirror to Teisha's jeans that fit snug, cuffed just above the heels of her silver mules. Some people say she look like Lil' Kim. Skinny waist with a big ass. You could put a damn coffee mug on that thing and it won't fall off. AnnMarie wished she had a butt like that.

Can't I come? I'll go home and change.

Teisha cut her a look through the mirror. Where Crystal at?

She with her mother.

Teisha didn't answer, didn't look at her again, so AnnMarie wandered back into the kitchen where Sunshine was saying to Niki: I'da kill you myself.

Niki flounced. But I ain't done nothing.

Who you foolin', Sunshine said. You need to keep your hands to yourself, yo.

AnnMarie slumped down for real now. She didn't know what they was talking about. She just knew she was about to get left. Well. She wouldn't tell them about the boy Darius and his studio. Didn't want to make nobody jealous.

The apartment door flung open just then and there was Nadette, standing in the middle of the room, glaring. Burning holes into the back of Niki's head. The room got quiet. Sunshine stood up, giving Niki a look but still Niki didn't move. She just sat there 'til Teisha came *clickety-clack* across the floor, looked at the two a them, told 'em to work it out, go in the other room and work it the fuck out.

Then Teisha left with Sunshine. Both of them dressed up fine, out the door and gone. Niki followed Nadette into the bathroom, closed the door, and AnnMarie sat in the stillness for a while, listening to the muffled sounds of their voices 'til it got quiet. AnnMarie stood, walked into Teisha's room, crossed to the closet where she reached up and brushed her fingers across the clothes. All them pretty clothes.

Last time she was in there with Raymel, he'd come up behind her.

He said, You gonna learn to dance?

Whatchu mean.

Teisha dance. My cousin saw her down at the club. She's good too, he said. They put mad money in her string.

But she hadn't been listening. She'd been touching the clothes. Oh, my gawd. Look at this, Raymel . . . Seventy-nine dollas, she ain't even take the tag off yet.

His hands had gone around her waist and she'd felt his lips brush her neck. She turned into him, put her hands on his shoulders and closed her eyes. She pretended she was Teisha, lifted her chin and waited for his lips to find hers.

The night air had cooled some but it still lay down and stuck to your skin.

She went along the ramp, passing the Beach 9 sign, and stood watching the couples move in and out the pools of light all the way down the boardwalk. Strolling slow, nowhere to be but here, appearing suddenly out of a patch of velvet dark where the lamplight broke and no longer shone. She looked for Raymel, itching now to see Darius' studio.

Spring out and touch something.

You never could hear the sound of the ocean, she thought. Not from up here. You had to go all the way down, all the way across the sand, put your foot in, you hear it then.

Darius Greene

4

Three days before her thirteenth birthday, AnnMarie took Central all the way up to the Nassau Expressway, waited for the flow of traffic to die, then hustled across the four-lane, leaving her neighborhood behind. She knew the shopping center was somewhere in Lawrence, where the sidewalks widened and the homes stood in neat rows, glass in all the windows, and grass that was green. Teisha had told her, take Central all the way. The whole while AnnMarie thought about Janet falling for Tupak, how she'd never get tired of that movie, that girl making her poetry, beautiful poetry to get around the sad feeling of life. A whole hour of walking until she saw the line of stores stretching out before her and she quickened her pace, excited now to have arrived, icy money ready to be spent.

She moved past planter boxes and colorful awnings, white ladies pushing strollers, sipping ice tea out of plastic cups. Glancing in all the big plate windows, she saw cream-colored mannequin girls with narrow waists and pointy breasts. Designer clothes, starched and tagged and beautiful. Perfume and candles, jewelry, candied apples, chocolate and stuffed animals. Up ahead some kids lounged outside a ice-cream shop, one of the girls giving her the eyeball, but AnnMarie just strolled on by thinking, Bitch, fuck you, I got money in my sock. She found the store Teisha had told her about called Madeline's, went inside and spent a hour trying on clothes. A salesgirl hovered near the changing room, making sure she ain't try to steal nothing. AnnMarie didn't care. She had cash money. Bought herself a brand-new pair of Diesel jeans size 2, hot pink Glitter Girl T-shirt and a black satin hoodie with the bright blue snake coiled around the left sleeve. Left off Madeline's, walked into the shoe store she'd passed on her way in, tried on a pair of Tims. Almost bought the pink to match her T-shirt, then changed her mind and got the Classic.

At Niki's house, she stripped out of her clothes and put on the outfit, head to toe, Niki watching the whole while, saying, Yeah, yeah . . . Girl, that hoodie is crack.

Word, you think so . . . ? AnnMarie turned, looking at herself in the mirror. A ripple of excitement rose up and made her laugh.

Mm-hm, she said. Those jeans too. You a It Girl now.

Niki leaned back on the bed, tossing her loose curls while AnnMarie waited for her to crack stupid but she didn't. She kept looking, halfways smiling and AnnMarie felt self-conscious all of a sudden so she cut her eyes away, unzipping the hoodie, saying, You want to try it on?

Hell yeah, Niki said, hopping up. She slipped it on, her fingers running down the snake. This look sick—you got the fashion sense, AnnMarie, true dat. I'ma make you my stylist.

AnnMarie laughed, watching her. Niki with her cinnamon skin and wash of freckles, stepping in front of the mirror, throwing up fake female gang signs. Posing, gangsta-ruff.

When they heard Niki's father leave off for work, Niki pulled a half-smoked joint from a matchbox and lit up, passing the roach to AnnMarie. AnnMarie took a hit, then another, feeling her lungs expand. Niki laughed at nothing in particular, fiddling with the radio and AnnMarie lay back on the bed, feeling a buzz coming on. I got to get home, she said. My mother got me on curfew.

Out on the street, new clothes back in the bag, Niki was talking nonstop like she do when she high, telling AnnMarie how Teisha partied with some homie named Uno, a MC about to blow up big on the mixtape circuit. He got a single out, Nadette heard it on the radio. We got to get on the radio. You know Ronald, he knows somebody at Hot 97, I'ma talk to him see how we can get something going.

Yeah, yeah, AnnMarie said . . . The weed making her head hum, heart pounding, mouth dry. Couldn't say much when she stoned, but Niki's words danced in her head, *You a It Girl now*, making her smile spontaneous, the start of 8th grade right around the corner. Maybe Raymel would finally take her to meet Darius, check out his studio, choir class with Mr. Preston . . . Then Niki's voice was cutting in again.

Say what? AnnMarie said.

I said, where the fuck that name come from anyway. Wu-Tang. Wu-Tang Clan, like Who-da-Tang . . .

AnnMarie bust out laughing. Niki snickered into her hand, saying Like Koo-da-Tang and Pootie-Tang. Both of them busting, bumping shoulders, all the way up Mott Avenue, a soft wind blowing, taking the punch out of the late-August heat.

No, I'm playing. Wu-Tang be dope, for real, for reals. You see they got a video out on MTV? Filmed it right there in Stapleton Houses. Goose-down, Champion hoodies, we got to make a video. The Night Shade, you wear your hoodie, I get one too, we all get 'em. Show some female swag, snake be our signature style, word . . .

AnnMarie laughed, saying, Hell yeah. Niki giving her daps. *You a It Girl now.*

Blessed was leaning on the walker when she walked in, a plate of cookies in hand, the plate resting on the walker like she'd stopped midstep, waiting like that for AnnMarie to appear.

Where have you been? Blessed asked.

Nowhere, AnnMarie said, her eyes cutting to the two strangers sitting on the couch, suitcases propped up one next to the other, crowded into the corner.

What kinda answer is that. Me asked you where you been, AnnMarie.

Shopping. I was shopping for my back-to-school. She raised the bag, showing it to Blessed. It ain't even eight o'clock yet.

Blessed frowned and the room went silent, AnnMarie waiting for the lash-down, but all her mother said was, You remember Carlton and Carlotta. Pinky's children.

AnnMarie glanced from one to the other, then said, Oh. Hey . . . Feeling their eyes on her as she took a step back and leaned against the door, glancing at the big-as-a-buffalo dude, thinking Carlton and Carlotta, who the fuck is they? His legs splayed, face wide-set, chin rolling into his fat neck.

You look grown, don't she look grown, Carlotta?

Mm-hm, she does.

You don't remember when you lived wit' us, AnnMarie?

AnnMarie'd heard of Pinky. Knew she'd stayed with her before foster care and Grandma Mason—but it was a memory her mother had given her, not her own.

She said, Yeah, okay, not really.

Carlotta laughed. The girl had her hair pulled back into a bun like Olive Oyl. Mad stupid hairstyle, got the rubber-sole wedges you see grandmas wear. Dang. She get grown, hope she never look like that.

Carlotta was saying, She used to love those Ninja Turtle candies. Sit in front of the TV and eat those candies. You remember that, Miss Blessed? Thought they gave her superpowers.

That's right, that's right, Carlton said laughing.

Blessed smiled. She said, Oh, yes. Yes. But AnnMarie could tell she was faking. Her memory partways gone since the stroke. All the little things. In one ear, out the other.

Thought she could fly back to Miss Blessed, Carlton was saying.

Mm-hm . . . his sister murmured. She'd stand at the window. You don't remember none of this, AnnMarie?

AnnMarie shook her head.

Well, Pinky's gone back to Trinidad, Blessed cut in. Gone to bury her father so they're staying with us for a while. Here, take these cookies, put them there . . .

AnnMarie crossed the room, took the plate from her mother's shaking hand, set them on the TV tray. Thinking, *for a while?* What that supposed to mean, *for a while*, all a them cramped together in this box of an apartment.

Out the corner of her eye, she watched Carlton lean back and stretch, his belly lifting away from the thin black belt cutting into his waist. She wanted to go past him into her room, close the door, try on her new clothes again, but her mother was talking, saying, You want Fanta? AnnMarie, go down get some Fanta from the store.

So AnnMarie went, glad to be outside again. She cut across the street, went up to Cornega, picturing Carlton's dumb smile, and tsked out loud. *Don't she look grown?* It bothered her they knew things she couldn't remember. Ninja-fucking Turtles. Superpowers. She thought hard, trying to picture Pinky's house, push pass the hazy space in her mind, when all of a sudden Kayla and Leela popped up, clear as day. They'd been her foster sisters at Grandma Mason's house. Twins, but not the identical kind. Both of them thin-boned and small, same age as AnnMarie, but tiny like twiggy birds. One of them had dry skin. Leela. Flaky dry skin, that girl had some kinda skin trouble. Grandma Mason catch her scratching, she'd beat that girl with the belt she let hang from a nail by the window. There'd been Shemar too. Another foster brother, a year younger than the twins. He got the top bunk 'cause Grandma Mason liked him best.

No Ninja Turtles up there in the Bronx, AnnMarie thought. Never any candy at all. Except when the older boys came upstairs. Grandma Mason's grandsons. With their Mars Bars and Nestlé Crunch. Grandma Mason would yank AnnMarie from the broom closet. Why you hiding, she'd say. They's your foster brothers too.

At the bodega, AnnMarie reached up and pressed the bell. She waited, knowing somebody inside watching the video screen, checking to see who out there. She heard the buzz and went in, past the old man buying a lottery ticket, down the aisle to the back where the soda was. She plucked a Fanta off the shelf when the A-rab start up shouting, *One at a time. One at a time.* AnnMarie turned. She could see him behind the counter, looking intently at the video screen, then heard the buzzer as the door swung open and in stepped Raymel, his face lighting up when he saw her.

Damn, girl, he said. I was just thinking about you.

Hey Raymel, what up . . . Happy to see him too, but trapped now 'cause all she had was the food stamp in her pocket. No way she pulling it out in front of him.

What you doing, you going to Sunshine's?

Sunshine, what they doing?

She having a little thing. Me and Jason headin' over . . .

She knew Sunshine lived with her boyfriend somewhere over there on Walcott, behind Redfern Houses. He a dealer or something, but he had mad swag. Drove a car and everything.

Who gonna be there?

Everybody.

And that's all it took. AnnMarie set the Fanta back up on the shelf and walked down the aisle. Yeah, yeah . . . I'ma go with y'all. Raymel grinned, said to the man, Let me get a Zig-Zag.

Ma! She said into the pay phone. Ma, I'ma go to this little birth-day party for Patrice. Patrice from choir? Her mother go to church with you, no ma, I just ran into them. Her mother throwing her a little party, please can I go. Since I ain't getting my own party . . . please ma. Please. There gonna be cake.

Her eye flitting over to Jason and Raymel who cracked up into they hands.

When she crept in after midnight, all the lights were off. She let her eyes adjust, listening to the low raspy sound of someone breathing. The buffalo on the couch. She slipped across the floor and stood in her doorway. Carlotta asleep in her bed, window fan blowing hot air through the room. She went into Blessed's room, unbuckled her sandals, left her shorts and T-shirt on and crawled in next to her mother, mad slow, careful not to bump her, even though she knew it took a thunder of elephants to wake her up.

She lay there for a long while, thinking about Sunshine's party. How she'd seen Darius come in with his homies through the haze a weed smoke. She tried to find Raymel but he'd disappeared somewhere, the room packed tight with people she didn't know. All a them older, outta high school at least. She wished she'd worn her satin hoodie. What would she have said to Darius anyway. Leaning up against the wall, looking mad fine. Some chick going up to him, talking in his ear. AnnMarie'd stepped on some girl's shoe. She cringed at the thought. The girl had reared back, glar-ing. *Bitch, watch where you walking.* The fella next to her snicker-ing. *Peewee like you, why ain't you home. Where your mother at.*

A wash of anxiety woke her. She felt Blessed next to her in the bed and she stayed still, laying on her side, staring at the wall. Thinking, almost thirteen and you sleeping with your mother.

AnnMarie rolled over. She felt her mother's hand against her side, felt the heat breathing off her skin. She used to love it, sleeping with her mother. Those first months in Far Rock, they'd had no furniture, just a chair somebody had left behind. At night, they made a bed outta blankets. AnnMarie'd crawl in next to her mother, listening for a long time until her breath evened out. Then she'd lift her mother's arm, set it over her waist, and the shouts and clamor rising from the street below faded into a vague and distant preoccupation.

In the living room, Carlton and Carlotta sat on the couch, eating cereal.

Well, ain't you grown, Carlton said with a fake-ass smile.

What you mean, she asked, going past him into her bedroom.

When'd you come home last night?

None a your business, AnnMarie thought, pulling open her drawers, digging around for a change of clothes. She heard him laugh, his eyes on her as she went into the bathroom. She locked the door, wondering how bad she gonna get it. Never knew with Blessed. Sometime she don't say nothing. She stood under the warm water. Sang the Brandy song she'd been working on. Sang the entire verse without stopping, then sang it again. She liked how her voice sound in the bathroom. Bouncing off the tile. Got mad reverb.

When she got out, her mother was awake, the two of them still on the couch, watching TV. AnnMarie stood in the doorway and held her breath, watching Blessed's face contort into a frown as she struggled to open a pill container. But all her mother said was, Open this for me, AnnMarie.

AnnMarie slipped across the room, took the pill bottle and unscrewed the lid.

This for your blood pressure? You know you got to eat food with it, Ma . . .

Her mother didn't answer, just took the pill and swallowed.

Pass me my Percocet.

AnnMarie hesitated. Percocet first thing in the morning. Her mother be sleeping before she wake. They used to do things. Go to the rec center. Cook food. Her mother humming a little tune. AnnMarie leaned over to look at the labels. Pills for cholesterol, pills for pain, tremor pills, depression pills. Pills for the heart.

Ma, why you need this, first thing in the morning.

Just open it for me, AnnMarie, my leg painin' me.

AnnMarie opened the pill bottle, then passed it to her mother, sitting down next to her on the bed. Her mother struggled to get the pills out with her shaky fingers but AnnMarie didn't move to help.

Instead, she bent and picked Blessed's wig up off the floor, bits of lint and a snarl forming. You want me to brush it out for you?

Just set it down, AnnMarie, her mother said sharply, and get out me room. Soon as me get me Medicaid fixed, Miss Jessica be back. She know exactly how me like things.

Her mother's accent flaring. What you got to be angry for, AnnMarie thought. Acting like a invalid. Fuck that. She stood up and stepped through the doorway, saying, Fine, I hope you get your Medicaid fix. Miss Jessica come back, all y'alls can have a fucking party.

You hear that, Carlton. You see how she talk?

I hear it, Miss Blessed. Back home she get a cut ass for that. A cut ass.

AnnMarie scowled. Sitting there like he some kinda crowned prince. She said, Who you. Who the fuck are you?

Then Blessed was trying to stand, her good eye glaring. What you say? What did me hear you say? You must want me to box you down. That what you want?

AnnMarie cut her eyes away but kept her mouth shut.

5

Her birthday came and went with the blow of a candle. August became September and there was no stopping school coming on. 8th grade, first day, AnnMarie strolled up to the yard, looking mad o.d. fine in her brand-new Diesels and black satin hoodie. First day easy, forgetting all about Carlton and Carlotta in the house, with all the *hey y'alls, what up, how your summer go* and fake cheek kisses, looking to see who got coupled up and who still alone. Kids filing into classrooms, teachers and their first-day speeches, the *what I expect from you* speeches, no one paying attention 'cept to each other—who gonna be best friends, who gonna be beefin', textbooks going around, pages ripped, marked-up and torn from the year before. Take one, everybody need a book.

Assembly, principal gave a speech, the expectation speech, the behavior speech, the *we're all one community* speech . . . Crystal was still gone so AnnMarie had taken a seat next to Patrice and Katelyn, girls she'd known since 3rd grade, PS 197. Choir girls. Good girls who could sing "Lord Take Thy Hand" and "Come to Me" on key, every note clear and beautiful. She spotted Brittany sitting three rows down front. What she got on. Fat bitch. Sitting between Shaquanna and Ashley. Tag-along 1 and Tag-along 2. Got her hair straightened, pulled up into a sweep. Spent some money on that, AnnMarie thought, but still she ugly. Suck-face ugly. Baboon-ass ugly. She watched Brittany lean in and whisper something to Tag-along 1, the girl laughing, her mouth moving 'til Brittany tsked and she shut up.

She didn't know why Brittany hated her, just that she did. It all got started sometime last year, Brittany saying, Stay away from Rashad. AnnMarie'd said, Rashad? Who the fuck Rashad? But it didn't matter, they jumped her anyway and it went on from there.

AnnMarie sat forward and re-tucked her Glitter Girl T-shirt, watching Brittany now, turn full around in her seat, her elbow flying. Tag-along flinched, cupping a hand to her cheek where Brittany had clocked her but Brittany act like she ain't done nothing, neck craning, eyes scanning the auditorium. Tag-along just sat there, dumb.

AnnMarie stared daggers into that girl. She hope they eyes meet so Brittany could feel the cut, all them blades slicing her apart. But Brittany didn't notice. Her arm shot up, waving to somebody across the auditorium. Fuck that girl.

Sixth-period choir. AnnMarie filed in with the other kids, called *Hey, Mr. Preston*, and took a seat next to the boy Crystal had been crushing on all summer. Wallace, who was leaning back in his chair with a new low fade and crisp white Polo. She said Dang, Wallace, you look nice, let me see. He turned his head, showing off the design the barber'd shaped into the side of his head—a swirly W ending in a curlicue. Is that a clef symbol, she asked. Nah, that be a dollar sign. Word, AnnMarie said, that is dope.

W$

Mr. Preston rapped his baton on the edge of a music stand and everyone got quiet. He didn't do no speech giving. He got right to it. Follow me one at a time, he said, and he sang a melody— high up for the girls, medium low for the boys. And when Brittany walked in ten minutes late, Mr. Preston just motioned her to the back of the room. AnnMarie ignored her. Eyes on Mr. Preston, she stood and took her turn, her voice rising sweet and clear until Mr. Preston said, We're gonna go again, AnnMarie. He didn't do that with none of the others. He said, This time we're gonna harmonize, you and Wallace. Then he counted out a beat and nodded first to AnnMarie, then to Wallace who took the cue, his voice coming up underneath hers, blending deep and rich and beautiful. AnnMarie felt the vibration, like a living thing passing through the room. She watched Mr. Preston close his eyes and listen, swaying like he gone to heaven.

AnnMarie smiled, pushing out the door, first day done. A few blocks from the school, she hooked up with Raymel and Jason who were walking over to Redfern, heading to 12-70 where they claimed a bench. Backpacks flung to the ground. High-school kids passing in clusters, and the air was warm and breezy even as the sun sunk behind the low-rise buildings, casting shadow blocks along the pathways.

Her mother had told her to come right home but there was no way she leaving 'cause in the midst of all the chatter and weed smell and laughter, Darius Green rolled up, taking a seat three benches down, joining a group of older boys, Bloods, in their own little circle. Raymel's hand went up in a *What up y'all* to somebody over there but no one seemed to notice, not even Darius, and AnnMarie wondered if they true friends or not.

She felt Raymel's arm go around her shoulder as he leaned forward to take the blunt someone was passing. She said, Ain't that your homie over there.

Who dat.

Darius.

Raymel didn't answer, sucked in the weed smoke and held it in.

Why ain't you introduce me.

Don't be a slut, Raymel said.

Say what? AnnMarie turned and stared. She shrugged off his arm, stood up and he reached for her, coughing up smoke, saying, I'm playin' with you, AnnMarie. I'm playin' . . . Off the bench now, he pulled her into an embrace, and she let him, 'cause she wanted the attention, even though she knew it was wrong, that it was Darius she was thinking of, feeling her brand-new Diesels snug against her skin, glancing now, down the path, past the kids roaming, to see if he was looking.

6

The days rolled up with change in the air, the October wind blowing damp and cool, night sky dropping early, sweeping daylight off like a blanket. They'd moved her bed next to the window, making room for the mattress they set out on the floor. She came home one day to find her room no longer her own, Carlotta's clothes hanging in the closet, Carlton's in the dresser, her clothes in a pile, spilling from a chair in the living room. AnnMarie blew up, screaming at her mother, Why you let them do that? What do you care, Blessed said. You never home anyway. Fuck you, I'm never home. Comatosin'. How would you know? Up in her mother's face 'til Carlton had clamped one of his big hands down on her arm and was beating her with the belt he'd wrapped partways around his fist. Or at least he was trying to 'cause AnnMarie yanked herself loose, screaming all the *fuck y'alls* and the *muthafuck bitch fuck yous* she could muster, her hands and arms getting lashed each time she reached out to stop the belt. Her mother leaning on the walker, yelling, *Whip she tail, whip she tail.* Whip she tail.

Carlotta got a job at BJ's working the register nine to five. Home by six o'clock, she'd sit on AnnMarie's bed, filing her nails down, listening to the gospel station on the radio. Carlton worked odd hours as a dollar van driver, sometimes the split shift, walking in at midnight with his heavy step. One night, she'd been dreaming.

She was asleep on the foam mattress in Grandma Mason house up in the Bronx. But in the dream she was grown, not a child, and she felt the sensation, like someone laying next to her, pressing up against her ass, a hand moving between her legs. Rubbing and cumming. She jerked awake and found herself alone on the couch. Carlton was standing in the kitchen, overhead light on, casting his face in shadow.

What's the matter, AnnMarie, he said. I wake you?

She said, Fuck you, punk ass. Stay away from me.

She couldn't see his expression as he moved toward her, shoving her back into the cushion, his knee grinding into her shoulder. Get offa me, she hollered.

Watch your mouth, he said, clamping his hand over her mouth. Or I beat you again.

A picture forming in her mind. Like heat folding over her, making it hard to breathe. Grandma Mason's belt swinging, cracking down across her spine.

At school the next day, in between 5th and 6th periods, Brittany came down the hall, bumped her shoulder, saying 'Xcuse me. AnnMarie slammed her books to the floor. She said, Bitch don't touch me.

Brittany nearly got her on the floor but AnnMarie yanked free and threw a solid, feeling bone against her knuckle. A crowd quickly formed, laughing with the *hooo shits* and the *ooohhhs, bitch fuck her up* 'til Mr. Preston pushed through and pulled the girls apart, his nose bloodied by one of their elbows. Then Principal arrived with security, asking for an explanation. AnnMarie stood staring at the floor, breathing hard, not able to look at Mr. Preston. She'd caught the disappointment in his eye, she'd seen it—an expression that made all the protest and rage bunch up in the back of her throat.

Principal gave them both five-day suspension. Her mother didn't know. School so stupid, never bothered to call. In the mornings, AnnMarie got herself up off Blessed's bedroom floor where she'd started to sleep. Five thirty, everything dark, made it into the shower and dressed before the light even went on in her bedroom. She'd slip out the door and hook into a group of kids walking up Gateway. In The Donut Shop, she'd take a seat facing the window and watch the sky brighten, late-pass kids trickling by 'til the street was empty and the lady in uniform start to hover, asking why she ain't in school. She need to get to school.

She made wide loops through the neighborhood, wandering down to the boardwalk, or in the other direction past the expressway; one day all the way clear up Mott Avenue to where the sidewalk ended and way over there, across the bay, she could see Inwood Country Club spread out like a bright green blanket.

One night she went by to see Niki. They hung out for a while but soon Niki got restless. She said, Come on. Let's go to Nadette's. So AnnMarie followed her out the door, the whole while Niki telling her about a new rap she come up with, spitting the verse while they walked and AnnMarie said, That sound dope. Then she told Niki about a song she was writing called "Avalanche" and do she want to hear it and Niki said, Yeah, sing it. So AnnMarie sang softly, stumbling over a couple lines she hadn't worked out yet but mostly it sounded good, Niki giving her daps, saying it was sweet.

But at Nadette's, Niki seemed to forget all about her. They smoked weed and Nadette put on some music, then started dancing in front of the mirror. AnnMarie cracked up, thinking she got to be joking, moving her silly ass like a stripper would but Niki wasn't laughing. She was watching, her and Nadette's eyes on each other through the reflection.

Then Dennis came home and Nadette stopped dancing. She

sat down next to Niki on the couch and said, Hey baby, but she didn't get up, even though he her boyfriend.

AnnMarie watched Niki and Nadette sitting there and for a little while no one spoke, the music playing from the stereo. But AnnMarie could tell they was talking, saying things to each other with they eyes. She wondered how you got like that. How you got close like that to someone else.

7

On Friday, she went back to school. After first bell, she saw Mr. Preston in the hallway moving through the swarm of kids, saying, *Get to class. Y'all need to get to your classrooms.* She pushed away from the locker, walking toward him, wanting him to take notice, ask how she doing, but she kept her eyes forward and when she felt a hand on her shoulder, she glanced up, saying, Oh hey Mr. Preston. He said, So you back, AnnMarie? Saying it stern, like he still angry. Right away, starting up a lecture, the *I expect more* lecture. *Stay away from . . . keep your head down . . . girl . . . trouble you get into . . . all that business . . . singing, am I right?* And when he let her shoulder go, she stepped back into the crunch and jam of middle-school life, one of a thousand kids who scraped back their chairs 5th period when the fire-drill bell rang, the whole school pouring out onto the sidewalk.

The air was crisp and cool. AnnMarie shrugged on her satin hoodie. She scanned the crowd and spotted Brittany's big head rising above the sea of faces, like a wave rolling toward her. She took a step back, then another, it was that easy, to slip away and be gone.

She wandered some, along Mott Avenue for a ways, until she finally got up the nerve to go into Redfern by herself. The housing project laid out in a grid with paths intersecting, lacing between the buildings, and up ahead she could make out a group of fellas hanging in a lazy circle by the benches near 12-70. She spotted Raymel among them so she cut across the path. But as she neared, she faltered, her heart skipping a beat as her eyes fell on Darius Greene sitting center stage, leaning back with his arm flung out over the bench. He was saying something and they was all listening. Too close to turn around without looking stupid, she told herself to chill, calling out, Hey Raymel.

Raymel turned. He said, What up, AnnMarie. And it got quiet all at once because Darius stopped talking and was looking at her now. She shifted, the only girl standing there in her snake hoodie and Classic Tims, all them eyes on her like, *who she* but Ann-Marie didn't care, all of a sudden she didn't care—she stepped right into the circle, and said, What's good, y'all . . .

Next thing she knew, she was sitting on the leather couch in his studio room, strobe light flashing, turning the white walls red, blue, green, then black. Raymel had slouched down next to her and she thought, Thank god for Raymel. 'Cause there was six of them and one of her. Darius doing his thing at the console, not once looking her way, all of them restless, red do-rags underneath they ball caps, eyes a mask of indifference until the weed came out, then finally the room start to soften. She told herself to breathe, took another sip from the bottle going around, coughed, then sipped again.

What's good, y'all . . . Someone had snickered, but Darius hadn't. He'd leaned forward and said, So you's AnnMarie. Her heart banging in her chest, like *You know me? You know me?* The way he'd looked at her—that's all it took. The sidewalk tipped and the whole world just fell away.

She glanced up at the posters on his wall—Busta Rhymes, Lil' Kim, Janet, all the superstars flashing in the strobe light. She got up the nerve and said, You heard Busta's new album?

Darius didn't answer but a boy she knew from up the block, he

said, That one sick and she knew she was taking a chance but she
went ahead and spit.

   . . . *Hey yo feel the bass line*
   Stack the overdrive . . .

One of the boys jumped in, start up a *thwaka thwaka thwaka*
and she had to laugh 'cause he was getting it right, then they all
laughing 'cause Raymel was on his feet, popping in the middle of
the room, his body moving like a badass mime, limbs like water
rippling. She let her eyes drift over to Darius, his fingers playing
with the keys of the console. Her skin tingled, watching him and
when he glanced over, their eyes met and she didn't look away.

A week went by and she didn't see him again. But she looked for
him everywhere, hanging out by the White Castle, passing in and
out of Redfern and even at Teisha's house, jotting lyrics in her
song book, or getting high with Niki and laughing 'til their guts
busted open, she felt it. Heartsick. Gawd, was she in love. Some
nights she stayed at Teisha's. Some nights with Niki. Some nights,
she snuck home after lights out, pulled the blanket off the couch
and lay there, drifting off on her mother's floor. She'd hear the
buffalo come in. Feel him standing in the doorway, watching her.
On these nights, she'd picture Darius punching him in the head,
smashing his face 'til it was bloody.

On Thursday, Teisha shook her awake. She sat up groggy, the
room still smelling of weed and cigarettes from the night before.
What time is it, AnnMarie asked. It's almost eleven, Teisha
said. Ain't you got school? AnnMarie got up, went into the bathroom, put toothpaste on her finger and brushed. Teisha appeared
in the doorway. She said, I got to shower, AnnMarie, hurry up.

When Teisha got in the shower, AnnMarie sifted through a

drawer, borrowed a scarf for her hair. Found her backpack kicked in the corner and went out the door, heading over to the school. But the closer she got, the more she slowed, thinking, What am I doing. All her energy slipping away, she was mad hungry. She looped past the school yard, looking across the street at the building, thought she heard the faint sound of the bell, what period was it, was it lunchtime? But no kids appeared in the yard so she kept going, wandering back up to Mott Avenue and the narrow sidewalks, the street choked with cars and an old lady creeping up the center lane, pushing her shopipng cart like a walker.

Past the Western Union and the 99-cent store and Tina's hair salon, she thought about weaves and braids and how ringlets be mad cute and soon she found herself on Nameoke where Darius lived. She slowed, glancing at the houses, thinking, Which one was it. She remembered the FOR SALE sign. Plywood covering the windows on the next, was it the green one, no, the one next to it yeah, there it is. What would she say. She'd pretend she looking for Raymel, see how it go. But passing the bushes and the stove dumped on the curb, she saw them up on the porch—three older dudes chillin'. She felt their eyes on her all at once, faces vaguely familiar, red do-rags hanging loose, so she cut across the street, the whole while feeling their stares like heat crawling up her back.

In Redfern, she found the bench where she first met Darius and sat down. She kicked out her feet, glancing up past the buildings, way up there the sky darkening. Clouds rolling in with the wind. She stood, tugged her pants out of her crotch, creased and re-creased the fold but knew she was looking ratty—wearing the same jeans for three days and needing a change.

The wind whipped up hard. She squinted against it but saw them coming. Finally.

School out, kids rollin' up. Patrice and Katelyn walking slow, backpacks half off their shoulders. Patrice got her hair down today. Her mother knew how to fix it. Patrice hair always look nice, even in this wind.

Why haven't you been at school, AnnMarie? Mr. Preston passed out the sheet music.

Word? How it sound, AnnMarie asked.

Oh, it's real nice. You heard a "Let Them Sing"?

Mr. Preston says everybody gotta bring five dollars for the trip.

What trip, AnnMarie asked.

Choir Academy, dummy. We all goin' on Monday.

AnnMarie pictured Mr. Preston on the first day of school. Closing his eyes, listening to her sing. Seemed like ages ago.

Brittany was asking for you, Katelyn said.

Talking how she's not done yet. How she gonna eff you up.

AnnMarie tsked. So. I ain't afraid a that girl.

So how come you been skipping—

AnnMarie heard the CRACK and saw Katelyn duck. Gunshot, close this time, close enough to make the school kids scatter all at once. It came from the far side of 12-70 and AnnMarie didn't wait. Got behind a tree and stayed still. She heard footsteps. Rubber on cement. Some kinda scuffle. Homies running. Then the rain came. Big wet drops, and a wash of sound like leaves rustling wild. *Pop Pop. Pop.* She crouched low, making herself gone. *Pop. Pop Pop.* She hugged her arms around her knees and the rain poured, sheets of rain, big drops falling on the back of her neck.

Still she didn't move but she felt her hands trembling so she clenched them together to keep them still. She thought to start her countdown. Now, she thought, but only got to seven when a boy dashed past with a gun in his hand, his white shirt electric in the sudden flash of lightning. She stared at her Tims. Watched the mud splotching there, and wished more than anything she could be home.

Ten, nine, eight, seven, six, five, four, three, two, one.

She slipped inside the apartment and stood listening. Saw her mother asleep under the blanket. Pulled off her wet shoes and went into the suitcase she kept under the couch for dry clothes. When she last ate something. Peanut butter crackers at Teisha house. Wish she had the sheet music. "Let Them Sing." Then she could practice. Maybe Mr. Preston'd give her a solo. She talk to him tomorrow. She'd go to school tomorrow. All the days gone, piling up one afer another, she felt a rush, like dread, spread across her chest.

She heard Carlton walk in with his heavy step but she ignored him, bunching up her underwear, hiding it under a clean shirt.

Where you been.

AnnMarie didn't answer.

Has your mother talked to you?

AnnMarie tsked. My mother ain't say nothing. Why should she.

Carlton laughed. You like a stray dog. If you was mine, I'd beat you again.

Fuck you, marshmallow.

He lunged and she stepped, putting the TV tray between them. Then she watched, waiting to see what he gonna do.

He went into the bathroom, slammed the door.

AnnMarie waited 'til she heard the shower go on, then went into her bedroom to change. She glanced down, saw a pair of his pants on the floor. She picked them up, dug into the pockets. Empty. Pulled open the dresser drawer, found some folded bills tucked deep in the back. She hesitated, then peeled off a ten. Punk-ass muthafucker. The front door opened. AnnMarie quickly shoved the ten in her pocket and hid behind the wall, listening to Carlotta go into the kitchen.

AnnMarie stepped into the living room and Carlotta jumped.

Dang, AnnMarie, you scared me.

AnnMarie watched her pull takeout from a paper bag, smelled the jerk spice rising from the container. Made her stomach groan. She turned, reached for her backpack and headed for the door.

Some boy called for you.

Say what?

I said, some boy was calling for you.

Who was it?

I don't know. He called last night, a couple times. I said you were out.

She heard the shower go off, saw the steam curl out the crack of the bathroom door like some kinda phantom-ghost.

When Niki opened the door, she looked at AnnMarie and laughed. What's the matter with you?

AnnMarie scowled. Nothing, she said. You gonna let me in?

Niki motioned her inside and AnnMarie followed. Niki leading the way, clunking down the hall in some shiny black combat boots, a Knicks cap riding high up on her head. AnnMarie knew how she looked—chapped lips, baggy eyes and hungry. She was hungry. Tears stung the back of her nose, any second she gonna lose it.

In the kitchen, Niki sat her down in a chair, put a sandwich on a plate and slid it across the table. Niki said, I comb it out for you but you know I can't do no braid, gotta get Nadette to do that. You see the zigzag she put in Dennis hair, now that be cracksnapple-dope. AnnMarie laughed. She took a bite of sandwich, chewed and allowed a single tear to pop out, run silent down her cheek. Niki didn't notice, standing behind her, stroking the comb through her hair, the whole time talking about the order a songs, how the order matter on a album, so there be flow.

8

The next day, she went to school. In through the blue doors, past the metal detector, clocking in before first bell. She went straight to Ms. Henley's class, took a seat. Ms. Henley looked up and said, Hello stranger.

Brittany breezed by in the hallway, did a double take then backed up, her big-ass frame blocking the doorway. She was wearing a too-tight velour sweat suit, matching, black on black with a neon purple zipper. Smiling now, staring right at her. AnnMarie just tsked and looked straight ahead. Knobby-kneed bitch. Cameltoe muthafucker. Better get yourself to the Big and Tall.

Second bell rang, Ms. Henley crossed to the door as Brittany danced away, laughing. Ms. Henley shushed them, then read aloud from a book about a girl who dress in cutoffs and T-shirts when all the other girls be wearing skirts and dresses, ain't afraid a nobody judging her. This girl can run fast, faster than all the boys and they hate her for it. Ms. Henley said, Write a paragraph about someone you know, use descriptive language, de-scrip-tive language.

AnnMarie took her pencil out and got serious. She thought for a moment, then wrote:

My home-girl Niki is like the karacter. Got the baggie jeans, white tees hangin down. She dont care what no body think she just is her self. Niki be comfertabul. Smile easy. Rah, rah, raspy voice, Niki got atatud for shore. Thats how the karact

Somebody belched like a sea lion and she glanced up, losing her train of thought. She drew a small heart in the corner, then turned it into a skinny-waisted girl. Lil' Kim came to mind, squatting in the bikini, that little pose a hers, up on Darius' wall.

At lunch, AnnMarie looked for Mr. Preston but he wasn't in the music room or the classroom where he taught math 2nd and 3rd period. She caught a glimpse of Brittany across the cafeteria and decided to cut out to Mel's for lunch. Took the ten-dollar bill from her pocket, slid it across the counter. Got herself a hero and a Coke.

AnnMarie kept her eyes open in the hallway. Drifted through pre-algebra, then earth science. Sixth-period choir. AnnMarie took a seat in the front row away from Brittany. Substitute teacher walked in five minutes late, said, Mr. Preston is out. Do homework 'cause I'm a sub, not a singer. Brittany slung her backpack over her shoulder, dropped a note in AnnMarie's lap and walked out the classroom. AnnMarie didn't bother reading it. She crumpled it up, let it fall to the floor.

Bell rang, school out. AnnMarie sprang up and headed for the doors. She knew what was coming but she went out anyway, Reeboks squeaking, lockers slamming, kids pushing out the doors, their voices loud and happy the day be done.

Outside, Mr. Stubbs was already on the street, walkie in hand, his eyes on a group of boys gathering across the street. Uh-oh, something up. Five, six, seven of them standing, ain't saying nothing, got that bored look they must practice in the mirror. AnnMarie glanced away, saw Brittany pushing out the door, Tag-along 1 and Tag-along 2 trailing in her wake like she the queen a queens. *Fuck* that girl. Ain't no way she backing down. AnnMarie's eyes cut to Mr. Stubbs who was crossing the street, moving toward the boys on the corner and it was then that she saw him, Darius Greene, leaning against the fence, looking her way, into the crowd where she stood.

Her heart just leapt up and hung in her throat.

What he doing?

Oh-my-gawd.

What he doing here?

Music blasting out a headphones, kids passing, but no one going anywhere 'cause you could feel it. Something in the air. Patrice and Katelyn at her side, saying, Hey AnnMarie. The two of them stopping 'cause everybody likes a fight, that's for sure.

Even Brittany had stopped to watch. Mr. Stubbs saying, Go home. Go home. Go home. But none of them budged, nah-uh, not for Stubbs in a guard uniform, no gun. They looked past him to some far-off point in the distance. Go home. Go home. Go home. Then, in one fluid motion, Darius pushed himself off the fence and was coming across the street, looking right at her now, and it was as if he'd signaled their release because the wanna-be Bloods broke up, swaggered off in a ripple, leaving Mr. Stubbs standing on the corner alone.

Go home. Go home. Go home.

All the kids felt it, AnnMarie was sure, their eyes glued on him as he stepped up onto the curb and touched her elbow. Hers.

Her heart flopping like a fish trying to breathe air.

How come you never home, he said.

She smiled, felt her lips dry against her teeth and she was about to speak when Brittany moved past, pretending like she don't see, pretending like AnnMarie don't exist at all.

Well.

AnnMarie watched her pass, then glanced up at him, saw the dimple his smile made right there on his cheek. Pretty smile.

studio time

9

After that, he started calling.

He'd say, When you coming back to the studio.

Sometimes they'd talk on the phone for hours, her mother giving her a look, like *Who that.* Who that on the phone again. But AnnMarie'd turn her back and listen to him telling her about the new one out by RZA, the raw sound, the hip-hop breakout.

You got to have a work ethic, feel me—got to know how to show your swag but also be a businessman. You want to go out to Jamaica, fine. Talk to JJ, Paul Red, gather up the young rappers, make a mixtape. Then you think distribution, you feel me.

Yeah, okay.

We was at the Palace last night. Big Mike, he step aside, let me have a go—we tore the place down. People went stupid for that shit. People went dumb.

Tha's crazy. I wish I coulda been there.

Yeah, yeah, he'd say.

And she'd wait, halfways holding her breath. Wondering what he gonna say next, wondering what gonna come next.

You work on your a cappella, I lay you down too.

AnnMarie smiled.

Stupid in the head with love.

She started to sing every day. Walking to school. In choir, math class, earth science—it don't matter, a melody floated through her head. At home, she started taking long showers, singing one song after another, sometimes switching up the rhythm of a cover song, letting a note hang in the air, stretching it out for as long as she had breath, Carlton banging on the door, yelling, Ain't you clean yet. But she didn't care. Fuck him.

She'd heard the stories. How Darius got into it. The fights, stabbing people in the head, sticking up stores. It was outlaw, Far Rock through and through. One day they was out walking. Heading to Three Kings for the steak and eggs he got hungry for. They passed a fella who glanced her way and before AnnMarie knew what was happening, Darius had stepped to him—*The fuck you looking at? The fuck you doing, put your eyes back in your head.* In the restaurant he slid into the booth, flipped open the menu and said, What you want, AnnMarie? I got you. And she'd smiled, her eyes swimming across the page. She'd seen the boy flinch. She'd seen it.

He showed her what was behind the door, pulled it open when she'd asked. It was a walk-in closet. No clothes in there. Just a bed on the floor, a perfect fit, no room for anything else but a orange crate with candles melted down and a bottle of E&J. No room for anything 'cept two bodies, laying side by side. When she turned in the doorway, he didn't step aside. They stood there, nearly touching, and it didn't take much to close the space between them, his lips on hers, drawing her in. First kiss. Sweet kiss, fingers brushing skin.

She thought it was funny, him throwing up gang signs shirtless in front of the mirror, *blat blat blat*. She watched him make his face hard, curve those fingers just so, the whole world afraid of him. Even Carlton musta heard who he was 'cause the day Darius came by to pick her up, he hid in her room. Darius said, Is that him and AnnMarie nodded, watching him cross the living room, push open her door and stand there, his back to her, saying something she couldn't hear. But Carlton stopped bothering her after that, stopped talking to her altogether. Two ships passing. She'd think, Who you now, punk ass. Who you now.

Three weeks they'd been together, getting serious for real, like candy and song dedications, when word spread that a house party going down at 36 Gipson Street. Teisha and Sunshine put her in this badass off-the-shoulder tee, skintight Jordache and a pair a heels she had to practice walking in they so high. They left without Niki, Nadette rsking, saying it's her own fault she late. And AnnMarie didn't care right then, her head buzzing, giddy 'cause she going out—the girls was taking her out and Darius had said, I see you there.

By the time they arrived, the party was spilling people, boys mostly, most a them old, high-school age and older. AnnMarie felt her heart thumping as Sunshine leaned in and said, See that fella next to Darius—that's Big Mike. We wanna get noticed, we gotta get to the mic.

AnnMarie watched Teisha and Nadette push their way through the crowd, moving toward the big man at the center of the throng. Sunshine nudged her, passing her a silver flask. Ann-Marie sipped, then sipped again, felt the heat in her throat. The house music had gone dead, feedback screeched and bounced off the walls, then a bass line start to thump and somebody up there freestyling. AnnMarie lifted up out of her heels to see over shoulders and sure enough a cypher had begun, loose circle forming, homies ramped up, rocking they heads to the rhymes.

She could see Darius up there too. What he doing. Behind the turntables, next to Big Mike—lifting vinyl from a crate. Getting ready for the next thing. Must be. AnnMarie felt Niki step up next to her and she turned, hugging her tight.

What up, what up, what up, Niki said.

We been waiting for you, AnnMarie hollered, then saw that she'd come with the plump girl Latania who she'd met one time before.

Sunshine flicked her gaze at Latania, then yanked Niki aside. AnnMarie couldn't hear nothing what they saying but Sunshine's mouth was moving like *What you doing? What the fuck you doing?* Niki back up in her face, both of them mad tight, then she gone. Through the crowd, gone, leaving Latania to follow after.

And as quickly as it started, the cypher ended, circle broke apart, fellas reaching for their cups, lighters hitting blunts, Big Mike's voice amplified, saying, Yeah, yeah, yeah . . . We got some fine young shorties in the house tonight, call themselves the Night Shade. Sunshine pushed AnnMarie from behind. Go on, go up there.

AnnMarie stumbled in the high heels but worked her way through the crowd to the front of the room.

Darius looked up and they eyes met but Nadette was saying, Where's Niki. Where she at? Sunshine in Nadette's ear and Ann-Marie saw all them fellas out there, staring, like *Who the fuck these chicks. What the fuck can they do.* Then the microphone was in her hand and Teisha was saying, We ain't got Niki. Go, go, go . . .

Out the corner her eye, she saw the needle drop and knew

the song before the first few bars reached her ears—a slow-jam instrumental Darius liked to play and he was looking at her now, nodding his head, *uhn, uhn, uhn,* so she raised the mic to her lips and sang.

Yeah, she hushed them. *"Goin' Down."* She sang the lyrics but made it her own, finding the backbeat as the pulse, her voice lifting, pushing toward the ceiling, spreading sweet and clear. And when she opened her eyes, she saw it—all the people sway, Darius stepping up next to her, his mouth close to her ear, he said, Damn girl, you made them dumb.

And then she was his. Feet tucked up on the couch, watching him behind the console. People coming in and out the little studio room. Rappers freestyling, some a them with pieces a paper, song words on a napkin, some a them good, but some rhymes so terrible, AnnMarie just had to cringe. It didn't seem to matter though, down there in the studio room, 'cause they all wanted it—the stripped-down beats, samples from "Renegade," "Die for You," "Phat Burn"—flowing from the speakers, Darius saying, Yeah, yeah, yeah, let's go again.

Wallace came by one day. His fade grown out, the *W's* covered by a black do-rag tied snug around his head.

What up, AnnMarie . . . How you feel, he said smiling, but he seemed nervous, shifting a old gym bag from one hand to the other. She stood up from the couch and hugged him. She'd heard his father was back in Far Rock, living again with his mother. Wallace hadn't been to choir in weeks.

Where you been, Wallace.

Nah, nah, nah . . . Call me Stack.

AnnMarie laughed. Oh, okay . . . you stacking now?

Word. Hustle for the stack, you know it.

How come you ain't been to choir. Everybody miss you.

Been working on a mixtape and whatnot, trying to put something together.

He pulled a CD from his gym bag, the zipper broke, and passed it to Darius. Here's the track I was telling you about. Check it.

Darius put the CD in the player and they listened, Wallace's voice like a grown man, rich and deep, his freestyle words weaving a story, a Redfern story about throwin' down and survival.

AnnMarie said, Dang, Wallace. You got a ill flow. I didn't know you was rappin' now.

Wallace smiled. Trying my hand and whatnot.

Word, Darius said, thoughtfully. Sound like a hit.

Wallace glanced at him, then ducked his head. Give it to Big Mike? I owes you.

Darius said, Yeah, I show it around. I give it to him.

But soon as he left, Darius tossed the CD in the trash.

AnnMarie looked at him, surprised. Why you do that? You didn't like it?

Competition, baby. Competition.

One Sunday before the party on Gipson Street, Darius had been out with his homies. AnnMarie wanted to jump out her skin, her mind on him 24/7, skin atingle, the memory of his touch, his lips on hers, locking her in a daze of love ache. No way she could stay inside with Blessed all day, so she wandered over to Niki's.

Niki's brother Bodie opened the door. He said, They in there.

She climbed the stairs, heard a soft rustling and pushed open the bedroom door.

At first AnnMarie didn't know what they doing, why Niki was pressed up against the plump girl like that. Then she saw Niki's hands draw away, her lips pulling out of a kiss and AnnMarie took a step back, startled.

What you want, AnnMarie? Niki said sharply.

Oh. Sorry, I was just looking for y'alls.

Niki snapped the pick from her back pocket and started working it through her cinnamon curls. Sorry, AnnMarie said again. She crossed the room and sat on Niki's bed. No one said anything for a minute, then AnnMarie pulled out a pack of Kools and said, You want one? Sure, I have one, the girl said and plucked a smoke from the pack.

She said, I'm Latania, who you? AnnMarie told the girl her name, then they lit up, blowing streams out the open window. Latania said, Turn on the radio, Niki, so Niki put on the radio and they listened to Hot 97 for a while, DJ Drastic playing a string of songs, and by the time "Waterfalls" came on, Niki seemed to've relaxed and they all started in about the hottest girl groups—TLC, En Vogue, SWV, Destiny's Child . . .

Later, Latania caught a dollar van back to Jamaica where her mother lived and Niki walked AnnMarie home.

They walked a ways in silence. Niki's shoulder brushing hers, cigarette smell still on her breath.

Don't say nothing to Nadette.

Nadette? Why would I.

Jus' don't say nothing to nobody.

AnnMarie said, I won't.

And she didn't. But she thought about all the times Niki had slipped off with Nadette, all the things she hadn't known, and it crystallized right then, how sometimes you grow up without nobody having to explain.

———

In the walk-in, Darius had said, Come lay with me a small little minute.

And when he eased himself into her slow, he whispered, You okay, you okay, baby . . . ? His lips by her ear, hands running down her body. Stroking. Licking, making her wet.

She'd said, Don't stop. Don't stop.

holdin' it down

10

If you asked her now, years later, she'd tell you it wasn't one thing in particular—a certain beef or comment dropped, the need for retaliation or an unspoken urge that made her life spin off the way it did. There'd been the studio room and the walk-in closet and the fact they was fucking like bunnies, AnnMarie thinking Darius was It—the be-all, end-all, the rope that tethered her. Coulda been the situation that happened in high school with the silver fox–lined coat or Carlton and Carlotta still in the house or the memories popping up outta the blue. Coulda been. Or maybe it was that she started to sense the smallness of her life, knew lines had been drawn but didn't know how to cross them.

Far Rock.

The Rock.

Lost Town, Ghost Town.

Niki had told her once, Far Rock was built on top of an old graveyard. Bones buried all the way from Bayswater to Bannister. She wondered if it was true.

There was no map.

She had no compass.

But she wanted to change things.

It wasn't a conscious thing, or maybe it was.

11

Eighth grade, spring semester, Brittany finally got kicked out for breaking some teacher's jaw. Gone for good. AnnMarie heard about it in the lunchroom, a hush falling across the table as Patrice leaned forward and told. She got shipped off to one a those juvie schools for violent kids, Patrice said. My mother friends with the teacher. Mr. Nobella, he in the hospital. He pressing charges. Good, AnnMarie thought. I hope he do. Fat bitch finally getting what she deserve.

AnnMarie walked around on cloud nine, having discovered orgasms, making Darius wait for her as she found the spot and felt the lapping sensation move through her body down to her toes. Daydreaming in school, the throb between her legs making her sigh into her hand. But mostly she focused on the words and numbers and passed her tests and sang for Mr. Preston in the front row.

In May, he took the choir class to sing for a school over in Cedarhurst, a rich neighborhood on the other side of the expressway. Mr. Preston knew the principal back when he went to Teacher College. He said, Consider this an opportunity, people. They didn't know what he meant and didn't care. Field trip meant no school for the day.

They walked in a cluster, Mr. Preston leading them across streets and boulevards and nobody skipped out, everyone curious to see what a white school look like from the inside. They weren't disappointed. Air-conditioning in the auditorium. Velvet curtains hanging. Spotlights mounted from the ceiling. AnnMarie tried to keep her eyeballs in her head as they filed across the stage. Never seen so many white people all at once. Mr. Preston shaking hands with the man must be the principal.

Down front in the rows of seats, all those mouths moving—she couldn't hear no specific words, just a sound like a unified rumble bouncing off her eardrum. Mr. Preston rapped his baton on the music stand and it got quiet. The choir kids straightened their backs the way they practiced, and when a paper airplane sailed through the air and landed at Mr. Preston's feet, they ignored it, singing first "Precious Love," then "Classic #45," and when Ann-Marie's solo came she dialed those kids out of focus, only thing matter was Mr. Preston's baton moving—one, two, three, four. She took a breath, pushed the air out her lungs in the form of a note, the right note in the right key and soon her voice was crashing off the walls, off the velvet curtains and those spotlights no one had turned on. When she got done they clapped. All the white kids clapping mad loud. *Respect,* thank you very much. She looked over at Mr. Preston and could see the relief on his face. Halfway bowing his head, Principal Man walking over to shake his hand.

The choir kids stepped down off the row of bleachers, gathering in a loose cluster, waiting for Mr. Preston to finish marveling. Beautiful space. Great acoustics. AnnMarie watched the Cedarhurst kids file out, taking all the air with them as they left the room. Principal Man rocking back on his heels, saying something. Something about a PTA to thank.

Then they were heading home, a empty feeling in AnnMarie's chest, she didn't know why. They'd passed through the hallways, peering in the classrooms where the doors had been left open, taking in the big rooms and the white kids staring, passing out the back where the tennis court was, kids doing calisthenics on a ball field. Walking past all the shiny cars parked in the school lot, trimmed bushes next to all those windows, no mesh bars blocking out the light. Blocks and blocks they walked, and when one of the choir kids kicked the lid off a garbage can Mr. Preston kept walking, stiff-backed, chin out, leading them back across the expressway.

All year she'd kept in touch with Crystal over the phone. After the hotel, Crystal's mother found a place to live in the basement of a house in Springfield. AnnMarie'd said, Springfield? Where that at. Crystal said, I don't know. Somewhere out here . . . Crystal told her how she found a cat dead in the street, its head mashed up and bloody. She asked about Wallace and AnnMarie told her he'd dropped out. How he a rapper now.

Sometimes she'd see him around the way, cyphering, putting all the other boys to shame.

Start of 9th grade at Far Rock High School, her mother switched out the walker for a cane and was moving around more. Ann-Marie would see her down on the street, sitting with Crystal's grandma on two lawn chairs, catching the last of the September light but still glaring when she went by with Teisha or Nadette or Niki. They a bad influence, she'd say. AnnMarie just tsked. She'd told her and told her, they a singing group. They singing. Blessed didn't believe her. She'd heard through the grapevine about the dancing and thought they was rude girls. Loose girls and vulgar.

She didn't say nothing about Darius. For some reason, Blessed didn't mind Darius. Even though they was smoking weed and making love and music, like Lauryn and Wyclef.

October came with rain and more rain. The whole world turning soggy and wet.

One school morning, AnnMarie got herself up early, threw on a sweater and ran over to Nadette's building to get back the coat she'd loaned her friend.

Nadette was sitting in the kitchen, wearing a low-cut leopard-print camisole, counting money, a huge pile a money spread out on the table. AnnMarie said, Dang Nadette, that's a lot a money. Nadette tsked, then stretched her arms above her head, yawning. She said, Girl, I earned it.

AnnMarie said, Can I get my coat back? Darius had bought it for her. Special for the start of high school. It was a cropped black leather coat, lined in silver fur and mad sexy. All the girls asked to borrow it.

AnnMarie found it laying on the floor next to a pair of five-inch heels and shrugged it on. She went out into a fine mist, holding her book bag over her head, walked the eight blocks up Mott Avenue to Far Rock High School, a place she looked forward to, knowing all the beefs of her middle-school years were behind her, where Darius waited for her each afternoon and no one dared mess with her.

She pulled open the door, went up the steps and got in line, kids slinging they backpacks up on the table, moving one by one under the metal detector, and when her turn came the guard waved her through, the alarm slicing the air, making all the kids turn and look. The guard saying, Empty your pockets but she was puzzled. What the fuck set that off. Her hands going into her pockets, all her pockets—her fingers feeling the cold slim piece of metal and she groaned inside, moaned inside 'cause there it was, Nadette's four-inch switchblade dropping into the plastic tray.

This time they called her mother. Two-month suspension. We have a no-weapons policy, Principal said. Blessed was furious. She said, What you doing with a blade. It wasn't mine, Ma, I keep telling you. It was Nadette's. She borrowed my coat and left it in the pocket.

Carlton said, Birds of a feather, Miss Blessed. You hang with ghetto, you gon be ghetto too.

Shut the fuck up, Carlton, AnnMarie said. Nadette got a job. She make more money than you, Mr. Nobody Driver.

He just laughed and walked away.

She wanted to poke pins into his eyeballs, she hate him that much.

Well, me na gon homeschool you, Blessed said. And you damn na hanging around here. The school don't want you, get yourself another school.

She went to Springfield High after that. Crystal told her to choose the school. We be together, she said. We'll have fun. But one week into the transfer, Crystal's mother moved again, this time out to Canarsie.

It took the wind out of her.

At Far Rock, she'd been reading *Where for art thou o Romeo* and sloping graphs in math, singing "My Sweetest Love." Coming in midsemester, she didn't know what was going on. No choir. Math teacher talking about *quadratic functions*. What the fuck a quadratic function? She start to feel anxious all the time, that feeling like she gonna up and blow away. Like a helium balloon let go in the wind, floating higher and higher 'til it wasn't nothing but a speck in the sky. You blink and it be gone.

At lunch she'd stand with her tray, wondering where she supposed to sit, all the kids at tables huddled together, she'd stand and stare. Where the fuck she supposed to sit. Gym came before lunch and there was a door there near the girls' locker room that led to the street. She started using it. Caught the bus back to Far Rockaway and to Darius, who was free most days—three years of high school and he'd been done.

They made love in the warm darkness of the walk-in, hips grinding, limbs entwined, and she felt that floaty feeling go away, his body like a anchor holding her down.

12

Two months into the transfer, she came home one afternoon looking for a notebook she'd left behind that had phrases and songs and little ideas written inside. She'd fallen asleep on the couch and when she woke, her mother was leaning against her cane, watching her.

You know why you so tired? Blessed asked.

Say what, AnnMarie said, blinking.

Me say, you know why you tired.

What, Ma, why you bothering me . . .

It was sweet going in, eh? Now it sour coming out . . .

AnnMarie stared at her.

That's right, the doctor told me, you pregnant.

It was true, four days ago AnnMarie'd gone to the clinic where her mother got her prescriptions filled. She'd taken a test. She'd sat on the crinkly paper in the examination room, just sat there, dumb. Couldn't move. Doctor talking, talking, she didn't hear a word he said. Even though it's what she'd wanted.

What you got to say, AnnMarie, Blessed said.

Fuck you and fuck him for opening his big mouth, AnnMarie said. Then she burst into tears. She hadn't told nobody. Not Niki, not even Darius.

AnnMarie had been skipping school all week when it happened. Lazing around at Darius' house, his mother at work, they'd been getting high and watching TV. AnnMarie felt moody and depressed. Bored out of her mind. Even with Darius, all the little dramas in the studio room. Tempers flaring over stupid shit. AnnMarie'd been flipping channels and found Oprah talking. Some doctor-type person up there on stage, the two a them talking about how to make a baby. A white lady from the audience start to tell her story, how she trying and trying with her man, how all she want in life is a child and a family and how that be the key to happiness. Then she start to cry. Ann-Marie felt sorry for that lady, pouring out her soul for everyone in America to see, and later, when she and Darius made love in the walk-in, AnnMarie felt the rhythm of his thrusts like a promise and she whispered in his ear, I wanna make a family with you. Darius said, Word. Just before he grunted and came.

Afterward she stayed on her back, like the Oprah doctor had said, raising her legs up in the air, to catch the sperm inside. What you doing? Darius asked. She folded her knees over her chest. Wrapped her arms around her shins and cradled herself, not stirring. She said, I'm making us a family.

Blessed crept across the room with her cane and sat down next to AnnMarie on the couch. She reached for her, pulling her into an embrace but AnnMarie felt the panic rising like walls snapping up around her. She shook Blessed off, crying, No Ma, don't . . . Stop touching me.

But Blessed held on, her arms tight around AnnMarie who struggled to pull away. God don't like ugly, AnnMarie, God don't like ugly.

But *Ma* . . . I got my singing, how'm I supposed to go to school. I ain't doing it!

You will. You'll go to school and have the baby. I'm gon help you. And I tell you this—if you kill me grandchild, I put you back in foster care and you'll burn up in hell.

Carlton walked in and stared at them.

What happened now, Carlton said.

AnnMarie felt a sudden rage and helplessness. Why you gotta be here, she screamed. Why don't you get the fuck outta my house.

But it was AnnMarie who left.

Walking mad slow over to Nameoke where Darius lived. She didn't know what he gonna say. Her eyes swollen, face blotchy. What he gonna say.

She'd seen him fly into a rage before. Seen him knock his mother down a flight of stairs. His mother, Darla, grabbing on to his arm to keep her balance, but he'd wrenched free and back she fell. Up in his sister's face. Beefing. Watched him clock some fella in the head, just a little thing set it off, and when the boy fell, he beat him bloody.

He was sitting up on the front porch with Raymel and Jason. Raymel glancing at her, then away as she approached.

Darius stood up and frowned. What happened, he said.

Inside the kitchen, away from the others, she whispered it, afraid of his reaction, even though he'd seen her do it, hold her legs in the air. Even though he never used protection, not once in the entire time they was together. Still she was afraid. But before she could look up, she heard him whoop, felt his arms go around her waist and he was swinging her around. AnnMarie's legs dangling off the floor, her arms around his shoulders, heart pounding.

———

They went over to the liquor store and bought a bottle of Hennessy to celebrate.

Darius telling everybody—we got Trinidad, we got Jamaican, we got Indian blood. Laughing and cheering. That gonna be one beautiful baby. And AnnMarie sat back on the porch, hearing the *clink-clink* of glass, and told herself to chill, feeling certain now it wasn't something she dreamed up on her own. He'd claimed it. They doing it together—making a family, a true family together.

And later, after he got drunk and told her he was wild with love for her, she didn't go home, she stayed all night with him in the walk-in. Fourteen years old, with her own man and a baby on the way. Right before he fell asleep she said, You gonna marry me, Darius, and he said, 'Course I marry you. You turn eighteen, we getting married.

He fell asleep but she didn't. She lay there looking up at the small cut of window, watching a patch of light move across the wall then disappear. She felt his arm over her waist and thought about the room her mother once had in the shelter.

It was a small little room. Very small with a twin bed and a chair. AnnMarie was living with Grandma Mason. In the beginning, her mother would come sometimes on the weekend and take her out of there. They'd go to the park, to McDonald's, sometimes to church. They held hands. In the evening, she'd take AnnMarie back to the shelter. But there was no childs allowed in the bedrooms after lights out, so Blessed would have to sneak her in. In the shower room, she'd set her inside a laundry bag she kept in a cart, pull the cart down the hall to her room.

AnnMarie sat scrunched up, clothes on top her head and she'd hear Blessed whisper. Quiet now. Shhhh. She'd sit in the bag, mad quiet, waiting 'til the lady check and leave. Then she'd feel her mother's hands lifting her out and they'd sleep together in that narrow bed. The wall on one side a her, Blessed on the other. Blessed's arm around her waist and AnnMarie'd think, I'm in my mother's bed, with my mother and everything fine. In the morning, Blessed put her back inside the laundry bag, pull the string, wheel the cart outta there. Take her down to the street, she'd go back to Grandma Mason house.

baby love

13

Like a thief in the night I was, running from your father. Like a thief in the night. Blessed leaned on her cane, giving AnnMarie one a her looks, like she mean business.

Except AnnMarie had heard it before. And it wasn't night. It was daytime. He was at the sugarcane factory when Blessed left, shoving clothes into a bag, screen door slamming.

You don't got something to say?

AnnMarie yawned. I heard you, Ma, I know the story.

Ever since Blessed had found out about the baby, it was like she was revived, on her feet asking AnnMarie how she feel, do she need something, asking where she going and when she coming back. And in between all the asking, she'd find a way to tell it, again and again—the story of her great escape. How he raped her. How he beat her with a pipe. A pipe used for plumbing.

You is a rape child, Blessed would say. But I kept you, you see how I kept you?

Like some kinda hero thief. Stealing past cornfields, past the houses made a concrete. Past the dirt yards and goats. Dogs barking, stray dogs so skinny they ribs show through. Snarling at any scrap a life that pass them by. AnnMarie pictured her without shoes on her feet, dress hem flapping, her neck twisted 'round, a look like fear turn to triumph in her eye.

'Cept she had shoes. Shoes and a bag full a clothes, AnnMarie remembered. A rainstorm had turned the dirt to mud, and there was ants, millions of ants clawing their way to sunlight. Blessed walked five miles to St. Margaret, caught the bus to Port of Spain, her feet itching and burning, ants crawling out her shoes, up her thigh, hungry for blood. Traveling papers fixed by a lady named Miss Deacon for three hundred dollars. She'd spent a year saving. A year of broken ribs and fat lips and eyeballs hanging out their socket. Clinic man patch her up, send her on her way. If she stayed behind, she'd end up like Jahar, her firstborn. That baby got shook and banged by AnnMarie's father. Shook and banged 'til he was dead.

You got his blood, Blessed said. But you see how I kept you.

Yeah, yeah. AnnMarie thought. 'Cept for all those years you didn't.

She remembered the first time her mother spoke about her father. In that narrow bed at the homeless shelter when she was a child. Wrapped around Blessed in the stillness, AnnMarie hadn't understood all the words. But she knew sadness. Felt it in her mother's chest rising and falling, in her eyes that refused to open. AnnMarie had reached up and patted her cheek, tried to pry an eye open, wanting her mother back.

When had her love for Blessed changed? AnnMarie couldn't remember.

Carlton and Carlotta had gone visiting, so AnnMarie went into her room to change. She could smell the food cooking. Her mother'd been a good cook once, before the stroke. Now she hardly cooked at all, fingers shaking, recipes turned inside out. Maybe that's what AnnMarie's father had liked about her. She'd cook up the rice and peas, macaroni pie, curry goat. There weren't no picture of her father. No way a seeing his face in her mind. Just a angry dude. She looked at herself in the mirror. Brown eyes staring. Was he in there?

AnnMarie heard the knock and let him in. Darius stood in the doorway, smelling like Irish Spring. She leaned against the frame, smiling, seeing the flowers in his hand. She took the bouquet wrapped in clear plastic. For your moms, he said, his hand moving to her belly where the baby was forming.

Blessed had sent AnnMarie to borrow a card table from across the hall and they all sat down, Darius' hands folded loosely in his lap. But AnnMarie felt the flutterflies bouncing around. What she got to be nervous for. What the fuck I care my mother like him. I love him and he loves me.

Are you in school, Darius?

Ma, let him eat.

No, I finished off with that. I'm interested in business opportunities and whatnot.

Oh, really . . .

Ma.

Shh, we're talking, AnnMarie.

Yeah, I'd like to own my own business. A recording business.

Oh, that's nice. AnnMarie says you have a music studio at your house, you making a living with that?

Little here and there but I got a fee schedule planned out, charge the artist for they recording time, and if I produce, I add on top a that.

A fee schedule?

You know, like money for my time.

Oh, that's smart . . .

Blah blah blah blah blah . . . AnnMarie wanted to tell her to please shut up. What she know about money anyway. Hadn't earned a dollar in her life.

But Blessed leaned back all of a sudden and went quiet, looking at Darius, like she takin' him in. Soaking him up with her eyes.

Finally she said, Well, AnnMarie, looks like you got yourself a good thing.

Ma, please.

Please, Ma, AnnMarie said, jumping up. 'Cause Blessed had started to cry. Tears coming out her eyes, running down her face, shaky fingers brushing them aside.

No, AnnMarie. I'm happy for you. You a sweet couple and I wish you the best in life, I do. I bless you both. You're blessed and I'm gonna help with the baby any way I can.

Thank you, Miss Blessed, Darius said. We appreciate it.

Go on, sit down AnnMarie and eat. Eat now.

Darius leaned over his plate then, and began to eat. Didn't matter the food mad nasty, salt for sugar, sugar for allspice—he dug in and ate. AnnMarie looked at him sideways and he glanced at her and smiled.

Blessed had a boyfriend once, before the stroke when AnnMarie was ten years old. His name was Prince. He had a table set up on Mott Avenue where he sold incense and statuettes and dolls the size of a grown child. Beautiful dolls with brown skin and long, cascading ringlets and eyelids that flipped open and closed. Blessed would pick AnnMarie up from school and they'd wander home, buy a thing or two from the fruit stand then stop to talk to Prince who wore a Muslim cap he called a kufi. AnnMarie'd peel back the mango skin and suck the juice, watching her mother and Prince talking. Blessed would tilt her head to the side, smiling, then laugh outright at something he said. Then Prince was Blessed's boyfriend, coming around the apartment, staying after supper to watch the TV. He went with them to church. For walks on the boardwalk. Sometimes he brought bags a groceries. He'd lean down, cup her chin in his big hand. He'd say, Hello Ann-Marie, how's you. Her mother'd laugh and say, She growin' what she is. Eating me out of house and home. And in these moments, AnnMarie'd lean against her mother feeling shy but happy, and Blessed would pull her into an embrace, like she was something special.

He had a house with black bars on the windows down by the water there on Healy Avenue. It had a big living room with a gigantic TV set on the carpet. Shiny clean kitchen, perfume soaps in the bathroom. Looks like you got a feminine touch, Blessed said, looking at him. Prince rocked back and forth on his heels and laughed. I like a clean house, it's true. He showed AnnMarie the room where he kept the dolls, opened up a big box and peeled away the sheet of plastic. Dolls the size of AnnMarie herself, laying faceup like soldiers in a row, their eyes open, staring at her. AnnMarie gasped. They so pretty, she said. Go on, you can take one. She'd never had a doll before, not even a stuffed animal. Grandma Mason didn't allow it. Thought it made them spoiled. She knew she was too old to be carrying a doll around, but Ann-Marie couldn't resist. They was too beautiful.

Prince turned on the TV and the room lit up all at once. Blessed said, Go on, sit down and watch. We goin' to talk. Then they went down the hall and disappeared into the room at the end. AnnMarie stood at the closed door and listened. She heard murmurs, then it went quiet.

After dinner was ate and the card table folded again, Blessed fell asleep sitting up on the couch. AnnMarie pulled Darius into the kitchen and pressed against his rock-solid body, locking lips, his tongue soft and spicy in her mouth and she felt herself go wet, hungry for him even with thoughts of Prince pushing their way to the surface. Prince who'd hoisted her onto his back to play piggyback, his fingers reaching under her dress, poking inside her underwear 'til she wriggled free. She ran into the other room where her mother was and told. AnnMarie couldn't understand why Blessed slapped her silly, saying *Look how you embarrassing Mr. Prince. No one wanna touch you, why you think everyone wanna touch you* but it was too late, Prince never came around again, and Blessed never had no man since.

AnnMarie never knew why. Whether Blessed had chosen her over this man. But she caught her one time, days later, standing in the bathroom, face to the wall, weeping. Shoulders caved in, head bowed in prayer, making small little sounds, like sorrow. Ann-Marie felt a stab of fear and ran to her, pressing herself against her mother's big frame, afraid Blessed would disappear into that black hole of sadness and never return.

She felt Darius' hands slide up her back, his arms engulfing her into a deep caress. She rested her head just under his chin and heard him sigh.

She said, We gonna have a baby.

Yeah . . . yeah, he said.

Ida B.

14

When the bus pulled up, she got on, walked down the aisle and took a seat, banging her knees against plastic, cramming herself in next to the window. Dang, she was uncomfortable. She sat up, unbuttoned her jeans which helped a little, she'd have to get some new jeans soon 'cause this just wasn't working.

Out the window the icy rain came down in sheets but it was moist inside too and she felt warm and wet all over—forehead, back, pits dripping. She wanted to take off her down coat but the nausea was pushing its way around her stomach, knocking up into her throat, bus lurching through traffic just made the bad feeling worse. She leaned her head on the glass and tried to breathe.

By the time she walked into Ida B. eight minutes past nine, the hallway was empty. Still she took her time, wandering into Room 5 where three girls sat at the long metal table, their bellies big, seven, eight months along and another girl, a new girl she'd never seen before slumped at the far end of the table. Hello, Ann-Marie, Miss Westwood said. We're reading from *Views of the City*, page 68. Go on, Camille, keep reading.

> . . . *What do we look at*
> *when we look out our windows?*
> *Is it an expanse of skyline,*
> *an array of rooftops,*
> *a sliver of green . . .*

AnnMarie's view was of the new girl. Got her hand cupped under her chin, head tilted, eyes on the ceiling. Girl need to get her braids worked on. Wash her hair, something. Dandruff there in the part-line.

Her eyes drifted up to the clock on the wall. Heard the heat hissing through the radiator. Only ten fifteen. English, math, then lunch. Her stomach pitched and groaned. She leaned back and unzipped her pants. Hand on her belly, she counted seven girls today, the last two drifting in just before ten, the room quiet now as they sat, doing silent reading from a book called *Desiree's Star*. AnnMarie brought the book up to her face and tried to focus, but her mind drifted to her stomach again and to her feet that felt too big for her shoes. Finally, she scraped back her chair and stood. Miss Westwood looked up, expectantly. I'm thirsty, AnnMarie whispered. Can I get a drink a water?

AnnMarie wandered down the hall to the drinking fountain. She filled her mouth and swallowed, burped then drank some more. Outside Miss July's office there was a bulletin board that AnnMarie liked to look at.

Eat Right, Live Right.

Are You Expecting?
Gynecology and You.

Teen Support Group.
Tuesdays 4:00 p.m. Join Now.

When AnnMarie returned, Miss Westwood was setting a bag of Golden Delicious on the table. Go on, girls. Fuel up. Chairs pushed back, everyone stood, stretched, yawned, then reached over and took a apple. Did everyone make it to the end of the chapter? Miss Westwood asked. How many got to the end . . . A couple of hands went up. Let's talk about what Desiree wants. Who is Desiree anyway? What makes her unique?

The new girl leaned over and whispered, They got a McDonald's out here?

Lunch bell rang, they left the building, walked down Liberty Avenue, the new girl taking her time, walking mad slow even though it was bitter cold outside. The streets frozen, heaps of snow crusted black with dirt and exhaust, refusing to melt. AnnMarie asked her name, where she from, how old she was and the girl said, My name Crystal.

AnnMarie's eyes went wide. She said, Shoot, tha's my homegirl's name.

Word?

We was gonna go to high school together, over there in Springfield but then she moved again and I was out there by myself. You know Springfield Gardens?

The girl didn't answer, shuffling along, her gaze on her feet.

Yeah, it was fucked-up, AnnMarie went on. I hated it out there.

Tha's too bad, the other Crystal said.

They stood in line, the girl playing with her lip, looking up at the menu board.

How many weeks are you?

Huh?

How far along are you?

Crystal looked at AnnMarie like she don't understand the question.

AnnMarie said, You pregnant, ain't you?

Huh-uh, noooo . . .

AnnMarie frowned. How come you at Ida B. then?

Crystal tsked. They made me go.

Tha's crazy, AnnMarie said. So you ain't pregnant?

My mother told me I got to go the doctor.

You do a pregnancy test?

I was supposed to go but I missed my appointment. I don't want nobody touching me down there. Huh-uh.

AnnMarie frowned, looking at her belly. Girl, let me see you.

Crystal pushed her jacket aside and lifted her tee. AnnMarie saw the skin tight around a melon-size bump. Oh, yeah. She definitely pregnant.

Can I help you? the boy in uniform asked.

I only got a dolla, Crystal said out loud.

AnnMarie glanced at her. Why she want to go to Mac Donald she only got a dollar.

What can I get for a dolla, Crystal asked the boy.

The boy swung around, looking up at the board. You can get a hamburger. Seventy-nine cent, but a cheeseburger put you over. That's a dolla five with tax.

Ummmm, the girl said, pulling on her lip.

Dang, AnnMarie thought. This girl got to be slow.

Go on, AnnMarie said. I got you. Get something to eat.

When she got home that afternoon, she sat on the bed and cried. Why she acting so nice. Spending cash money Darius had given her on this stranger. Only thing that girl got in common with Crystal was her name. She missed her friends. Niki spending all her time over in Jamaica with the plump girl, Latania. Nadette dancing nights. They'd stopped practicing almost completely. Last time she was over there, the nausea hit her like a Mack truck. She didn't even make it home, puking her guts up right there at the curb.

AnnMarie let out a moan.

Her mother came to the door, asked her what's wrong but AnnMarie didn't answer, just pulled the covers over her head and cried some more, the tears pouring down her face like she Niagara Falls. Her mother hobbled in, sat on the bed. Don't worry, Blessed chuckled, those your hormones talking. She pushed a tissue into her hand and told her to blow.

Blessed been doing that lately. Acting nice. Awake and on her feet. Acting like a mother to her again. Three weeks ago, she'd told Carlton and Carlotta they had to go. AnnMarie couldn't believe it. Pinky'd returned from Trinidad and Blessed told her, I'm gonna be a grandmother, *Praise be.* AnnMarie moved back into her bedroom. Got to sleep in her own bed again, close the door if she want to.

Around dinnertime, AnnMarie got a craving for oranges and ate two before her mother fed her curried chicken and rice, heaped the plate full and brought it to her on a tray. AnnMarie pulled out her homework, did two math questions then fell asleep in front of the TV. Woke with the fat feeling in her stomach so she walked over to Darius' house for some exercise.

He's out, AnnMarie, his mother Darla said, but come on in.

She waited in his studio room. After a while, she fell asleep on the couch and when she woke again, she lay there listening to the far-off sounds of the street, feeling warm and heavy all over. Darius' sister voice came through the floorboards. She was yelling something about a robe, where her robe at, something. Vanessa pregnant too except her baby daddy live in Averne, met him at a house party six months back. You lucky, she'd said to AnnMarie. Darius loves you.

Upstairs, Darla was in the kitchen.

She said, Where you going, AnnMarie, sit for a minute.

AnnMarie pulled out a chair and sat. Darla said, Are you hungry? I got these rice and peas over here. You want me to make you a plate?

AnnMarie said, No thank you, Miss Darla, I'm okay.

You sure? You look small to me. Darius' mother had a soft way of talking, always with the soft voice. It was no surprise Darius never did nothing she said. Still, AnnMarie liked her. Always asking, How you, you hungry, you thirsty? What you need.

AnnMarie said, Birth class start up on Monday. I hope he go with me.

Birth class, what kind of birth class?

They told us about it at Ida B. Wells where I go to school. Like a Lamaze class or something, you know Lamaze? They teach you how to breathe, contracting, when to push . . . That's what my teacher said.

When I had my babies, I never took a class. I just breathe on my own, she said chuckling. He gonna do that with you?

I got to talk to him about it.

Okay, then. Okay. Mrs. Greene slid a plate of rice and peas in front of her just as Darius walked in with Raymel. Raymel barely spoke to her these days. Ducking his head, looking the other way like he embarrassed. Upstaged and outshined.

AnnMarie turned in her seat, said, Hey baby.

Darius said, What up but kept going through the kitchen, down the stairs to the basement.

You goin' to these classes with AnnMarie, his mother called with her soft voice. Darius didn't answer. All AnnMarie heard was they shoes on the wood steps.

She wondered if she should follow him. She hadn't told him

she was coming but why should she've. She heard the *thump thump thump* of a bass line start up, lifting through the floor. Mrs. Greene didn't seem to notice, sweeping crumbs into her hand. AnnMarie got up and went downstairs. Raymel was lighting a blunt, the weed smoke filling the air. AnnMarie crossed to the window and opened it.

Darius said, Blow that shit out the window. Raymel glanced at AnnMarie, then took a step, exhaling toward the window, saying, So what you gonna do?

Darius tsked. I ain't gonna do shit. He want to trip like that, let him . . . He owes *me*.

AnnMarie sat on the couch and watched him hit the blunt. He said, Remember that night at the Palace. Those cuts was mine, he trying to take credit.

She wondered who they talking about. Probably Big Mike. Those two in some kinda rivalry. It bored her. Darius and his beefing. Who said what to who. Who down and who ain't. Not enough room on the ladder for everybody. She stared at the posters up on the wall. Lil' Kim with her skinny waist, squatting in that pose a hers. AnnMarie didn't have a waist no more. Just blubber and a baby.

She stood up.

Darius said, Where you going? Glancing at her now as she crossed to the door.

I'ma head home. She paused in the doorway, hoping he'd walk with her.

But he beckoned to her with his chin so she crossed the room and took the kiss he planted on her lips. She didn't say nothing about Lamaze or the weed smoke she knew was bad for the baby.

15

All the bus rides back and forth, AnnMarie had time to think. Out to Jamaica where the school was. The Ida B. girls housed on the ground floor of a three-story cement building used by Rainbow Academy, a suspension site for violent offenders. All the last-chance kids no school wanted. The bus winding along Snake Road past the airport, planes hovering mad low in the icy sky, one after another, their bellies looming as they made their descent. AnnMarie would turn her face from the window. She thought about the little things. Like how she had to pee all the time, how she felt bloated like a whale—face, feet, hands, stomach, legs— but she couldn't help herself. Pangs a hunger gnawing, she'd go through boxes of saltines with cheese spread, peanut butter out the jar, oranges, mangoes, cornflakes with milk. Song fragments drifted in. She'd try to piece them together, search for the words gone missing but was frustrated by her own fatigue.

She thought about the last time she got up on stage to sing. At the white school over in Cedarhurst. About Mr. Preston's expression, that look of relief. All the white kids filing out. Principal Man never made no introductions. A whole school full of kids but they shared no conversation, not even a hello. AnnMarie puzzled over it.

What difference do it make anyway. Your feet get swelled, you gain some weight. You buy a slow girl some french fries.

On Wednesday, Crystal was the only girl sitting at the long metal table when she walked into Room 5 at half past nine.

Where is everybody? AnnMarie asked as she dumped her backpack on the floor.

Leandra went to get a sonogram, Miss Westwood said. I don't know where the other girls are.

AnnMarie said, You okay, Miss Westwood?

I'm okay.

Ain't you sleeping?

Not so well.

Maybe you pregnant too, AnnMarie joked.

No, AnnMarie, I'm not pregnant. I'm disappointed. I expect you girls to accomplish something here. Now take out your math sheet from yesterday and let's go over the answers.

AnnMarie dug through her backpack, found the worksheet bunched up at the bottom.

She looked at it. I ain't finished mines.

So finish it now, Miss Westwood said sharply.

What she tripping for, AnnMarie thought.

She tried to catch Crystal's eye but that girl on another planet.

At Darius' house that evening, she sat at the kitchen table with Vanessa, watching two grown men carry first his turntables, then his speakers, up from the basement and out the front door.

What they doing, AnnMarie said quietly.

Vanessa shrugged. They been after him for a while. Phone ringing off the hook.

Who been after him, AnnMarie asked.

Z-Sounds. He got his shit on installment. Fuck if he making the payments.

AnnMarie felt a stab of panic. She stood, crossing to the basement door and listened. Installment? He never told her nothin' about installments. She thought he was fine with money. That they was fine. She heard his footsteps now and backed away as he strode past her and out the front door, the look on his face silencing her.

Vanessa got up and stretched. Then she went outside to watch. AnnMarie followed.

They were loading Darius' equipment into a black van. Another homie leaned against the driver door, hands folded loose over his crotch, just leaning and waiting, his eye on Darius who stood barefoot on the front porch.

Vanessa sucked her teeth.

Shut yo' mouth, Darius said. Why you even standing here?

Fuck you. I live here.

Vanessa was further along than AnnMarie, in her seventh month, and her sweatshirt rose up over her belly showing skin.

Look at you, y'all like some ghetto ho, Darius said as he went past into the house.

Vanessa tsked. At least I ain't getting repo'd.

AnnMarie turned, watching the van pull away with the equipment inside. She could feel the stillness settle on her shoulders, the van disappearing around the corner, Vanessa, quiet now in Darius' absence.

She went down to the studio room to ask him why. To say what happened, baby.

All the wires pulled loose from the walls, laying on the floor like black snakes uncoiled and lifeless.

Darius was putting on his shoes. He said, Don't say nothing.

AnnMarie tsked, frowning.

Did I? Did I say something, she asked, watching him. Seeing all the pent-up, unspoken inadequacy written as anger across his face. Things gone wrong and nothing to do to stop it. 'Cept a fight, maybe. A fight be good for something. She felt it coming.

The next day, Miss Westwood was happy again, six girls at the metal table when AnnMarie walked in. Camille was saying, Shoot, I get me a C-section. No way I'ma be ripped to shreds. My va-geegee too precious.

Pietra laughed, then groaned, laying her cheek flat on the table. I already got these pains back here, she said.

Miss Westwood reached over and rubbed her lower back, saying, Listen girls, her voice rising above the chatter, giving life is a beautiful thing. A woman's body is made to do this.

Yeah, but I ain't no woman, Camille said, I'm still a child, Miss Westwood, and I ain't gonna let no baby split me in two. Hell, no . . . Camille flounced down next to the teacher and leaned into an embrace.

Don't worry, you'll be ready, Miss Westwood said. Her eyes rested on AnnMarie for a moment but she didn't say nothing about the fat bruise on her cheek.

After the repo van had gone, Darius had chased her up the stairs, banging her up against the wall. Stop, Darius, why you *buggin'*? she'd said but his backhand slap knocked her silly, sent a flash a pain across her face. White dots popping, face on fire. For a minute, she'd been blind.

Muthafucka. She'd picked a point on the floor and made her blurry eye go there, even with his mouth right up to her ear. *You think you all that, up in my business all the time.* Then his hand went around her throat and squeezed. *What you got to say now.*

Maybe she don't notice, AnnMarie thought. Skin dark chocolate, maybe she don't see. Then again, this a school after all, not a police station.

Wings: Insect wings are found in many different shapes and sizes. They are used for flying, but also to attract a mate or hide from predators.

AnnMarie tried to focus but couldn't. Fuck him. Punk-ass muthafucka. Think he the bomb. Think he *it*. Fuck you, she thought. You no longer the father a my child. I do this my own damn self.

Most insects have two pairs of wings.

Most insects have two pairs of wings.

Most— AnnMarie stood up, walked out the classroom and down the hall to the drinking fountain. She took a sip a water, wandered down to the front door and looked out the window see what the weather like. Sun out, tha's good. Maybe she skip out after lunch. She went back to the drinking fountain, stared up at the bulletin board. Somebody had posted a flyer. Right in between ARE YOU EXPECTING? and TEEN SUPPORT GROUP.

MOVIE TRYOUTS!!

GIRLS WANTED.

ALL SHAPES AND SIZES.

NO MODEL TYPES.

COME AS YOU ARE.

AnnMarie stared and stared at that thing.

Two days later, she woke up not knowing where she was. She thought she was on a school bus, rumbling over some rough road somewhere way out there, far, far out at the edge of an island, the water glistening so bright she thought her eyeballs would split open but when she let her lids peel apart, the world was dark, everything around her dark and sleepy. She felt the bed beneath her, she was in her own bed, bladder full. She didn't want to get up so she snuggled deeper, looking at the clock radio. Three o'clock in the morning. That'd been happening lately. Three o'clock, she'd wake up with that anxious feeling. Couldn't go back to sleep.

She tried to push it aside but there it was: *I don't want this baby. I do not want this baby.* Usually she'd roll toward Darius, pull his arm over her waist, find his heart beating there and she'd be okay. But she hadn't seen him since the fight. Two days. She wondered what he doing.

She sat up in bed, peeled back the curtain and looked out at the gray night. Below her, she watched the streetlamp flicker. A woman came around the corner and passed beneath it, then suddenly ran off in a sprint. Was she running from something or to something? AnnMarie couldn't tell. There'd been no sound, no other person. What you running for, AnnMarie thought.

She reached over the side of the bed and felt around on the floor, found her backpack, pulled out the flyer she'd taken off the wall.

She read it again. She wondered where 404 18th Street was. Flyer said Manhattan. She'd never been to Manhattan before. She wondered if they needed girls who could sing.

16

She'd fallen asleep. Took a while, but she'd drifted off again and when she finally woke it was already past noon. She decided to skip out on Ida B. for the day, get some singing practice in. She called up Niki. Niki said, We going to Teisha's.

When AnnMarie walked in, Niki and Nadette were in the kitchen, laughing about something. Where Sunshine at, Ann-Marie asked. Y'all want to practice?

Teisha looked her up and down, How much you weigh now?

AnnMarie shrugged, I don't know. Why, I look fat?

Nah, nah . . . but why don't you get yourself some new clothes. You look mad sloppy.

Nadette bust out laughing. Niki too, snickering behind her hand, eyes glassy like she stoned underneath her Yankees cap.

Fuck all y'alls.

Teisha tsked. Just 'cause you pregnant, no reason to look like that.

AnnMarie slumped. Angry now, she sat silent.

Teisha came up behind her and started playing with her hair. I'm just messin' with you, AnnMarie. You should get your hair done, though. Sunshine do it for you. Y'all hear? She got a chair at Tina's. She doing locks, twists, twist outs, she cut that girl Allison, she gave her this cute style like a pixie 'cept kinda spiky. It be mad retro.

AnnMarie asked for a glass of milk, then ate some cookies Teisha found in the cupboard. Nadette and Niki walked out, saying they be back and AnnMarie started looking at hairstyles in a magazine. Then Dennis walked in with Darius and AnnMarie ignored him.

Y'all hear what happened to Wallace, Dennis said.

Who Wallace, which one, Teisha asked.

Wallace, what live at 12-50. He got mowed down last night in Redfern.

AnnMarie looked up. Wallace . . . ? You mean the boy go by Stack?

She heard Darius say, Word. Wallace Stack. *Blam blam*, mowed him down.

Nah, Wallace too sweet, I like that boy, what happened? Teisha asked.

They say he got mistook for someone. They apologizing now. Sorry muthafuckers.

Nah, nah, nah . . . I heard it some peewee, tryin' to show he got game.

AnnMarie stopped listening, felt her heart drop into her stomach, a sensation like the floor shifting as she stood and moved to the door. She felt Darius' hand on her elbow and he was following her into the hallway, Teisha's voice coming across the room, Peewee? What peewee . . .

They saying it was Levon's brother. How he want a rep.

In the hallway, Darius said, Where you going.

Stop, Darius, I'm going home.

He said, Come on now . . . I came to find you. You don't believe me? Look what I brought you.

He lifted up a plastic bag and held it out to her. She felt tears burning. She shifted, looking away. He shook the bag, coaxing. Come on now . . .

Her eyes went to the open bag and she saw the oranges. Oranges for her cravings.

Still she shrugged, fronting like she don't care, but she could feel herself giving in. Darius' arm went around her shoulder. He said, Forgive me baby. I don't wanna fight with you.

She closed her bedroom door, slipped off her jeans and crawled under the covers, his bare legs warm against hers. He leaned in, kissing her softly. She said, You going to birth class with me? He said, Yeah. Yeah, I go.

It's sad about Wallace, she whispered. I still can't believe it, you know we was in choir together . . . Word, Darius said, need to light a candle. They lay for a moment, AnnMarie drifting, thinking about the 𝒲𝓈 he got shaved into his fade, how she'd thought it was a clef symbol. Then she felt Darius' lips on hers, his hand moving between her legs, pressing gently, the way she liked. She let him roll her onto her side, lifting her leg from behind and they did it that way because there was the baby to think about.

First day of Lamaze class, she went looking for him. His sister Vanessa said he went to Raymel's. She walked the four blocks, took the elevator to the seventh floor, Raymel said, He with Big Mike. They working something out.

Well, let me get Big Mike number then, AnnMarie said.

When'd you get so bossy.

AnnMarie just looked at him.

Big Mike don't give out his number.

She tsked. Oh, so you his secretary now.

Fuck him. AnnMarie took the bus out to the rec center by herself, couples already seated on yoga mats they had spread out in a semi-circle. Girls in front, fellas cupping them from behind. Couple girls there with they mother or auntie, somebody. At least no one was giving her the eyeball. The teacher was smiling, going around, passing out a handout. She saw the boy Terrell from up the block walk in with a girl. Dang, she didn't know he gonna be a father. He was only a year ahead of her in school. She waited for their eyes to meet but he was busy, settling in behind his girl, looking nervous as hell.

She liked the instructor with her big voice and warm hands, she liked how she'd sat behind her and showed them all how to breathe. She said, All of you sitting here today need to get quiet inside, find the peace within you, we're going to learn many things during our time together . . . AnnMarie had drifted off at that point, her mind wandering to the future, to her due date, to Darius . . . Would he still claim her, would she ever sing again and then there was no stopping the tears from gushing out, the instructor's arms holding her, rocking her back and forth, saying, Go on now. It's okay. Breathe. Go on and breathe.

After class, AnnMarie took the bus home. She stared out the window at the dark sky and the passing sidewalks where the people was. Everybody heading home. She felt tired from all that crying and leaned her head on the glass. She wondered who the girl was with Terrell. She looked familiar, but AnnMarie couldn't place her. Maybe she was Katelyn's cousin. Everybody always related to somebody. You somebody's sister or brother or cousin. You a half sister, half brother, half cousin. Bloods in front of the White Castle. Look at Amani's brother over there. That peewee trying to act like he in the block. Wallace gone . . . She need to light a candle. Light a candle for Wallace.

House party. Block party. Rec center. Boardwalk. Bench. Storefront. You see it. Everybody making plans. You make plans.

She got off the bus at Central, walked over to the fruit stand. Bought a bag of oranges. Used food stamps 'cause no one around to see.

17

That Saturday she showered, lotioned, powdered, then inspected herself in front of the mirror. She looked like a damn pear, all that flesh sagging around her middle, no tight melon ball like the other girls, but her breasts were bigger and she kinda liked that. She lifted them up, holding each one in a hand, then stepped up to the mirror and studied the dark widening of her nipples.

She put on her favorite blouse with the cap sleeves and lace around the collar, looked in the mirror, changed outta that, put on a T-shirt instead. Too sloppy. She put the blouse on again, left a extra button undone. That looked better. Put on the black stretch jeans that stayed up without the button fastened. She sat on the bed and laced up her Tims, put on the down vest and looked in the mirror. Maybe no one could tell. Twenty-one weeks, she could still fake it.

She folded up the flyer, put two oranges in her book bag and walked out the door, didn't tell her mother where she going, just went. Up the block to Mott Avenue, over six blocks to the subway, she'd passed the entrance a million times but had never gone through the doors. 'Cept the one time when they first moved to Far Rock, her and Blessed. Riding all the way down from the Bronx, getting off at the end of the line. Other than that, she'd never had a reason.

She went down three flights of stairs, all the way down into the station, hesitated, then dropped a handful of change into the slot, asked the station man for a token.

She rode six stops without anyone getting on the car, 'cept a mother who look like she need a bath and four kids who climbed onto the seats next to her and sat mad quiet, overdressed in winter coats zipped up to their chins. One of the little boys turned, stretching his neck up to peer out the window but in a flash the mother whipped her hand across the others, yanked him back down and said, *Sit up straight and act right.*

AnnMarie turned and looked out the window. All the low-rise buildings out there, the empty lots with trash in piles, fences tipped on their sides like they been stepped on by a giant. Beyond that a cargo plane rose up, its wing tipping downward as it curved across the sky, and then without warning the subway car was gliding across water, and what a sight it was, so low were the tracks to the bay that it felt to AnnMarie they were defying gravity, floating instead of sinking into the depths of that wide blue water, soaring along in a box made of steel. Then the train car surged forward and plunged underground and AnnMarie had to take a couple of deep breaths right then because she thought she might throw up. She felt queasy, that queasy feeling like fear. Like, what the fuck she doing, what the fuck she think she doing.

Three days ago, she'd stood in front of Miss July's office 'til she got up the nerve, then went in and said, Miss July, what this be about? Miss July slid her glasses down her nose and looked at the flyer. She said, Oh, yes. A nice young man from the movie asked permission to put it up. I told him this was a school for pregnant girls but he didn't seem to mind. Are you going to try out, AnnMarie?

AnnMarie had stood there thinking, then said, They came all the way out here from Manhattan?

Miss July spread the subway map across her desk and showed her where to go. You don't even need to transfer. Just take the A train all the way—you see?

At Liberty Avenue, three Spanish-looking people got on and a family of Indians, the mother wearing one a those bright flowy-type dresses, silk draped over her shoulder, red dot on the forehead. Wonder what that dot mean, AnnMarie thought, wonder where they going, all dressed up, the man too, silk shirt hanging to his knees, little girl dressed just like her mother.

By Utica, the car was half full of Saturday shoppers. Saturday workers, everybody going somewhere. She felt hungry all of a sudden, so she pulled out one of the oranges, peeled it and ate it piece by piece 'til it was gone. She tried to picture herself in the room, what she'd say to the people there. I'm AnnMarie Walker. My name's AnnMarie Walker. In the 7th grade I sang "I Will Always Love You" at my school talent show. IS 53. You ever hear a the Night Shade, she'd say. We a singing group.

Hoyt–Schermerhorn

Jay Street

High Street

Broadway–Nassau

Chambers

Canal

She felt movement in her belly, was that a fart coming on? Dang. The oranges be giving her gas. Chinese lady glancing at her. What the fuck you looking at, oh, she talking to the other one, sitting across the way. AnnMarie glanced around the car, three, four, five—where all these Asians come from?

Spring

West 4th

14th

Miss July had said 14th and as the train pulled into the station, AnnMarie saw the number 14 painted on the wall and quickly stood up, filing out with a whole mess a people moving out the doors and onto the platform.

She stood for a long time on the corner of 14th and 8th Avenue, trying to figure out which way the numbers go, then finally she crossed the wide street, walked all the way to the corner before realizing the numbers were going down, not up. Turned around went back the way she came. 15th. 16th. 17th. Dang it's pretty up here. Look at all these pretty buildings.

Pushing through the glass door of 404 18th Street, sign in at the desk, no guard there but she signed in anyway, flyer said take the elevator to the tenth floor. Her heart wasn't beating fast then, but as soon as she stepped out, stepped into the big room, like a lobby with folding chairs and girls turning to look at her all at once—yeah, she felt it. Nervous as crap. Standing there like a swollen blob. Gas bubbles knocking around, hands clammy in her pockets. She heard the elevator door start to slide closed and she almost stepped back in. Press the button, go down the way she came. But she didn't. She didn't know why. A wish maybe. A wish. She took a breath and walked across the room, letting the fart rip right outta her, saying 'Xcuse me as she went past the folding chairs and the girls with their eyes glued to her stomach, past the sign that said CASTING in big letters and up to the desk where the white lady sat.

The white lady looked up and she said, What I gotta do now?

callback

18

When her turn came she walked into the room. Her mouth went dry, seeing five a them sitting at a long wooden table, light pouring in from the big window behind, their faces backlit and unreadable as she moved across the room.

You want me to sit here, she asked, trying to sound natural, not like she bugging out, noticing the Polaroid camera up on the table next to rows of casting pictures. Had to be thirty girl faces spread out across the table.

One a them stood up, reached out her hand, she said, Hi, I'm Alicia. AnnMarie shook it, said, Nice to meet you. Next one said, I'm Jenny, waving from her seat. AnnMarie waved back. Next one coulda said Mary for all AnnMarie heard, her mind going blank from nerves and a sudden self-consciousness. Grown-up white people, all looking her way—can they tell she pregnant? Punked-out lady with dyed black hair, saying she was the casting director. Her voice husky and deep. Go on, AnnMarie, you can sit, make yourself comfortable, do you want something to drink? Alicia, get her something to drink. Punk lady got a pile a bracelets that jangled on her wrist.

AnnMarie took the cup a water. She said thank you, then the man in the middle start talking. He said his name was Donald, Dean, something like that, and he was the director. AnnMarie shifted her gaze from her water cup to the tall white dude with glasses, looking mad serious as he asked his questions, How old is you, what school do you go to, who your favorite singer, what your favorite movie . . . And AnnMarie took a breath and answered. I'm fourteen years old. I go to Ida B. Wells, that's in Queens. My favorite singer is Brandy but I also like Whitney Houston for R&B and Missy Elliott for the more rap style she got going on. I'm a singer too. We got a all-girl group by the name of the Night Shade. In Far Rockaway. That's where I live, Far Rockaway, Queens. Y'all heard of it?

White dude was jotting things down on a sheet of paper, glancing up at her smiling, nodding his head. She wondered what he writing. What words he putting down on the page. *De-scriptive* language. Her mind drifting back to 8th grade, Ms. Henley class . . . when she heard him say, If you got stuck in an elevator, who'd you want to get stuck with.

She said, Say what?

Donald Dean said, If you got stuck in an elevator, who would you want to be with?

AnnMarie frowned. She said, I don't wanna be stuck in a elevator. That don't make sense.

And they all bust out laughing. AnnMarie felt the heat rise to her cheeks. She bit down on the urge to scrape back her chair and go. Why they laughing. What they laughing for.

But she looked him in the eye and said, What I miss. What's funny.

The man Donald Dean said, You didn't miss anything. We like your personality, that's all.

Then he stood, came around the table and pulled a chair up next to her. He showed her some pages with typewritten words on them. He called it a scene. He said, Take this home and memorize the words.

All of it? she asked.

No, just here—where the name Joycelyn is written. This is the dialogue, he said, for the character Joycelyn. We're calling you back to read. Just be yourself and you'll do fine.

Be myself, AnnMarie thought. I can do that.

19

Over the following six weeks, they called her back exactly four times. The baby getting big inside, her days filled with clinic visits and Ida B. schooling. Chasing down Darius who was out more than in. She hadn't told him about the tryouts. She'd kept quiet after she heard Teisha say to Nadette, Why they want to cast a girl who got a baby on the way. That baby doing flips and turns, bumping around in there. Sometimes she could see it, an imprint of a fist or a elbow, hard and bony, poking through her skin. But the movie people kept calling.

She'd practice the lines, trying them out different ways. Her mother looking at her outta her good eye. What you doing? Nothing, Ma. Nothing. Each time they call, she'd pick up the phone. She'd say, Did I get the part? Did I get it? But they'd say, We need to see you again.

So she went. Got herself up, put something nice on, took the train all the way into the city. She didn't always have money for the fare so twice she stood by the emergency gate, waiting for someone to come off the platform. Slip through when no one was looking.

Sometimes she'd read lines for the director—Dean was his name, she'd finally figured that out, not Donald. Sometimes they'd just sit and talk. Like regular people. She start to feel comfortable. The way he'd sit mad quiet and listen. Nodding his head, like he considering what she got to say. He'd ask her what her favorite subject was, about school, choir class and she told him about Mr. Preston from IS 53. About her baby father, Darius, and her due date. She even told him about the stroke her mother had and how she still recovering.

She didn't sing or nothing, she just was herself.

20

In April, Dean called. He said, I want to come out and meet Blessed.

She said, You wanna do what?

She thought maybe he thick—no one like Dean ever come out to Far Rockaway.

She said, Why you gotta meet my mother.

You're a minor, AnnMarie. You're about to have a baby. I have to meet your mother to see if we can do this.

So she cleaned the apartment, top to bottom. Shoved everything out the way, into the closet, into Blessed's room. Swept the floor, cleaned the bathroom, washed dishes, cleared off the sofa, making things nice. Baby kicking her in the rib, high up there, it was hard to breathe.

Blessed thought AnnMarie was crazy. What the hell you doing? She said. You gonna hurt yourself. Her mother only partways understanding what was going on. In one ear, out the other. In Blessed's mind it was like, Who coming out here? The director? Director of what.

But she got her mother changed outta her house dress, squeezed her into the purple dress she used to wear to church, combed out her wig, made her put it on.

Dean took the A train all the way out, all the way the fuck out to Mott Avenue. She knew how long it took to get here from Manhattan. It was the end of the line. AnnMarie stood at the station entrance, waiting. People glancing at her sideways, looking at her swollen belly, but she didn't care. When he came up the steps in one piece she smiled, satisfied, and they walked back to Gateway along Mott Avenue, AnnMarie pointing out the Thriftway, Tina's hair salon, the 101st Precinct and the Crown Fried Chicken on the corner.

She brought him upstairs, introduced him to Blessed who told him to go on, sit down. AnnMarie, bring him a Coke. You want a Coke, Mr. Dean? AnnMarie moving from the fridge to the sofa as Blessed got settled at one end, waiting for Dean to start talking. But he pulled out a box of cookies and a bag of baby oranges so she had to deal with the TV trays and setting out little plates and finding napkins and when he finally got to it, explaining the movie and AnnMarie's role, she held her breath, thinking, Don't switch up, don't switch up, please don't switch up and change your mind. She could hardly concentrate, picturing her life through his eyes—the mad small apartment, even with the kitchen window open the room felt stifling, her mother sitting there in that too-tight dress, lipstick on, one a her eyeballs not working, staring sideways. Do he even know where to look when he look at her face?

But then she heard him say, The shoot days are long and there are rehearsals, lots of rehearsals, Mrs. Walker. I need to know if we can do this with AnnMarie. She's got to show up on time, every day. Can I count on you? Can I count on your support? Blessed glanced at AnnMarie, then kinda leaned forward, looking at him outta her good eye. She said, I'm not going nowhere. I'm proud of my daughter. I'ma help her any way I can.

Dang, AnnMarie thought.

First time she heard that come out her mouth.

She proud a me.

Star blazing, blazing Star

21

She was eight month pregnant when Dean called rehearsal. Blessed start scraping the bottom of her purse for change, cashing in coupons for food, giving AnnMarie any extra she had. Subway rides out to Utica Avenue and back, money for lunch. She was big as a house. Wide load, peeps. Watch out. Baby poking around in there, letting AnnMarie know she was alive and strong. They met up in the basement of a church, across the street from Albany Houses in Crown Heights. It was AnnMarie. It was Sonia and Melody—those girls playing the parts of her best friends. Both of them marveling, reaching out to touch her belly. Oooh, when you due, what you gonna name her, you got a crib yet? Sonia was nineteen and going to acting school in Manhattan. A true professional. Melody was a Puerto Rican girl from the Bronx. A intellectual type, with long kinky hair and fair skin, always asking questions. They'd spend hours together with Dean. Memorizing lines, practicing the scenes.

Dean told them it wasn't going to be one a those big Hollywood movies you see with all the glitz and glamour and movie stars. It's an art film, he called it. Low budget. Everybody pitching in to make it work. There's gonna be a marching band and you girls are gonna learn an instrument or be on flags 'cause the band's a part of the movie too. The Crown Heights Steppers. AnnMarie and the other girls watched them practice one day. Those kids spinning the flags way up high in the air, keeping the beat. Turning, spinning. Stepping.

Dean would tell them, This is a story about friendship, it's about change. Your high school closes and you have the summer to figure out what you're gonna do next. Melody's character finds out she pregnant and decides not to go back to school. Word, AnnMarie thought, I can relate to that.

Even though Dean was the director, he act more like a coach. Giving them pep talks, cheering them on if they mess up. Talking about improvise. Stay loose, Dean would say. Don't worry so much about the lines on the page. You got your own story, use it. Put it back behind the words and let it flow. AnnMarie was in a daze of wide-open happiness.

She'd kept it from Darius. That first audition, the callbacks. Even Dean coming out to meet her mother. Ever since they'd taken his equipment, he'd been moody. Drinking Hennessy before noon, angry all the time. Not even the weed he smoke take the edge off. So she waited until the movie was a sure thing.

You doing what, he said.

She could feel the suspicion, then the jealousy pouring out his eyes and her heart just shrunk up. 'Cause she'd learned by now how he saw the world, how he thought there wasn't room enough for everybody on the come up.

She said, I'ma talk to the director. Maybe he can use some a your beats.

He looked at her sideways. What you mean?

She said, Every movie got music, right? Why not yours? Putting her arms around him then, looking up into his eyes, her belly bumping against him.

You got mad talent, Darius. Give me one a your CDs. I show it to him, she said. Because she loved him and wanted him to be happy.

He didn't say nothing for a minute but she could see the gears turning.

What you got to lose, she asked.

Yeah, yeah . . . he said. You could ask him.

She had to lay on her side now when she slept. Baby inside need to breathe, the doctor told her. She knew it was a girl baby 'cause she'd asked. She could feel the kicks and burps, the thrum of the baby heartbeat like the gallop of horses. Baby heart got four valves, doctor at the clinic told her, rolling jelly juice around her tummy, the sonogram wand pressed against her skin. A real live breathing thing.

She started making a list of baby names. Ashlee, Brianna, Makayla, Chasity, Dawn, Skye, Star. She'd show them to Darius. What you think, baby, she'd ask. If it a boy, I'd name him Blaze, he said. Oh, I like that. Blaze. She hadn't told him the baby was a girl. Could you name a girl Blaze, she thought. Blazing Star. Star Blazing.

Then the money start to appear. Out of nowhere. Cash money sitting out in piles in the studio room. AnnMarie'd walk in, her eyes going wide. She'd say, What you doing Darius. Where'd you get all that money. Sessions, baby. Recording sessions. He told her he was producing. Working out of Z-Sounds since his own studio wasn't more than a room with four walls. Maybe it was true. She wanted to think it was true. But later she heard through the grapevine—Dennis telling Nadette and Nadette telling Niki and

Niki finally telling her—Darius on a robbing spree. Sticking up strangers on the street. Going into any store ain't got plexiglass for protection.

Speakers appeared. Then a console. Microphones. All those piles of money turned into music gold.

She wanted to scream, *What you doing? We got a baby on the way and you robbing people? You gonna get caught, stupid.*

But he was happier. Hugging her more. Holding her at night. Drumming beats with his fingertips on her leg, a rhythm playing her to sleep. She'd murmur, You gonna get us a crib, baby? He'd say, You know it.

And then it went down, three days before her due date. A beautiful day. Sunny, no rain clouds, June 24. All day she'd been feeling fine, couple little cramp-type feelings here and there but nothing to get excited about. She took a bath in the afternoon, woke up still in the water, her body buoyant, realizing she'd dozed off. Watched TV for a while, called Darius, waited for him to come by, but she was restless, moving around the house 'cause the crampy feeling start to grow, like pressure building. Dean called. He asked how she feeling. She said, I'm fine, Dean. Everything good. Sonia called, asked if she had the baby yet. She said, No, Sonia, I still got three days. Then at nine o'clock that evening, she got the urge to eat Chinese. Darius was still out somewhere so she called up Niki and they went over to Lucky's for some Sweet and Spicy Chicken.

Niki had got her hair cornrowed, the cinnamon curls plaited in neat parallel rows, crown to nape. She kept rubbing with the heel of her hand. What's the matter, AnnMarie asked. Sunshine put 'em in too tight? Yeah, yeah . . . they's killing me. I think I have to take 'em out.

I do it for you, AnnMarie said. Niki got up to get their food, brought it back on a plastic tray. She start to eat. I decided to go for my GED, Niki said.

Yeah? That's cool. AnnMarie nodded, trying to be a good friend, to pay attention but she felt light-headed. She picked up her fork and start to eat. I can do a summer program, then I'ma get a job in a bank, Niki was saying, her voice sounding far away. AnnMarie felt herself expand, a feeling like she gonna burst so she put the fork down and leaned back, spice flavor strange on her tongue. She didn't feel right. Hot, like a oven had turned on inside her body.

Niki said, There go Darius. AnnMarie looked up and saw him passing on the street, Jason and Raymel trailing after him, moving up the block at a clip. In a second they gone. She got up, waddled to the door, pulled it open and stepped outside.

What they doing.

Darius! she called. But he didn't turn. She saw him reach up, pull his ball cap low over his eyes and enter the A-rab's store, Raymel a shadow behind him. Jason leaning up against the wall, his eye on the street. Muthafucka. He robbing that dude right now. All of a sudden she felt the pain, like a rope wrapping tight around her belly. She reached for the wall and leaned. Here we go, she thought. A contraction for sure. Gripping her like a vise and squeezing. Like pain she ain't never felt before. Breathe, she told herself. Lamaze teacher said, Breathe.

Then she heard Niki's voice saying, What up AnnMarie, you okay? She knew she supposed to count, look at a clock, something, time the contraction when the pain stop. That's what Lamaze had said. You got a watch, she asked. But before the words out her mouth another belt cinched tight and made her double over. She leaned both hands on the wall and could feel herself rocking, a moan coming out her mouth, then she was in the bathroom. All of a sudden she was sitting on the toilet, Niki holding her hand, saying, Maybe we should go to the hospital. She moaned, leaning forward, feeling the pressure build, a feeling like she got to push. Then she saw the blood and a wave of fear passed through her. Bleeding, why she bleeding. Nobody said nothing about blood. She waddled out the bathroom, Niki next to her, saying, Hold up, AnnMarie, pull up your pants but she was heading for the door and to the street beyond, she got to get to Darius. Up the block. Get Darius and go to hospital.

How she made it to St. John's six blocks away she didn't know. Everything had gone fuzzy. There was Niki's shoulder. Niki's arms holding her when she froze up, bracing herself against each tightening, the pressure like a boulder pushing down. AnnMarie moaning, She's coming . . . This baby coming out.

Next thing she knew she was standing in the lobby of the emergency room, water all over the floor, soaking through her Reeboks. Then she was in a room, up on a bed, hospital gown on one minute, undone the next, pooling there around her wrists. She was on her hands and knees, butt naked and sweating, her whole body wet with sweat but she didn't care—strangers all around, who was these people, someone strapping a belt around her waist, beeping sounds and the tight feeling coming fast and hard now. Pain like nothing else and she was breathing, breathing, low and deep, trying to get on top of the pain. She rode it. Her body swaying on its own, her head down between her shoulders until her elbows gave out and she was collapsing, no longer on all fours but on her back where the bed was inclined and she saw Blessed then, appearing outta nowhere. Ma, she said. Ma . . . and Blessed took AnnMarie's hand and said, Push AnnMarie push. And she bore down with everything she had, squinting past her knees, some doctor man between her legs, where the fuck did *he* come from? Saying, Okay AnnMarie, one more good one, one more like that . . .

Then with a strange slurping sound the baby was outside instead of in and she was crying out loud and the doctor was holding Star Blazing or Blazing Star, she didn't know which to call her, a nurse wiping off the mucus and fluid and traces of blood and AnnMarie could see her beautiful brown body through the blur of motion. AnnMarie was shaking, her whole body trembling from the aftershock but the nurse laid the newborn on her bare breast, skin to skin, and the doctor was poking around between her legs, her mother crying, *Praise be. Praise be.* But all she knew right then was the brand-new living thing pressed against her, flesh and bones and a beating heart.

22

Daruis, he missed the birth part, came rolling up first thing the next morning. Flowers in hand. Yellow roses. He brought a teddy bear and balloons and a little baby outfit in one of those bassinet-type things. White ribbons tied all around. It was pretty. He came into the room, passing the girl in the hospital bed next to hers, pulled the curtain closed around them. She was mad tired. Sore all over, shoulders, back, legs, even her face hurt from squeezing that baby out, but when Darius leaned over the bed and kissed her she reached for him. She didn't care that he'd been out robbing the night before. To see all the little things he'd brought for Star, to watch that dimple appear as she put their baby into his arms. All that hard shit he wore on his face all the time, all that hard shit just fell away. It fell away.

23

The doctor told her she'd given herself a front-to-back tear and that's why she in so much pain. AnnMarie laid back and cried. What my thing look like? There some huge gaping hole down there? The doc said, Don't worry, we stitched you up, you'll be fine. Blue ice packs cooling the swell, one after another, melting to mush between her legs. Stayed in hospital two days, then she out.

Back at home, she sat on those hospital-brand ice packs Blessed had to keep refreezing, crab-walking to the bathroom, trying to sit without wincing on the toilet seat. Star nestled in Blessed's good arm, her mother humming a little tune like she gave birth her own damn self. Getting phone calls from Dean and the girls. They're cheering, shouting, Congratulations. CONGRATULATIONS!

Dean sent flowers. Pink roses with white baby's breath. Sonia mailed a little outfit, Tommy Hilfiger on the label, with a matching baby hat and booties. AnnMarie squealed when she opened the box. All her friends came by bringing gifts, rattles and a silver spoon and a mobile for the crib. The room filled up with balloons. Everybody wanted to hold Star. She kept saying, Wash your hands. Wash your hands.

Two weeks 'til the movie, AnnMarie tried to relax. Tried to enjoy the little things, like the sound of Star's cry and her tiny toes, watching Darius nursing her with a bottle, his face bent close, eyes on her like she the most precious thing in the world. But she felt the panic at odd moments—in the shower trying to lift her leg without wincing, or when she was brushing her teeth, glancing in the mirror and seeing tired eyes staring back, hearing a door slam or a quiet settle over the room . . . In these moments, she felt the sensation like a hand squeezing her chest. How the fuck am I supposed to do this.

behind the scenes

24

Roll Sound
  Speed
  Roll Camera
  Scene 5, Take 3
  Mark It

AnnMarie heard the clap and Dean call *Action!* and they were moving down the school hallway, her shoulder brushing against Melody's, her eyes on the floor right in front of Bobby who wasn't more than a few feet ahead of them, walking backwards with the big-ass camera up on his shoulder. Her first line was *Why you bugging*, and when she said it Melody shoved her into the locker and AnnMarie laughed 'cause it was funny how she did it this time, her arm held in the air, wrist bent in a mock *fuck y'all*, and Ann-Marie was smiling inside too 'cause Sonia had stood up at the right moment, zipping her drum in its case—all of them getting it right, Bobby swinging around behind them as AnnMarie said, You coming or staying? Sonia said, I'm coming.

And AnnMarie thought *Now*, so she pushed the handle on the door and they went out to the school yard, felt the heat on their skin, Bobby trailing behind them but the camera still rolling. Out the corner of her eye, she could see the project kids hanging on the fence but no one was talking, all the crew peoples quiet too as Sonia slowed, knowing they supposed to let Bobby move in front again so the camera could capture their expressions when they talked about the birthday party.

What we gonna do, Lanisha? Sweet Sixteen, you gotta do something special.

They heard *Cut!*

Good job, girls, Dean hollered, then he turned and got in a huddle with Bobby as one of the crew guys lifted the heavy camera off his shoulder.

Sonia said, That felt pretty good.

I forgot my line, AnnMarie said. I was supposed to say, *What up, what up, what up.*

Sonia said, That's okay. It still sounded natural.

No one spoke for a minute, waiting for feedback from Dean, the three of them sweating in their band uniforms, the afternoon sun bouncing off the asphalt. They heard the neighborhood kids holler but their words were swallowed by a passing car, Nas thumping from the speakers.

Then Dean was approaching, telling them they gonna do it again, how they all need to slow down once they come out the door—Bobby needs to get in front of them, otherwise everything be outta focus.

And AnnMarie, try not to look at the camera, okay?

Oh, sorry. I didn't know I did that.

But she was embarrassed. Knowing she messed up. Hoping they didn't have to do Take 4 'cause a her.

She heard Sonia say, Are those kids gonna stay there all day?

Her eyes drifted to the fence as Dean turned, looking at them hanging there, nothing better to do on a Thursday, four o'clock in the afternoon, summertime in Crown Heights.

Dean said, Whatever's going on around you, whatever the camera can't see . . . ? Use it. Stay in the moment. Kids yell something, what would your character do?

You want us to beef wit' them kids, AnnMarie asked.

Melody laughed.

No, AnnMarie, I want you to stay in character and not lose your focus. Do you understand, girls?

Yes, I think so, Sonia said, thoughtfully.

Let's go again then.

The girls headed back inside, AnnMarie glancing over at the fence where Maya, the assistant director, had gone. She liked Maya. Got her hair up in a big ol' afro like those Black Power bitches. AnnMarie'd seen pictures in history class once but so far no one like Maya in real life. She had taken the walkie off her belt and was letting one of the younger boys hold it through the fence. He pressed his mouth up to the speaker and AnnMarie could hear him say, *Roll sound* as the others cracked up, grabbing for a turn.

AnnMarie yawned. She was tired.

25

Seven a.m., day six of shooting, AnnMarie felt like she was sleep-walking. Three weeks since the birth and she'd been living on Star time, not her own. Long days on set, sometimes twelve, thirteen hours. It don't matter. Every four hours, Star need formula. Twice in the middle of the night. She don't wake, you got to wake her, the doctor had said. She can't grow on her own.

Seven a.m., she supposed to be on set but everything had gone wrong the day before and all that wrong had drifted into those early-morning hours after Star woke and she and Darius had got into it. When the tiny cries pierced through the fog, AnnMarie groaned, her body dead. She nudged him but he didn't stir. She sat up, frowning, fighting sleep. She said, Darius . . . We gotta do a bottle. He didn't answer. Darius, she said again, the bottle. Then his voice came through the dark. You get it. She groaned, Please Darius . . . But he threw off the sheet, saying, Stop fronting like you somebody an' act like a mother. She tsked, Oh so you ain't in this. No, I ain't. I'm out. And when she reached for his arm, he wheeled around and punched her, rattling the teeth in her head.

She bit her tongue, spit blood in the sink listening to the door slam. Blessed didn't even stir. Three a.m. Mix formula. Heat water. Heat bottle. Feed Star. Star fussy, refusing the bottle, squirming in her arms. AnnMarie wanted to cry. Finally Star drank. Ann-Marie changed her diaper. Set her in the bassinet, rocked her to sleep. Four thirty, she got back into bed, the ice on her cheek turning to water in the plastic bag. Then the alarm was clanging. God damn. She had to be on set in forty-five minutes and hadn't even looked at her lines.

She called up Dean. She said, I'm sorry Dean, but I'ma be late.

She told him she need to shower, get her mother woke and ready for Star, three bottles mixed for the day and still she hadn't looked at her lines. Dean said, Calm down, AnnMarie. We're sending a car for you.

And when she arrived on set, a hour late, she felt a weight lifting, the whole ride out patting on the pancake powder where the swell was, forgetting about Darius and even Star, secretly happy to be here and not at home, the Lincoln Town Car pulling up to the curb where Dean and the crew people was waiting.

Before they got started, Dean gathered them. He didn't say nothing about her making them wait. Instead, he rallied them. He knew they was tired, he said. But they had to keep it together, each and every one of them, so they could get it right and make something special. He put a hand on her shoulder as she looked across at all the crew people standing together listening, and Maya the AD said, Remember, people, we're guests here in this neighborhood. Be respectful. Say please and thank you, 'cause they letting us be here—it's a privilege not a right. AnnMarie lifted her hands and clapped for that one.

'Cause in the beginning, she'd wondered how it would go down being out here in Crown Heights. Project kids hanging on the edge of things, riding their BMXs across the cables, passing the PAs and equipment or gathering on the benches of Albany Houses, watching with wary eyes as the movie crew bounced from location to location. Kids in the step band were all right. Mothers and grandmas coming by to pick them up after practice, or standing next to Maya watching a rehearsal.

Still, she wondered what would happen. Outsiders come in, thinking they all that.

When they broke for lunch, AnnMarie borrowed Dean's phone and called home. Her mother said, Star is fine. She drank off the whole bottle and is sleeping. AnnMarie hesitated, then asked if Darius had come by. Blessed said she ain't seen him. AnnMarie hung up and stood there for a minute, crew people mingling, going in and out of the church where they got food catering set up in the basement. She thought about the fight—not the three a.m. punch to the face, but the other one that had started the day before.

What he say about my mixtape, Darius had asked and Ann-Marie realized right then she'd made a mistake, dangling the possibility in front of him. Straight off, Dean told her the only music in the movie was gonna be from the step band. It's the style, Ann-Marie, sorry. It's called realism. She didn't know what *realism* was but Dean could be matter-of-fact like that. No bullshit.

She hadn't known how to tell Darius so she said, He ain't got time to listen to it yet which made Darius go quiet. Hostile quiet. She said, Why don't you come out to set, meet Dean yourself. Meet everybody. Maybe you could—but he cut her off. He said, I don't give a shit he listen to it or not. Who he anyway? Just some white dude making a chick movie ain't nobody gonna watch.

What the fuck that supposed to mean, she'd snapped.

AnnMarie stood in front of the church, watching a couple homies step out the doors of Albany Houses. Passing by the crew van, red bandanas wrapped around the leg of their jeans. Crown Heights don't look much different from Far Rock, AnnMarie thought. But at least a camera be rolling. Something she could tell Star about when she get grown.

26

The apartment they were using as a set belonged to one of the kids from the step band. It was hot up in there with all the lights and flags on stands, no fans or air allowed when the camera rolling— Albert with his sound cart stuck in the bathroom, the space so tight.

Today they getting ready to do the scene where she pick up Melody to go to the movies. The actress playing Melody's mother supposed to get up off the couch, get in her face the way mothers do.

MELODY'S MOTHER

The Bronx? Where your head at? You ain't going to school in the Bronx. You think you got wings, you gonna fly up there?

They did all the mother's lines first. It came out good. AnnMarie sat by the sound cart and listened with the headphones on.

In the hallway, they moved the camera to the bottom of the stairs and pointed it up at the apartment door where the girls would exit. Okay girls, Dean said. You're up. He reminded them that Melody was supposed to still be angry at her mother. AnnMarie's character supposed to be clowning around but supportive.

AnnMarie heard *Action*.

They moved out the door and down the stairs.

AnnMarie said, I woulda told her to go fuck herself.

Melody shook her head like she *over* it.

Dean called *Cut*. He said, AnnMarie, please don't improvise. Just come down the stairs, no lines.

You don't want me to say nothing?

No, I think it's better to *see* her anger, instead of using words.

Melody shrugged. I kinda liked it.

Yeah, but we're going to do it without any words.

They climbed the stairs to do another take. Melody said, Well I liked it.

AnnMarie said, Yeah but he in charge.

Melody said, So. You got a opinion, you can say it.

They went inside the apartment, closed the door and waited for Dean to call *Action*.

AnnMarie stood there, thinking. Then she whispered, You got a father, Melody?

Melody looked at her, puzzled.

Through the door they heard *Roll sound* . . .

Sometimes she forgot what the story was. Dean would tell her, it's about friendship, it's about change, you goin' your own way, making new friends, leaving the old behind. You're in this step band and the step band *is* the music. It's the rhythm. It's the flow. She'd be like, Okay, I got that. It's about the music *you* make, AnnMarie, and I know you understand that. Yeah . . . she'd say. Yeah, I got you . . .

She liked those conversations, and there were times in between setups or on lunch break when Dean would throw an arm over her shoulder and say, How are you, AnnMarie. Everything okay? She would say, Everything fine, Dean, and they'd talk about the small things, the day-to-day things, like Star gaining a whole pound or Blessed trying to string beads again. She didn't ask again about Darius and his music. Carrying the mixtape music around in her shoulder bag. Sometimes Dean would tell her about his neighborhood in the Village. How there be a rice pudding shop and a graffiti mural and a grown man who sang a cappella out on the corner for money. A picture start to form, slowly, like pieces of a puzzle falling into place.

When the AD called *Check the gate*, AnnMarie knew they be taking a break for a while so she drifted over to the sound cart where Albert sat on his apple box, messing with his cables. She said, You want your mic back now, or should I keep it on.

Keep it on, he said, you'll need it for the next scene.

She liked Albert. He was a big guy, big arms, thick-chested, with a Fu Manchu running down the side a his lips.

When you start growing that thing?

What, this?

Yeah—what they call that.

It's a mustache.

AnnMarie laughed. I know it's a mustache, Albert. I'm saying . . . It's like you Chinese or something but I can tell you ain't, where you from?

Born and raised in Arizona.

Word?

Yup.

Tha's cool. Where you live now?

In the West Village.

West Village? You live by Dean?

No, he lives in the East Village. West Village is West of Broadway, up to 14th Street. From Houston Street up to 14th.

Oh, that's cool. That's cool.

How 'bout you?

I'm from Far Rock. The Rock—that's Far Rockaway. Yeah . . .

That's out there, isn't it? What is that, the A train?

Yeah, way the fuck out there, excuse my language.

But you got the beaches, am I right?

Yeah, we got beaches.

We don't have beaches in Arizona.

Word?

Funny thing, whole time I've been living in New York, I've never taken the train out there. Never been to the Rockaways, not even Coney Island.

AnnMarie laughed. Word? Not even Coney Island?

Albert's walkie squawked. He pushed the button and said, Copy.

They listened to Maya telling everybody they moving out to Albany Avenue for the next scene. Albert glanced up at Ann-Marie, then pushed the button on the walkie and said, *Word* into the speaker.

AnnMarie cracked up at that man.

27

She had the next two days off. Forty-eight hours broke into four-hour stretches. When Star slept, there was time. Time to doze. Time to eat. To take a shower, sing in the shower, a melody coming to her out the blue, a song she knew by heart, carrying her over the tiredness and the waiting—the anticipation of Star waking, of bottle feeds and diaper change and lap play. Cradling her neck in the cup of her hand. Soft kisses. Blowing on her belly to make her smile. First smile, bubbles of spit, belly kisses and tiny feet. Forty-eight hours broke into laundry runs, four-week clinic visit, weigh-in, inches growed, feed schedule. Her own doctor visit skipped 'cause she had lines to memorize, a story to know and 'cause she wanted to be at home if and when Darius walked in, saying *Hey baby girl*, not to her but to Star. Then she would pass Star to him gently, using both hands to settle her flat on his chest where her lips would pucker and move in reflex, the suck reflex, tongue behind her lips rooting around for the tit or bottle that gonna keep her alive.

Next day, Maya the AD told her, Go on, work with Angie, she's waiting for you in the yard. Angie was lead drum majorette for the Steppers. A tall girl with dark chocolate skin and nice shoulders. Dean had told her she'd just graduated high school, made the honor roll. Clean white sneaks, that girl could toss a baton and never miss a beat. AnnMarie had to pass a group of kids hanging on the fence. She heard one of them say *There go the movie star* but she kept walking and didn't bother with no response.

Angie said, Forget about those haters.

AnnMarie shrugged. I didn't hear nothing.

Angie laughed, then tossed the baton up in the air. Where your baby at?

She home with my mother.

My cousin just had a baby. Gave her the name Clarissa Janelle Paris Preston Jackson.

Oh, wow. On her birth certificate she got Star Blaze Walker Greene but I just call her Star.

Word. Short and sweet. You got your flag?

Yeah.

Okay. Watch.

Angie tossed the baton, spun it high up in the air and caught it like it was nothing. Angie was pretty. Got a piercing through her tongue. The metal rod click on her teeth when she talk. Dean had gave her a part in the movie. Story goes, she and AnnMarie supposed to be new best friends.

First few times AnnMarie pulled her hand away instead of reaching for the pole like Angie was doing. Angie laughed. She said, That thing hurts if you miss.

But Angie taught her. They did the step routine first, practicing the moves over and over. Then they added the flag toss, Angie by her side, AnnMarie's eyes on her feet and on the pole in her hands as she flashed up down, up down, up down. She counted out loud, her piercing clacking against her teeth. Step step step step. They worked on it and worked on it 'til Angie said, Tha's it. You getting it. You *getting* it. And AnnMarie forgot about the kids roaming in and out the yard, sometimes calling out stupid shit, and after a while, a ball game got started down where the hoop was, everybody just doing they thing.

When they took a break, Angie said, You got a man, AnnMarie?

Yeah, I do. My baby father.
Well, we having a cookout this weekend. Y'all should come.
AnnMarie said, Yeah, I come.
Music, dancing—my boyfriend likes to bust it up.
AnnMarie smiled. Word.

28

AnnMarie had fallen asleep. She came awake blurry-eyed, harsh light beaming down from the mega-bulb up on the stand. Didn't know where she was for a minute, then it all came into focus. Dean there, sitting on the edge of the couch in somebody's living room where they'd been filming a scene.

He said, Someone get a soda to wake her up.

She looked around. Where the girls at?

I told them to go to wardrobe, Dean said.

Why? We finished in here? I thought we was gonna do more takes.

You don't know your lines, AnnMarie.

Yes I do.

No, you don't, Dean said, sounding angry. You keep messing up.

She felt around on the couch. Where my pages at.

Someone get AnnMarie her lines, he yelled.

Then he said, Here's what we're gonna do. I moved up Sonia and Melody's scene. We're going to shoot that first. I want you to sit here 'til you know your lines.

She could tell he was PO'd but she was angry too. Far as she knew, Dean didn't have no baby, no child at home to take care of. No baby father fucking with her late at night when she trying to get a few minutes' sleep, putting his hands on her, wanting sex. She'd tried to keep Darius offa her but he kept at it, guiding her head down, then forcing her head down until she gave in. Cum taste in her mouth. She had to get out of bed, rinse her mouth out. Then Star woke again, needing a cuddle and a bottle. What Dean know about raising a baby.

A PA brought her the scene. She forced herself to concentrate. Looked at the pages, saying the words over and over until they were locked in her head. Still she thought about it, how she'd put Star back in the bassinet and went to sleep on the couch instead of the bed where Darius was, not wanting to touch any part of him.

She went to watch the girls. It was a walk and talk on Bergen Street. Bobby had the camera set up to follow them and she watched on the monitor, like a video screen.

With the camera rolling, she heard them talking about AnnMarie's character. How she hadn't been coming around no more, how she be hanging with Angie and what up with that. Then the conversation drifted to Melody taking the test, finding out she pregnant and how she don't want nobody to know, not even the boy who got her pregnant.

When AnnMarie'd told Darius, he'd picked her up and spun her around. Whooping. Her legs dangling off the ground. She'd laughed and said, Put me down, Darius. Put me down. Hell, no, he'd said. I ain't letting go.

Dean had them do the scene three, four more times. AnnMarie went and sat by Albert, watching the sound tape spool through the machine. She felt a loneliness creeping in, settling in the pit of her stomach. She wanted to tell them they just words on a page. Words on a page. How could they know.

Next day was better. Call time wasn't until ten a.m. and Darius had stayed at his mother's. She got Star bathed and dressed in a little outfit, yellow ribbon in the curl of hair, white baby shoes on her feet. Packed a diaper bag she got from the hospital, made sure she had dipes, wipes, three bottles of formula. Then she called Darius, woke him up. She said, You want to come to set with me? I'm bringing Star. He said, I got things to do.

She called up Niki. Niki said, Hell yeah. I come with you.

When AnnMarie opened the door, she could tell Niki'd got herself dressed up. Starched white tee hanging low over ankle-length baggies, but pressed, with a crease down the middle of each pant leg. Brand-new ball cap on her head, bright red. Looked good against her cinnamon skin. Brought out the freckles. She helped AnnMarie lift the stroller down all the stairs to the subway platform, hopped the turnstile, opened up the emergency gate so the stroller could fit through, rode the hour out to Crown Heights. All the crew people coming over to marvel, to make faces at Star, touch her fingers, say how pretty she was. AnnMarie introduced Dean to Niki and Dean said, So you're Niki. Female Rapper Extraordinaire. And Niki bust out laughing, ducking her head, like she embarrassed. But AnnMarie could tell she liked it. Getting props from the movie director.

At lunch break, Dean said it was okay to leave if AnnMarie came back on time so they pushed Star in the stroller and walked over to the Golden Palace on Nostrand Avenue. Niki told her how she got into it with Nadette again, how Nadette jealous over this that the other thing. That girl always jealous, even though she still living with Dennis. AnnMarie said, Girl, maybe it's time you change things, you know, 'cause this just ain't working. Niki thought about it. Then she asked, What up with Darius. Where he at these days. AnnMarie hesitated, then said, He in and out. But she didn't want to talk about it. She just wanted to eat, Star fast asleep in the stroller, she could use both hands. And when they finished off all the Kung-Pow Chicken, Sweet and Spicy Shrimp and egg rolls, AnnMarie picked up the check and said, I got this. Pulling cash money from her pocket she'd earned from working.

Walking back to set, Niki said, You want me to take Star home? I was gonna stop off at the Target there on Flatbush. They got the Subway Series tees. I could pick up some dipes for you.

AnnMarie hestitated. She trusted Niki but not enough to take Star home alone. Someone cough in her face, that be mad nasty.

You don't wanna stay 'til we wrap out, AnnMarie asked.

Niki shrugged. They let me wear the headphones?

AnnMarie laughed. Hell yeah, they let you.

29

AnnMarie was getting mic'd inside the sound truck when Maya came up to the back end and said, Y'all should stay in the van.

Albert turned and looked at her. What's up?

Some fool has a gun. We're dealing with it.

AnnMarie said, What? Where.

Stay in the truck, AnnMarie.

But as soon as Maya disappeared street side, AnnMarie leaned out to get a view of things. Didn't look like nobody had a gun—kids sitting on the benches by the kiddie playground, woman pushing her laundry cart along the path. Everything look normal 'xcept for the crew people standing half hunched behind a car in the middle of the street.

AnnMarie could see Angie sitting over there on her boyfriend's lap. Mayfield, Tyrone, Jonah. All them, just lounging in the heat, laughing about something.

Then she saw the boy. Couldn't be more than thirteen, fourteen years old, looking mad sloppy, swinging the gun around and talking to somebody on the far side of the playground.

She ducked back, her heart banging in her chest. She hated the boy right then, the power he had to make her afraid. She felt Albert come up behind her and they watched him without speaking. Then Albert said, Have you seen those PSAs in the subway? It's a picture of a toy gun next to a real gun. The words say, Can you tell the difference?

AnnMarie shook her head. No, I ain't never seen that.

Cop car cruised slow up the block, then stopped in the middle of the street. Project kids don't move. They eyes on each other like the flashing lights don't exist. Maya and Dean leaning in the driver-side window but AnnMarie couldn't hear nothing what they saying.

When she looked again, the boy was gone. Maybe it'd been real. Maybe not. A toy gun the way everybody acting, even the cops—even the cops didn't get out the damn car.

She felt hot, her scalp tingling, and Wallace flashed in her mind. Her friend shot dead in Redfern projects. End of March when it was still cold, frost on the ground first thing in the morning, you see your breath in the air. Darius said he got mistook. Muthafuckers. Mistook for who, AnnMarie had wondered. His blood dried black on the cement in front of the D'Jantes' ground-floor window. That's all that'd been left.

There was a burst of laughter. Someone had turned on the sprinkler. The crew people moving between cars, stepping up onto the sidewalk, going about their business.

Albert's walkie crackled: *All clear.*

I guess we're clear, Albert said.

AnnMarie nodded but she didn't say nothing about the boy who'd changed his name to Stack.

30

It'd been a good day all around, her mother up and on her feet, moving slow but without the cane. You gonna be okay listening for Star when she wake up?

Blessed said, We be fine.

She called Darius, left a message saying they should leave by six o'clock. Hit me back, baby.

Then, just to make sure, she rolled the infant stroller right up to the couch, prepared two bottles of formula, set out Pampers, wipes and sanitizer—all of it on a tray ready to go. Making it easy for Blessed.

She got herself dressed, high heels, denim dress with the snaps you could leave unbuttoned if you want to. Dabbed Glow on her wrists, behind her ears, was putting on mascara when Darius called.

She said, Hey baby, you ready to go.

He said, Why you want to go out there.

His tone stopped her cold.

She said, What you mean, why? I told you. Angie's having a cookout. You said you go with me.

Darius didn't say nothing.

She could hear him doing something where he was, rustling around, something.

Darius.

What.

Come on, let's go. Come get me.

Why don't you come over here.

AnnMarie tsked. Oh, so you just switch up, last minute—you not going now?

No I ain't.

AnnMarie sighed. They hadn't seen each other for three days. He'd been staying out, and it'd been a relief almost, to be alone, just Star to worry about.

Well, what we gonna do then.

What the fuck, AnnMarie . . . You so special, you gotta know what we doing. You can't just hang with me. You got to be *doing* something.

I'm just asking, 'cause if we go to Angie's house, they gonna have food, music—

Nah, nah, nah. Me and Raymel got something.

What the fuck you talking about, me and Raymel. You just said, Come over. Since when you got plans with Raymel.

Ain't got nothing to do with you. If you wasn't always thinking about yourself maybe you see I'm trying to put something together.

Darius left that to hang in the air.

Trying to confuse her with his bullshit.

AnnMarie hesitated, then she said, Well what if I go out there myself, then you and Raymel can come later, you know, when you done with your thing.

Darius tsked. Raymel don't know nobody out there, he ain't interested. You so stupid sometime, don't even know why I bother. Then he hung up the phone.

Fuck you, she thought. Y'all never leave Far Rock anyway, don't know why I bother asking.

She took the train by herself, late in the evening, sun dipping, nearly gone, turning the sky an electric blue. The house was on

Kingston Avenue. She found it easy, and went around the side where the music was coming from.

Angie hugged her, told her she look nice, come on in, come on back. Weed in the air, *I'll be missing you . . .* blasting from the speakers. AnnMarie said, I love this song. And she didn't care she didn't know nobody, she start singing like Faith Evans, Angie's mouth dropping open. She said, Dang AnnMarie, I didn't know you could sing. Then they start dancing, everybody dancing, the whole backyard filled with people having fun. Wings and dogs cooking on the grill. A case full a wine coolers. Star at home safe and sound, AnnMarie went ahead and took a sip.

She left at midnight, Angie and Mayfield walking her to the sub-way, saying it ain't safe out here, all the thugs lurking. Mayfield's arm around Angie's shoulder as she told AnnMarie about a dance competition she trying out for—if you a finalist, you get to dance backup in a Def Jam video.

Wow, AnnMarie said. That's cool.

Yeah, Mayfield said, kissing Angie's cheek. Tha's my girl.

AnnMarie took the train all the way home, thinking about Angie dancing, tossing her baton and catching it the way she do. A melody flowing, AnnMarie slipped her feet out of her shoes and rubbed her toes together. She pictured Star swaddled in a blanket, eyes closed, breathing. Dancer, singer, drum major, flag girl. Which one she gonna be.

31

Just a stupid ol' thing that started around a couple words, turned into taunts about how people from Far Rockaway be mad stupid.

Melody tsked. She said, I'm not from Far Rockaway and I say *it's bleeding* too. Why does where you live make you stupid? How is your neighborhood an indicator of intelligence.

AnnMarie was nodding 'cause Melody be mad smart like that. She could cut you down if she want to.

But the Crown Heights kids just looked at her, then bust out laughing, all a them, all at the same time laughing in her face. One kid said, *How is your neighborhood an indicator of intelligence* . . . in a fake white-person voice and Melody ain't even white. She's Puerto Rican, both sides a the family.

AnnMarie had to step to that boy. She didn't care he was bigger, bumping her shoulder like she need to back the fuck up.

Melody with a hand on her arm, saying No, AnnMarie. Leave it.

But AnnMarie heard herself say, *Huh-uh* . . . This punk-ass bitch gonna insult you like that. Come at you with some bullshit. Fuck you, she spit. *What you gonna do? I fight you right now.*

And in a deep part of her mind, she wondered what she was doing. She a grown mother now. What the fuck she saying. She hadn't been in a fight in two years, if you didn't count Darius.

All the kids pressing in, shoving their bodies together in a tight circle, adrenaline pumping, the boy slamming his chest into hers but hesitating about taking the first punch. And when Maya and Dean broke through the circle, AnnMarie was aware of the relief she felt, Dean's voice lifting above the mayhem saying, *Okay, okay. What's going on, what's going on here.*

Nobody said anything for a minute. Maya standing there like she superfly, hands folded over her chest, her eyes cutting across their faces like a mother you don't want to cross. Some of the kids start to scatter but Maya said, Don't nobody move. A couple kids tittered but they stayed put. Ain't got nothing better to do, Ann-Marie thought. A fight always good for something.

Sonia said, We were just talking about whether you say *it's bleeding* for when it's hot outside or when it's cold.

And then they start coming at us with *you stupid* 'cause a where you from, AnnMarie said.

Dean sat down on the bench. He laughed. But that's good—is it bleeding hot or is it bleeding cold . . .

He said, Why don't we put it in the movie.

All the kids stood there dumb.

Huh?

What?

We gonna have a fight? On camera?

No, no, no, no, no . . . You girls discuss it.

Discuss it?

Talk about it . . . The three of you will be walking and one of you says something like *It's too hot out here* and the other one says *Yeah it's bleeding*. And you say *Wha—? You don't say it's bleeding hot, you say it's bleeding for when it's cold* and you kind of argue—you go back and forth but it's too hot to argue so you just kind of let it go. Then you stop at the ice-cream truck and all you guys over here— and he pointed to each and every one of them Crown Heights kids—you're getting ice cream too. You're at the truck getting ice cream. Do you see? Do you see how it will work?

So they did the scene, walking through the courtyard, the

three girls from the movie, Crown Heights kids by the ice-cream truck, mad quiet, listening to the lines and waiting for their cue. And they only had to do it three times—Bobby walking backwards, the camera up on his shoulder, Albert there with his boom mic off to the side, giving her a wink and a thumbs up when they wrap that shit out, and she felt happy inside, sitting back eating her ice cream—Dean bought ice cream for all the kids out there that day and AnnMarie was about to tell him about Blessed doing the same thing a long time ago but she thought, Nah. I'm good. Right here, right now, staying in the moment with Sonia and Melody and all the other kids whose names she didn't know but who'd come up with a scene about bleeding without spilling a single drop.

that's a wrap

32

August came and went, another birthday gone. She turned fifteen that year and felt proud, opened up a bank account, first bank account for the Walker family. Put the movie checks in, signed her name on the back the way the teller said. Drew cash money out, paid down the Con Ed bill for her mother, bought a Rocawear outfit for Star—a all-white jumpsuit with button snaps and white booties, soft as velvet. Dressed her up and took her out in the stroller- —she'd outgrown the infant one, pushing the new blue-and-white-striped Maclaren Techno up the block. To the grocery store or over to Niki's—AnnMarie feeling certain that everyone who saw them pass would know she was a good mother, doing it right.

Yeah, she'd often think. Making the movie was fun. It was mad fun, like her life had finally sprang open and even when it came to an end, crew wrapping up cables, light stands returned to the crate, big-ass camera tucked back in its cushioned box, she held on to that good feeling.

It took her a month before she discovered the roll of film she'd lost in the bottom of her makeup bag. Got them developed and sat on the couch looking at pictures with Blessed. Her mother smiling as she pointed out Sonia and Melody. Angie, Maya, Dean,

Albert—the last day of the shoot Albert shaved that Fu Manchu off. Looked like a entirely different person.

The new me, he'd said.

She'd call up the other girls, say Heyyyy, what up, what y'all doing, how you been. They'd ask about Star, and she'd tell them how she trying to sit up, grab on to every little thing, drooling, clapping her hands together. Melody started work full-time in a office and Sonia, right away that girl got cast in another movie. A movie about a white girl starting up at a all-black school. Sonia got the part of the new best friend. AnnMarie said, That's nice, Sonia. I'm happy for you. You deserve it. And they'd reminisce about all the fun they'd had but she felt lonely sometimes, missing the rhythm of those days—missing Darius too. He slept over once in a while, keeping clothes in the closet but mostly he out. Telling her he busy doing this that the other thing—saying he getting ready to MC at this block party, that club, talking about putting a mixtape together for a record label. By now, she didn't believe him. Knew it was mostly bullshit—things don't go his way, he'd drop into one of his moods, coming over, wanting to mix it up. Like the time he popped up, wanting to get some. She said, I ain't in the mood, Darius, but he pushed her down on the bed anyway, got a knee between her legs and spread her wide.

Other times he'd be his self, weed on his breath. Drifting in with takeout, or a new mixtape he said he made special for her listening pleasure. He'd say, Where my baby at? AnnMarie would turn and look at him. Check his face before she took a step. There was the occasional shopping bag. Pull the ribbon loose, she'd open up the boxes to find Puma and Baby Phat and Tommy outfits nestled inside. Tiny shoes made of real leather, little socks with lace around the ankles and beanie hats in baby pink and yellow and green.

Late October, she got a call from Ida B. Miss July said, Hello Ann-Marie, we've been trying to reach you.

Miss July told her she ought to come by, get her records taken care of, think about her GED . . . She said they got a life-after workshop—like a reunion with the other young mothers, share stories, birthing stories and how to get by. AnnMarie said, Thank you, Miss July. I be there . . . But she never went. The idea of that place was like a step back instead of forward—picturing that long metal table and the sleepy feeling that had always crept into Room 5. There'd been the slow girl. Crsytal. AnnMarie tried to picture it. Do she want to sit next to Crystal? Hell no. She wanted to talk to Dean and Sonia and think about the movie and what was around the corner. She knew they was in the edit room, putting all the scenes together on a machine Dean called a Avid.

She'd call him up. She'd say, How's it going? Is it done yet? How do it look? Is it good, what's happening? When's it coming out in the movies?

Dean'd have to cut her short, saying Patience, AnnMarie. Patience.

In November she missed her period. She didn't think nothing of it at first 'cause her periods had been spotty after she gave birth, sometimes blood, sometimes no. But when she went to the clinic for Star's six-month checkup, the clinic lady asked her how she feel. Clinic lady said, Star is healthy but how are you, Mom? Anything you want to talk about? AnnMarie said, Everything good. Everything fine. Clinic lady said, Have you become active again? What you mean, AnnMarie asked. The clinic lady meant sex. Wanted to know if she been fucking again. AnnMarie hesitated before answering. She hadn't been in the mood, felt no real desire for Darius so she said, No, I'm taking a break from that right now.

The clinic lady said, Okay, just make sure you use protection.

Even if you're not getting your period, you can still get pregnant. AnnMarie thanked her for the information.

When she left the clinic, she thought about the time Darius had made her fuck him. Yeah, he'd come inside her. She remembered that. She'd waited for him to leave before she got up, went to the bathroom, wipe his shit off.

Few blocks from Gateway, AnnMarie stopped and went inside Evelyn's Pharmacy, pushing Star down the narrow aisle 'til she found the section for females, her eyes passing over the boxes of douches and tampons and maxi pads, finally spotting the tests. But she couldn't bring herself to pick up a box. Not with Star only six month old. What they gonna think, *She stupid, or something?* So she backed down the aisle, past the counter where the sisters from 3D, Eve and Adrienne, sat with their matching sweat suits and crimped weaves—one a them saying, You didn't find what you need, AnnMarie? Leaning over the counter, eyeballing her as she backed out the door with a clatter.

She left Star at home with Blessed, took the bus all the way to Five Town mall, went into the CVS, plucked the test box off the shelf, got in line at a register where the salesgirl was a stranger. Got home, peed on the wand, staring at the purple plus-sign slowly emerging. Yeah, she pregnant. Fifteen and pregnant again. She sat down and cried.

33

A week went by, then another. AnnMarie spent them chasing him down, going by his mother Darla's house, walking over to Raymel's or Dennis', somehow missing him. Always just missing him.

She needed to talk to him, tell him about the anxious feeling, about the purple plus-sign and the nausea creeping in. His sister Vanessa'd say, Sit down, AnnMarie, let Star play with her cousin. His sister having given birth to a baby boy who she named Rocco James. His mother Darla panfrying potatoes in the kitchen, the onion and garlic smell wafting through the room, making Ann-Marie's mouth water. She'd say, He over at the studio, you want breakfast, AnnMarie? Why don't you eat something . . . Ann-Marie'd lift Star from the stroller, saying, Studio? What studio? Darla'd shrug. I don't know. I just heard something . . . You know how he is. Crossing to the table with a plate of fried potatoes and AnnMarie'd feel the hollowness expanding so she'd set Star in her lap and eat.

Days went by. Monday, Tuesday, Wednesday, AnnMarie with the morning sickness, waves of nausea crashing. Star start up crying, AnnMarie'd look at her and groan. On Thursday Dean called. He said, The movie got into a festival. An important festi-val, AnnMarie, called Sundance.

He said, It's great news. Really great news.

What's the matter, AnnMarie. Why aren't you excited.

No, that's great, Dean. I'm happy for you. I'm very happy for you.

No, AnnMarie, be happy for you. Be happy 'cause we're all going. We're going in January. We'll go to the screenings, you'll talk to people, talk about your experience, see other movies if you want to . . . It's going to be a great time.

AnnMarie sat down and took a breath. She said, We going where?

Utah, AnnMarie. We're flying to Utah.

Flying. On a airplane? She didn't know where Utah was but she heard the excitement in his voice, the enthusiasm like a dose of medicine. She pressed the phone to her ear, she said, I don't got money for a airplane, Dean.

He said, Don't worry, AnnMarie, all you need is a warm coat.

And she smiled then. 'Cause it was good news and what she'd been waiting for. She tried to picture it. A film festival. In Utah. Utah . . . ? Where that at. She'd have to look on a map.

The next few days floated past, AnnMarie daydreaming, a little bubble of excitement knocking around inside, blocking out the image of the plus-sign. She called up Sonia and Melody, left messages on their answering machines. What you gonna wear, what you gonna bring. Can you believe it? We going on a airplane. The phone start ringing off the hook, calls back and forth. She went by to see Niki and Niki let her talk, going on and on about the news, AnnMarie bugging with excitement. Niki leaned back on the bed and grinned. Word—you a movie star now. AnnMarie threw her arms around Niki and squeezed, Niki laughing. She said, Dang, AnnMarie, calm down. AnnMarie let her go and said, I just can't believe it. I can't believe it. I never been on a airplane before.

Niki said, What you gonna do with Star. You bringing her with you? And AnnMarie realized she hadn't thought that part out so there were more phone calls and messages left, waiting for Dean to call back and when the phone rang on Saturday afternoon, she ran across the room and picked up.

She heard a operator's voice saying, Will you accept the charges from Darius Greene. She thought, Charges? Who this on my phone. Then she heard his voice thin and faint in the background, saying, *AnnMarie! AnnMarie . . .*

Darius?

The operator cut in, Do you accept the charges? No speaking unless you *accept the charges.*

AnnMarie said, Yes I do and get off the line. She heard the click and said, Darius? Where are you?

I'm in jail, baby. They saying I robbed a store. But I got mistook, you know how they do—I ain't done it and these muthafuckas beat me upside the head with a book, tryin' to get me to confess. And his voice faded a little at that point 'cause she was thinking about the movie festival and the plus-sign she hadn't told him about and how she need to get Star on jar food and what did he just say, they beating him in the head with a book?

I need you, baby . . . Come get me out.

Come where, she asked. Get you out how?

Was he crying? The line start to crackle and his voice broke up but she'd heard him.

I need you, baby. You all I got.

AnnMarie stood there for a long while after she hung up the phone. Then she ran into the bathroom, brought to her knees by an upswell of nausea. Vomit from lunch turning into dry heaves and after she finished off, she rinsed her mouth, then walked back into the room where Star was, crawling across the floor of the Pack 'n Play. She watched her daughter lace her fingers around the lip of the playpen and pull herself up. Just like that. All in one motion, Star was standing, her eyes shining, smiling like she the Cheshire Cat. AnnMarie tried to be happy, scooping her up, smothering her with kisses. Deciding right then to keep the phone call a secret. She said, Ma, you know what Star just did? Ma, come out here and take a look at this.

34

On Monday morning, she went down to the bank and withdrew the last of her movie money. Closed out the account. It was exactly seventy dollars. Folded the bills and slipped them in her pocket. She'd called up Raymel. He told her how it usually went down. Probably a sentence hearing, he'd said. Bring bail money just in case. She made up an excuse and left Star at home with her mother, caught the dollar van and rode it all the way out to the Queens County Courthouse. Stood in line at security, then followed the flow of people up the stairs and into the building. Saw a window and a sign that said INFORMATION, but the stool was empty behind the plexiglass. AnnMarie waited, peering into the big room with a low ceiling, tiles missing in places, a couple of women talking in a corner behind a desk. 'Xcuse me, AnnMarie said, pushing her mouth up to the slatted talk hole. 'Xcuse me, she said again. One of the women turned, moving her round ass mad slow across the room where she plunked down behind a desk, not the stool by the window, and pulled open a drawer, hunting for something. AnnMarie said, How can I find out about sentencing. Without looking up, the woman said, Window 5. Up the stairs, second floor. AnnMarie climbed the stairs and found the line of people, snaking all the way down the corridor, shoulders slumped, a dead feeling in the air, music blasting from somebody's headphones.

Next.

Next.

Step to the line.

Come to the line.

Come to the line.

Come to the line.

When AnnMarie's turn came, she stepped to the window. What courtroom I go to for sentencing? she asked.

Name.

AnnMarie Walker.

The man behind the desk had his eyes on the computer screen, his finger tapping at a key. Tapping. Tapping.

There's no AnnMarie Walker. What was the arrest date?

No, wait, AnnMarie said, confused, you want *my* name?

The man glanced at her. He said, Name of the defendant.

Defendant?

Who got arrested, the man said, impatient.

Oh. Darius. Darius Greene.

Arrest date.

I don't know, he called me on Saturday but I don't know—

Precinct.

I don't know.

The man looked up again, his eyes on her like she stupid.

I don't know the precinct. Maybe the 101 . . . ? You don't got his name in there?

He said, How old are you?

I'm fifteen.

He shook his head, went back to the computer screen, tapping on the key with his finger.

Come on, mister, you don't got his name in there? Darius

Greene. G-R-E-E-N-E. He said to come here and bring him bail money.

Courtroom B.

He looked past her then and said, *Next. Step to the line.*

AnnMarie stood at the back of the courtroom and scanned the half-filled benches. Right away she spotted Raymel's dented-in head in the back row and knew she'd come to the right place. She excused her way past a old grandma holding a toddler in her lap, stepped over two women who'd fallen asleep, heads drooping into they chest.

Raymel looked up as she approached, then turned to the girl next to him and told her to scoot down.

AnnMarie said, What up, he come out yet?

Nah . . . We been here waiting.

AnnMarie glanced past him to the girl on his left—she was about AnnMarie's age, with blue eye shadow and a mouth shiny with lip gloss.

How long you been waiting, AnnMarie asked.

Mad long, the girl said. A hour at least.

Raymel stretched. He said, I'm getting hungry.

Word, the girl said.

AnnMarie looked to the front of the room. The judge up there, his face patchy and gray, eyeing one black dude after another as each one shuffled out the green door in city-issue jumpsuits. Landing at the table where a white man stood in a loose-fitting blue suit. AnnMarie couldn't see his face, only the way he stood, like he needed a iron and a press to straighten his back, communicating with the judge.

Who that? AnnMarie whispered.

He the lawyer, I think, Raymel said.

Say what? He look mad sloppy.

The girl laughed softly. AnnMarie glanced at her and their eyes met.

I hope he ain't here for Darius.

Drug possession. Domestic violence. Illegal weapon. Resisting arrest. Disorderly conduct. Disorderly conduct. Disorderly conduct. Robbery. Attempted Robbery. Resisting Arrest. Assault. Hearing dates passed out. Bail set. Bail denied. But no Darius. Then the judge was standing, scooping up his robe from around his ankles. Smacked the gavel on wood. Lunch break. Raymel stood up and stretched. He said, I be back. And then he was scooting past the girl and gone.

Where he going, AnnMarie asked.

The girl shrugged. They sat for a moment in silence as people started to file out the courtroom. AnnMarie wondered what she should do. Others had stayed put, lingering by the benches, standing and stretching, then taking a seat again.

She glanced at the girl.

Where you from? You live in Far Rockaway?

The girl said, Yeah . . . I live with my aunt.

How you know Raymel, you his girl?

The girl shook her head. She said, I'm CeeCee.

Okay. I'm AnnMarie.

The girl said, I know who you are.

AnnMarie looked at her.

Darius told me about you.

AnnMarie frowned. Darius?

And her heart buckled right then, hearing the words come outta that lip-gloss mouth, saying, Yeah, he my boyfriend.

———

Excuse me? What you mean he your boyfriend—you know I'm his baby mother . . .

I know, he told me all about you. He said y'all ain't together anymore.

AnnMarie stared in disbelief but CeeCee kept smiling, sitting there like it ain't no thing.

No, we're still together, AnnMarie said. He lives with me at my mother's house.

CeeCee ignored that. She said, Did you like the clothes I got for Star?

Say what?

The outfits I got for Star, did they fit?

The girl had opened up her bag, her hand inside searching for something.

The Baby Phat and little Tommy outfits . . .

You bought those?

Um-hm, she said, pulling out her wallet. The Puma booties, I chose the 6-to-9 month so she had room to grow. Ann-Marie just looked at her in shock. Muthafucker. This girl buying clothes for Star? CeeCee flipped open her wallet and held it out to AnnMarie.

AnnMarie saw Star's face staring up at her, the picture tucked beneath the square of clear plastic. It was the same picture Ann-Marie carried in her wallet, this girl rambling on about how Darius said she could be Star's stepmother and how happy she is to be there if Star need anything, how she can't wait to meet her, that baby so cute, she such a cute baby. AnnMarie's head spinning, her whole body going numb.

'Cept the thumping of her heart. She wanted to rip it outta her chest. Crack her rib cage open, yank it out her own damn self. She felt a rustle next to her, the girl moving past down the aisle, but she kept her eye on the door. The green one that had opened and closed a dozen times, all the boys and men walking through in they jumpsuits. She looked down at her hand, pictured a gun there, a gun she'd raise up and shoot him with.

By December, that little plus-sign became a negative—she start bleedin' in the middle of the night, AnnMarie curled up in a ball a pain, the crampy feeling taking her breath away. Blessed said, Throw the sheets out. They ain't worth keeping.

Darius, he never even knew. She never told him. Muthafucker. Let him rot in jail. He tried calling. Do you accept the charges. She hung up the phone.

And the days went by like that. Rolling past in slow motion. A feeling like she underwater. Like she'd never been in a movie, never done nothing special at all.

family tree, remix

35

She woke up, blurry-eyed, four forty-five in the morning, the space on the bed next to her empty, Star standing in the crib, wet with pee. AnnMarie stumbled over, lifted her out, got her nightie off, onesie off, diaper sagging, searched in the dark for a clean one and found the pack empty. She brought Star into the bed anyway, pulling the covers up to her chin, hand on her belly the way she liked, and they slept again until the clang and hiss of the radiator woke them for good.

Later, she sat on the couch, Star in her lap sucking on a bottle while she called Darius on his phone. She knew he'd worked the night before, his shift ending sometime around one, but she didn't know where he'd gone after and now all she got was the music beat he'd recorded before the sound of the beep.

She called again at seven, then again at seven fifteen. This time he picked up, music in the background, people's voices, party going on somewhere. She said, Where you at? Star need diapers.

I be there, he said.

Darius had stayed in lockup for twenty-three days and when he got out, he told her the story. Showed up at her door one morning and she let him hang out to dry, telling her about the day the judge heard his case and how the store clerk and only witness never showed. Case dismissed. Judge gave him a lecture. Saying, You lucky this time. I don't want you in my courtroom again. Change up. Act right. Get a job. You on probation. She heard him out, her foot holding the door open, waiting for him to get to the part about CeeCee. And something musta scared him, maybe it was jail time, maybe it was that she wasn't letting him in 'cause he said, No more robbin', no more fights. I want to live with you, Ann-Marie. Let's live together and be a true family. The girl CeeCee ain't nothing.

She a stalker, AnnMarie.

You think I'ma let some bitch buy clothes for my child?

You think I can't provide?

And he said it with such disgust that she believed him.

He started asking around. Somebody knew somebody who knew somebody worked at Puffy's restaurant in the city so he got him-self a job as a line cook and started bringing home takeout in a glossy copper-colored bag.

It was mad classy, he said, describing it to her one night when they were laying in bed side by side. White tablecloths, white couches and chairs, white marble counters. Chandeliers hang-ing. Waiters in white suits who took care of all the playas walking through the door. She had rolled over and kissed him. She said, When you gonna cook me something.

I cook for you, he said. Chef Supreme.

What's that.

Darius laughed and rubbed her thigh. It's my specialty, what you think. Cut a beef this thick, off the hindquarter, choicest part a the meat. Potato au gratin. Skinny beans, steamed down four minutes tops.

Listen to you, she said. You been schooled.

Yeah . . . yeah, he said, laughing. I cook for you.

Half past nine, Darius still wasn't home. Diaperless and naked waist-down, Star peed all over the couch, leaving a big wet mark on the cushion but Blessed wasn't up yet so AnnMarie covered it with a towel and let it be. She snuck into her mother's room, found her purse, took the three dollars from her wallet, got Star bundled up in the stroller, got herself bundled too and took the elevator down to the street.

It was cold. Fingers burning, January wind whistling through the crumble-down building on the corner, whipping up dirt and fine dust, pushing it out into the street. Dang. She pulled her sweater sleeves down over her fingers, then set out, pushing the stroller with her knuckles, taking 20th to New Haven, the wheels popping over the cracked cement, her breath coming out in bursts of white cloud.

At the entrance of J&B, AnnMarie navigated the stroller in through the doors, shivered in the warm air then grabbed up a shopping basket and moved toward the aisles.

The store was mostly empty, a fella cutting up boxes in the cereal aisle, Frito man restocking chips on the shelves. She went past him to the canned goods, found the row of baby food. Seven months old, Star going through the jar food, three a day.

Peas, apple, sweet potato. 39 cent.

Pureed chicken. Beef and potato. Plain beef. 49 cent.

She did the math, put one jar back then headed to the diaper aisle, Star being good, playing with the bottle of apple juice, saying Yah, yah, yah, yah as she teethed on the nipple.

She paused in front of the Pampers, took down two packs of size 6-to-9 month and pretended to read the fine print. She set one of the packs into the shopping basket, then bent over Star, stroked her cheek, saying Yah, yah, you a good girl and with the other hand slipped the second pack into her shoulder bag.

She fussed with Star for a second longer, then laced her arm through the basket handle and pushed the stroller down the aisle to check out.

Breathe, she told herself. *Star need these. Just breathe.*

How much the Pampers? There's no price on it.

AnnMarie plucked the Pampers from the basket and handed them to the checkout girl who scanned the bars.

$13.95

AnnMarie tsked. There ain't no sale on? I thought there was a sale.

The girl snapped her gum.

There a sale goin' on at Thriftway. Box a Pampers cost you $18.99.

Word?

Yeah. Eighty in a box. It's a good deal you think about it.

I'ma go over there then. I'll just get the baby food.

The girl set the pack of Pampers off to the side, rang up the baby food.

AnnMarie handed over the three dollars, collected twelve cent change.

She took her time, looping the plastic bag onto the handle of the stroller, tucking the blanket around Star, making sure she snug. Her heart lifting out her chest when the manager step out from the raised booth at the end of the aisle, but all he said was, *Can you work a double?* Talking to the salesgirl as AnnMarie pushed Star out the door into the cold, bright sun.

Breathe, she told herself. Just breathe. Ain't nobody know. But Dean popped into her head right then and she felt a rush of shame. Stealing like she some kind a ghetto trash. Sonia and Melody— she'd be seeing them soon enough. Movie playing at the festival. Two weeks, they flying to Park City, Utah. First screening for the people, Dean had said. It got her excited but nervous too. She'd asked about the money, she ain't got no money. He said, Don't worry, AnnMarie. We're gonna take care of you. This made her smile. The thought of getting on a plane. Staying in a real hotel. Red carpet. Watching herself up on the big screen.

Fuck it. Ain't nobody gonna know.

Near the corner of New Haven, she stopped, pulled her sweater sleeves down over her hands and when she looked up she saw a girl emerge from the bodega across the street, a phone pressed to her ear. For a moment, AnnMarie couldn't move. Even from this distance, AnnMarie knew who it was. *CeeCee.*

What she got on. Little bitty miniskirt, flimsy sweater, no coat. Bitch must be crazy. Her lips moving, saying something into the phone, moving this way now, her shoulders up by her ears, hunched against the wind.

AnnMarie lifted the front wheels of the stroller and swiveled Star around. She thought she heard her name but she didn't look back. *Don't go there*, she thought. It ain't worth it. You got things to do.

When she walked in, the pots and pans were piled on the couch which meant something in the oven and she could smell it too, something good like mac and cheese cooking. She parked the stroller by the door and let Star sleep.

What you cooking, Ma?

Blessed was sitting in the chair, still in her housedress, nylon cap but no wig, pill bottles open on the TV tray.

Not me. Miss Ondine.

In the kitchen, Ondine didn't turn around. She said, It's not for you, AnnMarie, it's for my nephew's party. He's turning two.

AnnMarie tsked. Ma, why you let her *do* that. She supposed to be working, she come over here and cook food for her damn family, skinny-ass bitch.

AnnMarie!

Ondine turned from the stove with a plate of scrambled eggs and toast. She set it in front of Blessed and said, Here your food. And you better do something about her or I'm leaving. I won't have some little girl cussing me like that.

AnnMarie reached for the phone and punched in Darius' number, listening to it ring, the whole while glaring at Ondine, her mother saying, Did you go to Family Services?

AnnMarie looked at her like, *Can't you see I'm on the phone.*

Her mother waited.

I told you I did, AnnMarie said. I did it yesterday.

She heard tsking sounds from the kitchen.

What is wrong with her she always in my business?

Blessed ignored her. She said, You meet with Miss Patterson?

No, some other lady.

Did they give you food stamps?

I told you I ain't asking for that.

She heard the shower go on. AnnMarie hung up the phone, scowling. Whyn't you tell me he was home?

She went into the bedroom and looked around. Yeah, he home. Tokens and phone up on the dresser. She picked up his sweater, put her face to it and breathed. She hesitated, then picked up his phone and went scrolling.

Darius came into the room, towel around his waist, smelling like Irish Spring. She sat on the bed and watched him dress.

I saw that girl.

Who.

CeeCee, coming out the deli on New Haven.

Darius gave her a look, halfways smiling. I told you that girl stalking me.

He lay back on the bed, stretched an arm out for her to come close.

She lay down next to him, put her hand on his chest.

You got any Q-tips?

In the bathroom.

I looked. There ain't none.

Why don't you change your number.

Why.

AnnMarie shrugged, glancing at him, checking for guilt on his face.

AnnMarie! her mother called.

AnnMarie sat up, then crossed to the door.

It's Family Services, Blessed said.

AnnMarie put the phone to her ear and listened. Lady said they got an opening at a playgroup. You don't got day care? Ann-Marie asked. No, it's a playgroup run by a licensed caregiver. She's covered under our plan. It's five dollars a day. AnnMarie took down the name and address, told the lady she go check it out.

When she went back into the bedroom, Darius was under the covers, asleep. She sat on the edge of the bed, flipped open her notebook and found her to-do list.

School records from Ida B

Get GED

Day Care

Star clothes

New Coat/Glove

She crossed out *Day Care* and wrote *play grupe/lisens care giver* then wrote the name and address from the slip of paper into her notebook.

Her mother'd been on her to get herself on welfare, get the food stamps coming in, money for bills but AnnMarie just looked at her like, *And end up like you?* Huh-uh, no thank you. I got a movie festival to go to.

She pictured it. Like on *Entertainment Tonight.* Microphones up to her mouth, flashbulbs popping. Paparazzi ask, she in school, getting her diploma. Her daughter, Star Blaze Walker Greene—she in a playgroup.

She hadn't told Darius about Utah. Two weeks to go, she still had time. She turned, put her hand on his back. She felt his skin warm against hers.

36

The next day Niki came over, said *Gladiator* playing. Come on, I take you. AnnMarie said Darius sleeping. She supposed to wake him at three o'clock for his shift. Niki said, You ever heard of a alarm clock.

So they folded up the stroller, hopped a dollar van and went out to Jamaica. When they got to the theater, they pushed Star around the block a couple times 'til she fell asleep but when they got up to the booth, the ticket fella said, You can't bring a baby in here. Niki looked at him like he stupid.

She said, You see she sleeping?

The fella hesitated, then said, Go on but if she starts disrupting . . .

Yeah, yeah, Niki said, go sell some popcorn.

The whole time watching, AnnMarie pictured herself up there with Russell Crowe, wearing that beautiful gown. All that trickery and violence. It was mad violent. Slaves getting ripped apart by lions. About three-quarters through, Star woke up and started squirming. Niki held her, shushing her softly and she was okay again until the end.

They walked out the theater into the cold, talking about how badass all them slaves was, about the lions looking mad real even though you could see how they faked it 'cause what actor gonna get up in there with some live animals. They kept talking inside the dollar van, chatting up a storm, rewinding the movie in they minds, busting up over the perverted brother and his lecherous ways, and by the time they stepped out the van, AnnMarie'd decided Darius had to see the movie, how she'd drag him there if she had to. But when they got back to her building, AnnMarie slowed, then froze completely.

Inside the first set of doors stood CeeCee—don't know how she got in but there she was, *inside*, shivering in that same flimsy sweater.

Hey AnnMarie, CeeCee said, her teeth chattering she so cold. Blue eye shadow and that lip-gloss mouth.

AnnMarie spun the stroller around, got the key in the second door and said, What you want, CeeCee.

CeeCee dropped into a squat and smiled, touching Star's toes through the blanket, looking up at Niki now, saying, She so cute ain't she?

AnnMarie pulled the stroller away. I said what you want, CeeCee?

CeeCee stood up and straightened her skirt. I need to talk to Darius.

He ain't here.

He said he be here playing with Star.

You see he ain't here, don't you.

Niki shifted, looking between the two of them.

Okay, but I got to talk to him.

He ain't here. He ain't here. He ain't here. Get it.

CeeCee seemed to shrink. Skinny and frail in that sweater hanging down her thighs and for a second it looked like she gonna cry.

But AnnMarie couldn't help herself. She said, You know Darius says you stalking him. You know that, right? He says you ain't nothing but a stalker bitch.

CeeCee tossed her head like it ain't no thing. But AnnMarie saw her eyes narrow.

Then she said, He says the same thing about you.

AnnMarie didn't know how she got upstairs, but there she was, on the couch, that sick feeling lifting through her chest, Niki on the floor playing with Star, saying something but all she could hear was CeeCee's voice in her head. *You know we's having a baby together. Didn't he tell you?*

She'd wanted to punch that girl, stick a knife in her eye but she hadn't. She'd just stood there like a fucking retard, unable to move. Niki's eyes on her, making the whole thing worse.

What? AnnMarie asked Niki now. What you say?

I said, She's a dancer at Crush.

Niki stood, setting Star in AnnMarie's lap. That's how I know her. Crush. Remember that place Nadette work at for a while?

AnnMarie didn't say anything.

Niki stared at her. She waved a hand in front of her face, laughing.

I'm out, Niki said.

What, where you going?

I gotta go, she said. I'll check you later.

Before she left, Niki kissed two fingers and blew her the peace sign.

AnnMarie barely looked up. The disbelief and shock spinning itself into a mass of burning rage. Star half bouncing in her lap, batting at her face with her little hands until AnnMarie took hold of her wrists and stopped her. Stop, she said, pushing herself up off the couch. Swinging Star onto her hip, she headed for him.

He was in the bathroom, brushing his teeth. AnnMarie shifted Star onto the other hip.

You know who was downstairs?

Darius didn't answer, his eyes on his own reflection. She said, That bitch CeeCee. She's telling me you says *I'm* the stalker. She says soon as she has her baby, you goin' off to live with her.

Darius frowned but still didn't speak.

Did you hear what I said?

He kept brushing.

She pushed him. Ain't your teeth clean yet? Spit that out.

And she saw him do it. Purse his lips and spit the whole mess into her face. She felt it land wet and disgusting and she couldn't speak she was so shocked, hearing him say, Bitch don't *touch* me.

She walked into her room, set Star in the crib, came back at him with one of her high heels. She coulda killed him she so angry, tried to gauge his eyes out, draw blood, something. Star was screaming, watching from the crib as they spilled out into the hallway. Her mother yelling from the other room, *What is going on, why that baby crying* but Darius didn't care, he got the shoe away and threw her down. She tried to get away, scooting back across the floor, kicking at his arms, thrashing but he got hold of her leg and yanked her forward 'til he'd straddled her, had a fistful of her hair and held her fast. The backhand slap made her eyeballs rattle but it was the punch to the nose that did it. Blood gushing and pain like nothing else, not the birth of Star, not Carlton's belt, not the beatings from Grandma Mason. Somehow this was worse.

No one called the police. No neighbors banged on the door. Blessed barely made it out her bedroom, leaning on her cane, say-ing *AnnMarie . . . AnnMarie, what the hell going on . . .* Maybe 'cause it was over before it started. Darius walking out. She couldn't remember screaming, maybe she had, maybe she hadn't. All she knew was her heart breaking into a thousand pieces. Didn't matter her body was battered. That last kick to the kidney, silencing her, leaving her gasping for air, she was used to that.

37

She woke up feeling like she'd been hit by a truck. Bruised and broken, her face swollen, ribs aching—it hurt to breathe. Couldn't even brush her teeth her mouth hurt so bad. Got back into bed and went to sleep. Blessed stood in the door with Star in her arms. Five days, her mother came to the door, sometimes coming in to set a TV tray on the bed, or to take it out again. Five days a her saying, Why you keep taking him back, he treat you like that. It's your own fault, AnnMarie. When you take him back.

Shut the fuck up, Ma. Please. Just shut the fuck up.

The address they gave her was 3244 Butler Place, number 34. The caregiver name was Princess Jones. That her real name? Ann-Marie had asked. Family Services said, Yeah, that's what it says.

AnnMarie wound her way through the long corridor, pushing the stroller left then right until she found number 34 at the end of the hall. Her face had shrunk back down to size and she looked herself again, could smile without nothing hurting.

Princess Jones opened the door and let her in. It was a big room with a checkerboard rug and there was bricks made of cardboard for stacking and books in the corner and a plastic kitchenette and three children, maybe two years old, playing with a plastic tea set.

AnnMarie glanced at the woman as she spoke—she was short

and squat with hair going white, combed back flat against her head. Little tendrils of gray curling by her ears, black moles scattered across her neck.

Princess Jones was saying, I have a routine I follow. Playtime, snack, outdoor play, lunch, rest, playtime, book. Some mothers need extra hours, the children stay for dinner. I give them a snack at ten o'clock, something healthy like an apple or an orange, and another snack at two. You provide lunch.

AnnMarie was thinking, Star ain't eating no apple yet, and as if she could read her mind the lady said, You can leave baby food with me and I can feed Star that. Any formula she take, leave that too.

She reached out both hands and said, Let me hold this child. Come, Star, let's see if we get along.

Star went into her arms easy, held on to the lady's shirt, legs wrapped around her hip as Princess showed AnnMarie the bathroom, the bedroom where three cribs and a Pack 'n Play stood and the kitchen where a toddler's table and chairs had been placed under the window. The rooms were bright, the floor clean, ain't nothing bad here. Little ones playing with the tea set.

As she walked home, she thought about Princess Jones and the playgroup. Maybe she do it. Maybe she would. Time for school, get her GED. Call up Dean, make another movie. *Roll sound. Roll camera.* The director call *Action.*

Get the fuck outta Far Rock. Anywhere but here.

When AnnMarie came home, Ondine was on the phone.

Where my mother at?

Shhh, she sleeping.

Did you take her out?

She *sleeping.* Now hush. I'm on the phone.

She said, Miss Jeffers? Hello Miss Jeffers, this is Ondine Jackson. Your Avon order came in, how you want to pay for that.

AnnMarie went into the bedroom and slammed her door.

That night she dreamed of Princess Jones, woke with a start and reached for Darius. But the bed was empty and she remembered they were done.

She lay awake, staring into the darkness. The apartment quiet except for the raspy in and out of Star breathing. She thought about those car rides with Grandma Mason to the agency for the monthly check-ins. It was the only time she got cheese and crackers, her favorite snack. Flat-footed bitch. Grandma Mason coulda beat her five times the day before, but if it was agency day, AnnMarie got cheese and crackers and she kept quiet.

AnnMarie tried to block out the memory but the shame rose and fell with each breath she took. She got up, went into the living room and turned the TV on. What a fool she was, little girl six, seven years old, didn't say nothing to her mother. They used to blindfold her, those boys. Grandma Mason's grandsons. It was Gerome. It was Jay. Tie a do-rag over her eyes. Lift up her dress, pull her panties down. Press up against her crack. Rubbing and cumming. Rubbing and cumming. She tried to hide but they always found her.

She missed Darius all of a sudden, an ache so strong she didn't know what to do. How could she miss him. She didn't understand it. Wanting his arms around her right then, like a warm blanket. She wandered in and out of her bedroom, flipped on the kitchen light and stood, staring at the floor. Out the window, she saw the streetlamp flickering on the corner and a figure passing underneath.

She got back in bed, closed her eyes but there it was, the shame like a beast mocking. You nobody. Worth nothing. Piece a dust. Speck a dirt. She sat up, crossed to the crib and scooped Star, still sleeping, into her arms. Brought her into the bed and laid her down close to the wall so she wouldn't roll off. She put her cheek up to Star's mouth, felt the warm air moving across her cheek. AnnMarie watched her, chest rising and falling, like waves crashing, like a star blazing across the night sky.

Push back, she thought. Push back.

38

It'd come to her in the night, the only thing she knew for sure—
ain't no way she leaving Star with a stranger in a strange house, no
matter how neat and tidy. But when she woke the next morning a
feeling of apprehension still hovered, leaving her moody and restless so she packed Star up into the stroller and went by to see Niki.

Niki's brother Bodie opened the door and let her in. Niki was
sitting on the floor, an arm laced over her knee and she didn't
look up.

What you doing, AnnMarie asked.

Shhh, I'm posing.

She glanced at Bodie who had sat back down again, a sketch
pad in his lap. AnnMarie shifted Star onto her other hip, then
leaned over to look.

Dang Bodie, tha's good. I didn't know you could draw, when
you start drawing?

Tha's 'cause he gay.

AnnMarie start to laugh, then realized Niki wasn't joking.

Cedrick don't let him draw. Think it make him more gay.

Oh, AnnMarie said.

Cedrick was their foster father. Bodie and Niki weren't related
by blood, just by Cedrick.

You like boys, Bodie?

Duh, Bodie said, his tongue coming out, stabbing at his lip in concentration. His eyes on Niki's face, hand moving across the page.

You hear, Bodie? Niki said. AnnMarie's going on a airplane. To a movie festival.

AnnMarie caught the edge in her voice, and for a second she was surprised. When she first told Niki the news, she'd acted happy—they'd spent the day talking about it, AnnMarie on cloud nine, Niki right there with her, dreaming about stardom and the path to get there. She wondered when the hate start brewing.

AnnMarie said, Ain't no thing. I still gotta get a job. Get my GED.

Niki tsked. Why you need a job. Roll out the red carpet. You a movie star now.

Bodie glanced up from the drawing. Shut up, jealous. You should be glad for AnnMarie.

Niki didn't say nothing, just sat there, her face empty of expression. Which crushed her, a feeling like loneliness sweeping through the room. A line dividing them. AnnMarie glanced at the drawing. All shade, no lines. It was Niki alright, looking mad beautiful.

Then she heard Niki say, You should draw Star next.

Bodie shrugged. I draw her, but she got to sit still. Can't be climbing all over the place.

So Niki helped AnnMarie strap Star in the stroller, gave her a bottle to suck on, took her down to the street. AnnMarie singing a little melody soft under her breath as Niki walked along beside her, their shoulders brushing.

Niki said, You know I watch Star for you.

AnnMarie looked at her. What you mean.

When you go to Utah, Niki said. You know I'ma help Blessed out.

AnnMarie smiled. You know I'ma bring you something.

Like what.

A souvenir.

Like what.

How 'bout snow.

Niki bust out laughing. Took four times around the block, but they did it, got Star to fall asleep.

39

Nine in the morning, she finally got past the busy signal and got someone on the phone. The man said, You don't need an appointment. Welfare open eight a.m. to five p.m., Monday to Friday. You want food stamps you go to Room Number 3. We at 219 Beach 59th Street, first floor.

The night before, Star had woke up crying. AnnMarie dead tired, third night in a row, Star'd been fussy. Doctor had told her, Get her a teething ring. She teething. So AnnMarie'd gone into the Thriftway, walked the aisle, slipped one into her pocket. She'd used it each night, Star sitting up in her lap, drooling as she gummed the soft plastic.

Star finally fell asleep again, but she hadn't. She made a list. Formula, quarters for laundry, baby detergent, baby food, diapers, wipes. Star need clothes, onesies stretched tight, had to cut the toe part off to give her room. Coat. Pair a boots. Snow boots. Scarf. Gloves.

By nine forty-five, AnnMarie got Star fed and bundled up, ready to go, put the slip of paper with the address in her pocket. Went back for the teething ring, made Star clutch it with her fingers. Down the elevator, out the doors and fuck all if Darius ain't out front, talking to his homies, pretending he don't see her but soon as she go past, he followed.

Where you going.

She kept her mouth shut. Fuck that. She kept her eyes forward, hands on the stroller, pushing it along over the uneven sidewalk, then she stopped, stood for a minute, pulling her sweater cuffs down over her hands. Darius kept walking, not even realizing she ain't there and inside she smiled at that little stupidity until he turned, raising his hands like, *Come on now . . .*

He stood there 'til she caught up, then he reached over and put a hand on the stroller.

Hol' up now. Hold up and let me talk to you.

No, Darius. Let go the stroller.

What you mean *let go*, this my child. You gonna beef wit' me on the street, that what you wanna do?

AnnMarie didn't answer.

But she dropped her hands from the stroller, left Star there for him to push and walked away. She didn't have to turn around, she could tell he was right behind, the stroller wheels squeaking as they rolled over the frozen sidewalk, all the one-way streets circling, Brookhaven to Grassmere, taking one turn after another until she found herself in front of the kiddie park that'd been closed for construction. Darius came up behind her, tucked the stroller in next to a bench and sat down. Hunched up against the cold, AnnMarie waited.

He blew into his hands, shoved them back into his pockets.

He said, I got paid.

AnnMarie tsked. That all you got to say, you spit in my face, you beat me and that's it—*I got paid.*

He shook his head like he embarrassed. Now that right there was stupid and I admit it. I know I did wrong and I'ma apologize to you.

Why you do it, Darius, why you think you can treat me like that. That girl coming around, saying you having a baby with her.

He reached out and played with Star, her fingers batting at his hands, saying *da da da da da da* and when she kicked off the blanket, he rose, leaned over and tucked her back in.

I mean, what you gonna do?

I ain't gonna do nothing.

AnnMarie tsked. You a fucking dog, you know that.

He was quiet for a long time. He so quiet AnnMarie wondered if they be able to fix it.

He blew into his hands, his thighs trembling from the cold.

She said, Well, what you gonna do. You gonna be with me or her.

He said, CeeCee gonna have her baby whether you like it or not.

He said, I know I act stupid. I'm a flawed individual, feel me. But we's a family. You, me and Star. That ain't never gonna change.

She studied him for a moment. Star got his mouth and chin. She could see it.

She reached up and adjusted her do-rag. She need to get her hair done soon. Festival roll up, she need to be ready.

Darius shoved his hands in his pockets, bracing himself against the wind. Then, he looked at her sideways. You wanna go to Three Kings, get something to eat?

She thought about it. Welfare could wait.

lift off

40

She finally told him. A few days before the flight, she said it flat out. I'm going to Utah, the movie's playing in a festival there, ain't it crazy? She didn't tell him it was a big deal, how Dean was gonna try to sell the film, how there'd be people there wanting to talk to her. Darius glanced up from the TV screen. He said, Utah? Why the fuck you wanna go there. Don't you know they got white muthafuckers shoot a black man on the street.

AnnMarie looked at him.

Ignoramus. Trying to mess with her head.

Blessed sucked her teeth.

AnnMarie glanced at her. She was staring hard at Darius who didn't seem to notice but when he walked out a few minutes later, she shook her head. *Finally*, she said.

AnnMarie had to smile.

Taking her side for once. Thank you very much.

They worked it out that Niki would come over, run errands for her mother, bundle Star up in the stroller, take her out once in a while to get some air.

Day of the flight, Niki hugged her and she held on, listening to Niki's raspy voice in her ear, saying: Don't forget my snow.

First time she been on a plane. She thought she gonna be sick, that roller-coaster feeling tying her stomach in knots. She had to pull her eyes away from the window—the wing vibrating like it gonna break off as the plane tilted and made its turn, heading west over the city, the ground below patched and squared, homes and buildings and roadways like paper cutouts.

She reached over and clutched Melody's hand. Melody laughed, saying, It's okay, AnnMarie. We won't fall. But all AnnMarie felt was the bumping, the high-pitched hum in the cabin—any second they going down. She could feel Melody leaning, looking past her out the little window so she cracked her eye and saw that they was cutting through a haze of white, the wing jutting out, flicking the mist in fine swirls, the whole world obscure. She shut her eyes again and kept them closed until the bumpiness went away and she got used to the hum. When she looked up, the plane hostess was moving down the aisle, her blond hair brushed back neat and tidy into a bun, a voice making a announcement that they serving refreshments.

AnnMarie glanced around the plane. Ain't no black people go to Utah, Darius had said. Besides her and the assistant director, Maya, sitting two rows up with Dean, everyone else was white. No one looked mean or angry though, no one had tried to take her seat when they first got on the plane—she got a assigned seat. 17D, the ticket said, right next to her name. The plane hostess came by pushing a cart filled with juices and sodas and water. She said, What can I get you girls? AnnMarie looked at Melody. That cost money? she asked quietly.

Melody said, Do it cost something? No, sweetheart, the lady said. Not unless you want a mixed drink but you don't look old enough for that. What can I get for you?

AnnMarie got a can of Coke and a bag of pretzels, the plane hostess passing her a little napkin. Melody showed her how to

unlatch the knob so a tray table fold down over her lap. Ann-
Marie looked out the window. She couldn't see nothing now but
blue all the way, all the way clear off forever. 'Cept there was one
cloud over there off to the side—looked solid like a bed made of
cotton. Like it could catch you if you fall. You could just lay down
on it, AnnMarie thought, take a nap if you want to.

By the time they found their suitcases at baggage claim, rented a
van from Enterprise and drove along the winding roads through
the mountains, stars had appeared, stretching out across a vast
velvet sky, stars twinkling like she'd never seen before.

The place they staying was called a condo, Dean said. Looked
more like a house attached to a bunch of other houses, with
angled roofs all covered in snow, icicles hanging from the eaves,
mad tall trees spread out wide, so many trees, looked like they in
the middle of a forest. They entered through a long hallway and
she saw the ceiling way the fuck up there, a antler-type chandelier
hanging down. Moose head sticking out the wall, its nostrils flaring. AnnMarie said, Dang. She'd never been in a house this big.
It was five bedrooms and three bathrooms, a full kitchen with a
stove and fridge and counter looking right onto the living room
with a fireplace and a ledge to sit on and real logs in a pile. Melody
leaned over the railing on the second floor and looked down to
where AnnMarie stood. She said, What bedroom do you want? I
don't care, AnnMarie said, smiling. I do not care.

She asked to borrow Dean's phone and called home, excitement pouring outta her mouth. She said, What up y'all. We made
it. How everybody doing? What's going on? How you feel?

She talked to Blessed for a while, telling her about the house
and the moose head and the queen-size beds and the quilted blankets and goose-down pillows—how they all staying in one place

together like a family. Blessed said, That's nice, AnnMarie. That sound nice. Then she put Niki on the phone. Niki said, You ain't gonna believe this, AnnMarie.

What happened.

You not gonna believe this . . .

What happened, Niki, tell me.

We was playing, me and Star, and you know how she been pushing herself up and wobbling, well I kinda had one hand reaching out, you know, helping her and guess what she did—she took a step, swear to god AnnMarie, let go my hand and took a little step.

And AnnMarie didn't know whether to laugh or cry. She said, Oh, my god. How she do that, she only eight month old—put that girl on the phone. Let me talk to her.

AnnMarie said, Hi Star it's your mommy and I miss you and I'm proud a you and are you walking, you gonna walk for me when I get home?

But Star started to wail and AnnMarie heard the phone drop, commotion on the other end. She sat down on the bed, felt her shoulders slump and a tiredness creep in, she felt tired all of a sudden and a little pang of loneliness, listening to Star screaming on the other end of the line. She pictured the apartment, Blessed standing in the middle of the room, leaning on her cane, Star's face wailing, and when Niki got back on the line, she said, Word. I guess she missing you. Blessed got her though . . . she be fine.

When AnnMarie got off the phone, the house was quiet. She wandered through the condo, looking in the bedrooms, smelled the little soaps in the bathroom, went downstairs. She felt a cool draft where the sliding door was cracked open, heard voices on the deck.

She stood at the glass watching Maya in a one-piece bathing suit join the others, lifting her bare foot off the snow as she climbed into the hot tub. Steam rising off the surface, jets bur-bling the water, they breaths coming in little puffs. They was talking softly, Dean's arm slung over the side. He look different, AnnMarie thought, his chest bare, glasses fogged over. Melody climbed out and sat on the ledge, steam swirling off her skin. Sonia wasn't there. Last minute, she had to stay and do pickup scenes for the other movie she making. But everyone else was in the hot tub—Dean, Maya, the cameraman Bobby, Albert the sound man. She heard Melody say, Come on, AnnMarie, get in. AnnMarie glanced up.

Y'all crazy, she said. It's freezing outside.

But they all turned, calling her name, saying Come on, Ann-Marie. It feels good.

Later that night, when she crawled into bed, she couldn't sleep. She lay there for a long while thinking. She'd gone ahead and stripped down to her tee and undies, stepped across the deck, the snow burning her feet, and climbed into that tub. They'd been right, her body slowly adjusted to the piping hot water, her toes lifting, bumping into Melody's under the water. It had felt good. Underneath the covers, she pulled her knees up to her chest. She pictured Star taking her first step, how it'd been Niki's eyes and not hers to witness and a sudden longing for home swept through her. To be home and not here, in the big bed with soft sheets and a extra goose-down pillow under her head. She stared into the darkness, wondering if other actors and actresses felt this way too.

41

The day of the screening, they drove together in the crew van to the little town called Park City where the movie festival at. Out the window, AnnMarie saw mountains and snow everywhere and a ski lift cutting two black lines across a hill.

Look, Melody said.

People way up there, zigzagging through the powder, little tufts of white springing up behind they skis. It was mad beautiful.

Dean was driving, tires crunching, a fresh snow falling, wipers blowing flakes from the windshield and when he rounded the corner, she could see the little town up there, like a fake village from a fairy-tale story.

This is Main Street, Dean said.

Banners hanging, flags flapping from poles, all different kinds of people walking along the sidewalk. Look like a black dude over there, standing by the curb. Sure was—one, two, three, four more stepping from a restaurant, looking mad stylish in big puffy coats with fur on they collar and mirrored sunglasses.

Who those people, Dean, AnnMarie asked.

Dean followed her gaze out the side window and said, I bet they're with the movie *Love & Basketball.* Looks like Omar Epps over there.

AnnMarie turned full around in her seat as they drove past, trying to catch a glimpse of that movie star. Her eyes scanning the group until she saw him, plain as day. Even from a distance, he was mad fine, standing with the others, talking on his phone. She'd seen all his movies—*Higher Learning. Scream 2. The Wood.* Dang, she didn't know he gonna be here. He was too fine. Wonder if he coming to see her movie.

Dean pulled up to the curb and AnnMarie heard someone slide the van door open. Everyone started to pile out but she didn't. She couldn't move, her heart pounding, it was like she stuck to the seat. The front of the theater was crowded with people, a line forming, bunching up the block, all the way to the corner. Her eyes fixed on the movie posters, a whole bunch of them spread across the wall—her face blown up big in between Sonia and Melody. Little twinkle in her eye, dang—she'd never seen herself macro-size like that . . .

Dean leaned in. You okay, AnnMarie? You coming?

Yeah, I'm coming. She took a breath and slid out the van, keeping her head down as she moved through the crowd on the sidewalk. She was mad nervous, crunching through the snow in her boots, feeling hot all over. Aware suddenly of her stonewash jeans up in her crack, and her hair—wondering whether she should take off the North Face earmuffs she got on. Which way more stylish. On or off. She bumped into Melody who had turned and was reaching for her hand as they entered the theater. More people inside, so many people, their voices swelled around her. A section of seats in the middle had been roped off with ribbon. Reserved. Reserved. Reserved.

Sit here, Dean told them. I'm going to check on the projection system.

AnnMarie took her coat off and tried to get comfortable—people filing in, finding seats, getting settled, cell phones pressed to their ears. She spotted Dean in the aisle, shaking hands with somebody, a small crowd forming around him. Who was all these people? Couple rows down, two white dudes sat, both a them with long sideburns and hair on their chin like goatees. Was these yup-

pies? AnnMarie didn't know but they looked like college type—
black-rimmed glasses, turtlenecks, wool scarves around they necks.
She turned and looked over her shoulder, had the *Love & Basketball* people come in?

White sideburn dude had put his boot up on the seat back in
front of him, his arm slung over his knee, looking around. Blessed
never let him get away with that, AnnMarie thought as she stared
at that fella. He was kinda cute, his hair spiked up in front, his
jeans cuffed just above his Tims. AnnMarie's eyes drifted back to
his face and saw that he was looking at her, smiling. She ducked
her head, embarrassed and Melody nudged her, saying, Take off
your earmuffs. So she pulled them off and tried to fix her hair,
brush it back behind her ears.

Feedback bounced off the walls as the festival people started
to make their announcements and there was a shift in the room,
AnnMarie could feel it, as the crowd settled down, the room growing quiet. The festival person talking about the movie and the
director, Dean, and how happy they was to debut the film. Ann-
Marie turned, glancing around to see if Omar Epps had made it
inside. Didn't see nobody—where'd Dean go, everyone clapping
all of a sudden so AnnMarie raised her hands and clapped along
with them, then the lights went down and the movie start to play.

She could barely pay attention, felt the flutterflies, her stomach
bubbling but she held her eyes to the screen, watching herself act.
Walking down the hall of the school with Melody, Sonia bent
over her drum case, heard her voice say: *What up, what up, what up.*
She thought, Dang. Is that what I look like . . . That what I sound
like . . . ? And she smiled, remembering the moment—Bobby with
the big-ass camera up on his shoulder, walking backwards out the
door, three four five times they had to do it—all the project kids
hanging outside. Maya passing them the walkie-talkie through
the fence. She heard the audience laughing here and there but it
was hard to get lost in the story because she kept thinking about

everything she'd done and been through to get there. The lead drum majorette, Angie, teaching her to toss the flag high up in the air and catch it with both hands. How Darius had plucked her in the eye and made her suck his dick and all the sleepless nights with Star, those hazy hours of night, feeding time, diaper change. She wondered how Star doing. That girl took her first step and she'd missed it. She'd missed it. And before she knew what was happening, she felt tears burning—Sonia up there on the screen in the last shot of the movie. Riding on a train, just sitting, staring out the window, thinking about something. She could hear how quiet it had got—a hush like no one was breathing. Then the picture cut to black and names start to pop up in the credit roll and everyone was clapping. Clapping, clapping, clapping, mad loud.

Melody reached for AnnMarie and pulled her into an embrace. AnnMarie hugged her back and they rocked each other, laughing, AnnMarie's chin on her shoulder. She could feel all the people in the room, felt their eyes on her as the lights went up, but she dialed them down and scanned the room, like radar—looking for Omar Epps. Tried to spot his fine brown face in the crowd.

42

They went that night to a fancy restaurant to celebrate. It had crisp linen tablecloths and cloth napkins and two forks instead of one and wineglasses on the table, even before Dean had ordered the wine. It was the whole family—Melody, Dean, Maya, Albert, Bobby . . . Eating and laughing, having so much fun.

The menu was in French but Maya leaned over and told her to get the linguine type thing with cream sauce. AnnMarie looked at her and said, You speak French, Maya? Maya laughed. She said, Only menu French, AnnMarie.

People who'd seen the movie start dropping by the table. Just regular people, strangers coming over to say congratulations. Pulling up chairs, sitting down next to Dean, talking in his ear. Melody got up to use the bathroom just as a old white couple, like old in they fifties, dressed in matching ski coats and corduroy pants, tapped her on the shoulder. They said, We just wanted to tell you, we loved the movie. You were wonderful. We sooo enjoyed it. Smiling real big. Beautiful work, the man said. I'm a professor of film studies at USU. We drive in from Salt Lake City every year to attend the festival and this is one of the best movies we've seen.

Thank you thank you thank you, AnnMarie said.

It was so real, the lady said. And kind of sad if you think about it . . .

Yes, the professor man said, it reminds me of that ethnographic film we saw recently, what was the title . . .

Sad? What's sad about it, AnnMarie thought.

But she said, Yeah, Dean? He's the director—he said our type movie, it's called realism. That's the movie style.

Oh, they said. My goodness, a talented actress and smart too. Then they started asking AnnMarie questions, all kinds a questions—Who is she, where do she come from, you so young, what it like to be in a movie. And when Melody returned, they all got into a conversation about realism and the facts of life and how some girls choose to keep they babies, the professor and his wife pulling up chairs, leaning in to listen and Melody said, She a mother too, nodding to AnnMarie. They gasped, looking at her. You're a mother and you acted in a movie? You're so young. Oh my goodness . . .

Two waiters had to come over, bring a extra table, put it at the end 'cause it was one big party all of a sudden—all the people spilling off the sides, Dean coming over to introduce himself, pulling up a chair, and for a long time the linguine with cream sauce sat untouched on her plate. It wasn't until later, much later, when things had died down, that she got to it, picked up a fork and ate the whole thing cold.

43

The movie came out in Manhattan.

It played for a month at a theater there in the West Village. Limited distribution, Dean called it. But it had a great run, great audience response, he told her. People loved it. It did so good that they moved it to another theater on Houston Street where it played for three more weeks. She remembered Albert, the sound man, talking about Houston Street near to where he lived by NYU. She took the train into the city one Saturday afternoon, just to see. To see the film title up there on the marquee. To look again at her face blown up big next to Sonia and Melody.

It played in San Francisco, Los Angeles, Seattle, Atlanta. It even went to Hawaii. She got her name in the *New York Times*, in the *New York Post*, in some other newspaper she never heard of called the *Village Voice*. They said she was compelling. *A compelling performance. Authentic.* Hell yeah, she authentic. When she met Dean for lunch, he brought her the clippings and she put them in the scrapbook that she'd started when Star was first born. Sonogram pictures, Star as a newborn, Star's first birthday, pictures from the movie set.

But it never played in Far Rockaway—ain't no theater out there anyway. Got to go to Jamaica you want to see a movie. Take the dollar van to Green Acres you want to see a picture. And she realized there'd be disappointments.

There gonna be disappointments.

the brass ring

44

She never went back to high school. After stepping out, flying to the festival and having the time of her life—she never went back. She did some acting—a couple little roles here and there, but no starring role like Sonia.

It wasn't that she didn't have her eye on the prize or that she'd lost track of the direction. But it was simple. Far Rock didn't have no superhighway to Hollywood and one little art movie ain't got enough gas to get you there. So when all the activity died down and the apartment on Gateway Boulevard shrunk back to size, she knew she needed to get herself a backup plan.

It took her a whole year before she gave in and went out to Ida B. for a job training seminar. Her and three other teenage mothers sat on folding chairs underneath the hum of fluorescents in a basement room of the building. The job counselor told them there was lots of alternatives for girls like them—training programs and career paths and options. It was up to them to reach up and grab the opportunity. The lady presented a slide show, pressing the little clicker button, swapping out one picture after another, advertisements for various training schools, teenage graduates frozen on a pale yellow background, all of them dressed in uniforms, all different kinds of uniforms—hospitality, housekeeping, janitorial, customer service, food service, health industry. The lady passed out a information packet. AnnMarie flipped it open and stared at the glossy pages with the same teenagers smiling, teeth white and triumphant.

Then she rode the bus home. She thought about how *hospitality* be code for maid training and *janitorial* be code for toilet scrubbing and how *food industry* meant McDonald's. Do she want to have a career at McDonald's. You work hard, the career lady said, climb the ladder, next thing you know you're the manager, you're running the restaurant, do you see? Do you see how it works?

Do she want to be a manager at McDonald's? How she gonna get another acting job if she working full-time at fast food. And where the fuck Darius. Hadn't seen him in nearly two weeks. She knew his other baby mama, CeeCee, had given birth to a baby boy. Nadette had told her about it after he'd shown up at Crush one night, showing off a picture of his newborn. CeeCee back working, Nadette said. She on the money train, dancing, Darius don't gotta do shit. Fuck all if he gave AnnMarie any money for Star. Last time was when she turned two. Took a twenty out his pocket, set it on the kitchen counter. She just looked at it. What the fuck she supposed to do with twenty dollars.

By the time she stepped through the door, AnnMarie was in a foul mood, feeling sorry for herself and cranky. She dropped the information folder onto the couch and picked up Star, scowling.

What's the matter with you? Blessed said.

AnnMarie ignored her. Why her pantie's wet. You didn't put her on the potty seat?

She refuse.

AnnMarie tsked, walked Star into the bathroom, stripped her down and sat her on the potty chair. She said, You gotta learn,

Booboo. You ain't wearing a diaper no more, you got to pee on the seat. Now sit there 'til you go . . .

I don't gotta . . .

Just sit there.

Why? I don't gotta go.

AnnMarie groaned. I'm trying to teach you something. Now sit.

Niki walked in right then, said, Hey y'all what up.

Blessed glanced up. Don't bother with her—she's in a bad mood.

Niki laughed, looking at AnnMarie. Why, what's the matter with you.

AnnMarie tsked. They telling me about options.

Who telling you?

Ida B. That job training thing over there . . .

Blessed had been holding one of the flyers close to her face, her sight blurry, trying to read the words. What this say, Niki. Do it say *Nurse School*?

Niki sat down on the couch, took the flyer from Blessed's hand. Yeah. It says *Caring. Nursing Aide Training Program.*

Blessed nodded. Um-hm. You got a brain in you, AnnMarie. You could be a nurse aide. Get yourself a job in a hospital.

Hell yeah . . . Help out all the injuries, Niki said. Take a pulse . . . find a beat. Find a beat, take a pulse. Niki turning it into a rhyme.

AnnMarie cracked up. Shut up, Niki. Crazy.

AnnMarie shifted, thinking about it. Niki'd gone ahead and got her GED. Took her a year to do it, but she made it happen. Still didn't have no job but she was looking. Wanted to work in a bank. Be around all that money. She'd even gone into TD Bank, asked for a application but they told her she need to get a degree first. Next step. Always a step.

Do the nursing program, AnnMarie. You make a good nurse, her mother was saying, sounding positive.

Niki said, I let you take my temperature.

AnnMarie laughed. But it gave her a boost of confidence. *Nurse* sounded better than *janitor* or *french-fry maker* so she called up Dean and asked to borrow the money, got herself enrolled in Caring.

45

It wasn't a regular school with kids her age going eight a.m. to three p.m. Didn't need no GED, just the tuition money up front, eight hundred dollars. There was twelve people in her group, mostly older women in their twenties and thirties, from the West Indies. She didn't know when exactly she realized *nursing* meant home health aide. Same job all the women had coming in and out the house, taking care of Blessed. But there was no backing out, her mother hollering—*Since when you think you better than everybody else?*

They met twice a week six–nine p.m. on Lefferts Boulevard. She got trained in how to do blood pressure, how to check vitals, how to feed somebody if they eats from the stomach, how to clean the tube so it stay sanitized. And when the eight-week program ended, she got a recommendation from the teacher and a placement at a agency that sent her out to neighborhoods and into apartment buildings all over Queens and Brooklyn. Old people mostly. They bodies fallin' apart with something. Diabetes. HIV. High blood pressures. Depression. In pain. Slow moving. Slow talking. Most of 'em cranky to be alive and living this way. So they'd yell a lot. In her head she'd think, You screamin' at me? For $8.50 an hour? Huh-uh. This ain't worth it.

But she went. 'Cause she needed the paycheck coming in. Eight in the morning go in, make they breakfast, clean dishes, clean bathroom, sweep floors. Wash clothes. Made sure they took their medication. Went to supermarket. Took them out for walks. When the day was done, she'd go home to Star and Blessed, sometimes Niki was there, all of them hanging out, waiting, on Gateway Boulevard.

For a while she got placed with this one lady, Miss Beatrice. She was funny. A butch type, hair shaved off clean to the scalp and hefty. Wore the baggy clothes. Miss Beatrice had arthritis in her joints, had to use a walker to get around, just like Blessed. AnnMarie'd help her into a wheelchair, they'd go down to the street, stroll around. Miss Beatrice was different from the others. She was easygoing and liked to talk, they was always talking. AnnMarie would tell her things about her life and Beatrice would do the same, telling AnnMarie about her favorite Chihuahua that had died and her sister who ain't spoke to her in ten years and the neighbor she had one time, smoke so much weed you get high just breathing in his exhale.

Yeah, Miss Beatrice was cool. After a few weeks, AnnMarie felt they more like friends. Sometimes she start laughing about something and AnnMarie'd see her gums. Beatrice didn't have no teeth in the front, only on the sides where the vampire teeth be at. AnnMarie'd think, Oooh, please close your mouth. That is disgusting.

One time AnnMarie said, Miss Beatrice, what happened to your teeth? As soon as she said it though, she knew it was wrong 'cause Miss Beatrice sat back on the couch, and went quiet.

I didn't tell you about my teeth? She finally said. I used to have a set the dentist glued in. They fit good. I had a nice smile, real nice smile. See that picture over there? That's me with my teeth in.

AnnMarie crossed to the kitchen where Beatrice was pointing.

She peered at a very small photograph, like the kind you use for a ID card. It was Miss Beatrice all right, with all her teeth, hair short but not butch-like, more like a cute afro, kinda spiky in the front with reddish tips.

You like nice, Miss Beatrice.

I got that picture took about six, seven years ago, when I got my visa renewed . . . That's where I met Bertrand, Bertrand Gold. I ain't never told you about him?

Huh-uh. So Miss Beatrice told AnnMarie about the man Bertrand Gold who she'd met in the waiting room of the visa building and dated for a while. He'd taken her out to Coney Island to have some fun. They went on all the rides—the Scrambler and the Tilt-A-Whirl and the Cyclone, one of the rides whipping her back and forth so hard her teeth popped out her mouth, gone for good.

AnnMarie felt the urge to laugh but didn't. She said, Miss Beatrice that's terrible.

Um-hm. I'm looking around, all over the place, searching for my teeth. This fella Bertrand asks me what I'm doing. I don't want to tell him but I do. I say, My teeth fell out and he kinda backs up, you know, like he disgusted. Then he goes and gets a hot dog. Didn't help me. Nothing. I guess he didn't like a girl with no teeth.

AnnMarie watched her shoulders rise up in a shrug. But I'd just as soon known then what kinda man he is, rather than later, you know, if I fall in love . . .

AnnMarie wanted to reach over, pat her shoulder, give her a hug, something. But the moment passed and Miss Beatrice was saying, They made me a new set but I lost those somewhere. So now I'm stuck with this. Smiling wide, showing off her teeth holes.

Yeah, AnnMarie liked that lady.

Dean would call up, he'd tell her about an audition he heard about, or he'd pass on her name to another producer or casting director—they'd call her in to try out for some little part or another. Miss Beatrice let her go in the middle of the day. She'd take the train into the city, do her thing—Beatrice would cover for her, sign her card nine to five, agency never knew.

That's how she got cast in another movie. Got a role playing a ex-felon at a halfway house. The main character was played by the actress Maggie Gyllen-something, Maggie Something. A white girl. She was nice, had a pretty smile. AnnMarie liked her. The director was nice too—a female director this time. AnnMarie was only there for one day but it made her feel good just doing it. Being on set again—*Lights, Camera, Action.*

Go back to work, Miss Beatrice'd say, how it go? How you do? Any big stars there? Anybody I know.

And AnnMarie would tease her. She'd say, Well you know me, Miss Beatrice. And Miss Beatrice would laugh and laugh, her teeth holes all black and shit.

One day AnnMarie showed up to work, Miss Beatrice wasn't there. She stood at the door knocking, calling out, Miss Beatrice, you in there? A neighbor opened up his door and said, Cops came by, took her out in handcuffs. AnnMarie said, What? The neighbor said, Yeah, cops came by, they was hauling her out the door, she was crying, saying, You hurting me. You hurting me. AnnMarie said, That's terrible. She knew how much the arthritis hurt, the stabbing pain Beatrice got when she tried to walk. But the neighbor man was chuckling.

That old girl finally got caught. Passing all those bad checks. She finally got caught.

AnnMarie looked at him surprised but he didn't say more, just closed the door.

———————

AnnMarie stood for a long time in front of Miss Beatrice building. Then she found a pay phone and called the agency. They said, Go home. We call you with another placement.

AnnMarie said, Well, am I getting paid, 'cause I can't take no time off. They said, Go home, we call you.

46

Two weeks and three days, AnnMarie was home with Star, that child giving her more trouble than she worth. She want, she want, she want—when they say Terrible Twos they mean it. Star getting her hands into everything, pushing a chair into the kitchen, climbing up onto the counter, getting into the bag of cookies. Pulling open the fridge, trying to lift the Fanta bottle off the shelf. What you doing, AnnMarie'd say. You can't have that. *No.*

Star'd say no right back at her. She don't get what she want, she throw herself down, start screaming.

Niki'd sit there, laughing. AnnMarie glaring. You getting a time-out. She'd scoop Star up off the floor, put her in the crib and close the bedroom door.

What you doing, Blessed' ask. Pick that child up.

Hell, no. She need to learn.

Star's screams knocking against the door, Niki trying to keep a straight face.

AnnMarie tsked. Y'all think you know better?

She'd decided against the home-style playgroup she'd been offered by Family Services. Problem was, when AnnMarie was at work, Blessed hardly ever went out. Had her in front of the TV all day, watching *Sesame Street*. AnnMarie knew, almost three years old, Star need to be out, not in—walking, talking, playing with other kids. But she hadn't been able to do it. She just couldn't bring herself to leave Star with no strangers.

Two weeks and three days. The agency finally called up, sent her
down to Beach 96th Street, name on the card was Doris Pullman.
Her hair gone to white, small and frail, her brown skin speck-
led with age spots. AnnMarie soon learned Miss Doris was angry.
Always angry over the smallest thing. The way AnnMarie chop
up the garlic, the way she stirred the food or set the wood spoon
on the counter. Hovering, saying I hope you clean that up. Having
her mop the floor every day. Every day. Who needs to have they
floor mopped every day?

AnnMarie'd go to work. Do chores, cook food, give meds, five
o'clock go home.

It was boring as hell.

Some days she'd try to track Darius down. By then, she didn't
care so much about CeeCee, whether he with her or not, whether
he lying or not, whether he back sticking up stores or making
music. She didn't know why—she just knew it'd been a while since
she listened for his knock or his footstep on the stair. Maybe it was
'cause of Omar Epps, seeing him that day on Main Street. She'd
caught a glimpse of a black man who'd done something with his
life. Omar Epps. She never got to meet him but was okay with
that. Dean had found a poster of him and gave it to her as a birthday present. She taped it up over her bed.

Still. She'd take Star with her, popping the stroller over cracks
and potholes, she'd say, Let's go say hi to Grandma Darla, see
where your daddy at. His mother had moved into Redfern Houses,
a two-bedroom apartment over there in the grid of low-rise buildings. His sister Vanessa and her child went with them, taking one
of the bedrooms. Darius got the couch. Once in a while she'd
catch him home. She'd take Star out the stroller and give her a
nudge, saying Go on, say *what up* to your father. Star holding on
to her pant leg, not moving. Darius would laugh, bending to scoop

her into his arms. The question of money and child support inevitably leading to a beef—fat lip, bruised arm, teeth rattling upside her head.

Sometimes he'd pop up at Blessed's and she'd let him in. Sometimes they even made love.

'Cause she wanted Star to know him.

Like, This your father. This is your father. Even if he is a fucking retard.

Niki'd look at AnnMarie and shake her head.

Ways a the heart and alla that.

flipped

47

She'd never kissed a girl before but Niki was kissing her now, her mother in the other room, home health aide doing something, washing dishes at the sink. Star napping right there in the crib.

A breeze pushed through the window. She could hear the clink of metal and water running, feel Niki's tongue swirling in her mouth but it was hard to concentrate since all she could think was how Niki her best friend and what Darius gonna say if he find out.

Niki musta sensed something 'cause she pulled away and AnnMarie could tell she was looking at her so she opened her eyes. Niki's face seemed different all of a sudden, unfamiliar, so AnnMarie closed her eyes and kept them closed until she felt Niki's lips on hers again. Niki's hand brushed her nipple, then slid down her waist until she found the spot between her legs and AnnMarie couldn't help it—a moan came out even though she didn't know for sure what she was feeling, she just knew it was something.

AnnMarie! Her mother's voice made them jump and Niki sat up quick.

Then Star stirred in the crib, her eyes coming open, sleepy eyes looking through the bars at her mother.

AnnMarie crossed to Star, bent and scooped her up, the child yawning.

Blessed always be doing that, Why she gotta do that, Ann-Marie said, even though inside she felt relief.

AnnMarie!

AnnMarie tsked, set Star on her feet and said, Go tell your grandma how she woke you. Star turned, pressing her forehead into the fold of AnnMarie's lap and said, No.

No, go on—go in there, stubborn, and tell Grandma how she woke you with her yelling.

Star started to whine, shaking her head back and forth 'til Niki picked her up and carried her into the living room.

Blessed looked up from the couch.

Where you off to, Niki, where AnnMarie at?

She in there. You want me to tell her to come out?

AnnMarie leaned in the doorway and looked at her mother.

Blessed said, I need you to go to Thriftway, get this prescription filled.

I need to feed my daughter first.

I'll feed her. You get my prescription. I need to take my medicine.

Why'nt Ondine go. It her job, ain't it.

Ondine act like she don't hear. Leaning against the counter, staring at Niki, eating a bowl of something she heated up.

Ondine said, What I want to know is if there's a girl underneath all that boy clothes.

Niki looked at her like, *I fuck you up, bitch.* Which made Ann-Marie laugh and then they passing out the door, Star curled up next to Blessed, one happy family.

They walked to the drugstore, the whole time Niki acting as if the kiss ain't happen, talking her ear off about this girl Paloma she want AnnMarie to meet, this girl who live out by Latania's mother, a feminine gay girl, real pretty, wear the mule shoes, skin-tight Calvins, how she know all these interesting people in the fashion world.

AnnMarie kept saying, Um-hm. Okay. Yeah, that sound good. And in her head she was glad Niki wasn't making a big deal outta it. In her head thinking she can't believe what just happen. Niki was her best friend but *now* what she gonna do. Be Niki's lover? She ain't gay. She love Niki, but she ain't gay. Was she?

Plus Niki had Nadette. She knew they was still messing around even though Niki denying it ever since Dennis finally caught on and told Nadette he want out. Moved in with some other girl on the other side a Central. Some ugly chick, Nadette had said, with dyed red hair like clown hair, and a skinny ass. Sounding jealous, which made Niki stare at her hard like she stupid—the whole thing turning into one big soap opera. Coming to the corner now, she sensed Niki go quiet. Three fellas standing in front of Mott's Famous with they red bandanas, teeth shining.

Too late to switch up and cross the street. AnnMarie tried to act natural.

She glanced at Niki. What you say?

Nothing.

You just asked me something.

No I didn't.

One a them smiling at AnnMarie now, getting ready to make his play. She could see it in his eyes before the words came out: Hey there shortie, you look fine today.

Sure she do.

Why don't you hold up a minute and let me talk to you.

Mm-mm-mm . . .

What's your rush, girl.

One a them she knew from around the way, always on one corner or another mouthing some type a bullshit, thinking he Don Juan. Same dude Darius stepped to one time when they first hook up, but the guy don't seem to remember that now.

Hold up now.

She with her boyfriend.

Ho, shit!

Laughing, laughing.

Excuse me sir—sir. Yeah, you . . . Turn around and . . . did you see that look? Bitch just looked at me.

Redbone gave you the death stare.

Shrivel your dick right up.

Laughing, laughing.

Their voices chased them all the way into the cool interior of the Thriftway. Down the aisle all the way to the back, Ann-Marie cussing: Fucking retards. The ugly one—did you see his teeth? Horse-mouth muthafucker, Darius beat the shit outta him one time—muthafucker looked at me, *bap*! Darius said, What you got to say now . . .

But Niki like she deaf. Eyes forward, hands in her pocket, she don't say nothing. AnnMarie glanced at her, then left it alone.

At the pharmacy, AnnMarie slid the script across the counter. Niki found a empty chair next to a old woman who kept looking at her sideways like she trying to figure out what she is. Sitting with her legs spread wide, black do-rag underneath her Yankees cap, extra-large hoodie hanging loose over her shoulders.

Coulda been a sir, like the fella said.

AnnMarie knew Niki was used to it. Had to be. In the past year, Niki'd switched up her style, got her cinnamon curls cut into a short afro, shopping now at DJ Rays, urban style for men. Still. She looked comfortable, sitting there as if she the only one in the store, earbuds in, bopping her head to the music.

Niki be okay. Niki tough.

Gawd, she can't believe they kissed. Niki's hands running down her body like that. They'd just been talking, that's all. Ann-Marie'd been stretched out across the bed, playing with the curtain, Niki next to her, staring up at the Omar poster on her wall. She said, Why you got that up there. 'Cause he fine, AnnMarie said. It's creepy, Niki said. Fella looking down at you while you sleeping. AnnMarie sat up, laughing, and when she turned her head, Niki'd leaned in and kissed her. Just like that. AnnMarie hadn't pulled away, she didn't know why, Niki's lips on hers, lingering, soft and tender. A breeze lifting the curtain while Star napped right there in the crib.

She wanted to tell somebody, talk it over, but she didn't trust Teisha no more. Teisha or Sunshine. Walking into the apartment, two weeks ago, she found Darius chillin' on the couch, sipping from a bottle a St. Ides. Teisha'd been laughing about something but she glanced up and said, *Hey, AnnMarie* . . . acting like it ain't no thing, him sitting there. She wondered why they let him in, acting like they friends. Behind his back, they was always talking shit, how he ain't worth her time, telling her he a dog. She need to get herself a new man. Asking why she let him beat her when he don't even provide.

She hadn't stayed long and when she got back home, she thought how things had changed. How the hours and days and months had passed in that walk-in, how he'd held her down. Couldn't tell if she still loved him. Somewhere in the periphery, he was hovering.

In the Thriftway, lady behind the counter called her mother's name.

The lady said, Make sure she drink lots of water. This one here, take with food or a glass of milk. No alcohol. No driving, okay?

AnnMarie nodded. Yeah, yeah . . .

When she turned from the counter, Niki was watching her. AnnMarie made a motion to go but Niki just sat there. She crossed to Niki, reached down and pulled a bud from her ear.

Let's go.

Niki looked at her. She said, Oh, so you the boss now.

AnnMarie felt her skin grow hot. Something had shifted and AnnMarie didn't know why.

Whatever, Niki—we done, that's all. AnnMarie held up the prescription bag. Still Niki don't move, nudging the bud back in her ear, turning up the music.

AnnMarie tsked. She said, Later then . . . Walking up the aisle toward the front of the store. What the hell wrong with *her* . . .

AnnMarie paused near the cosmetics and pretended to look at the Revlon shades, lifting out a eyeliner, then another. She glanced toward the pharmacy but Niki was gone.

AnnMarie felt her heart bang hard for a second. Then she headed for the exit.

The automatic door swung open and AnnMarie stepped outside, blinking in the bright light, looking now to the corner where Horse Mouth had been. The corner was clear but Niki was there, leaning up against the wall of the store.

AnnMarie approached, trying to read her face. What the hell you doing?

Niki didn't answer, looking off to some point in the distance.

AnnMarie groaned inside, then said, We going or what?

Niki lifted her hand and fake coughed into the palm, saying, *You a tease*, the words coming out half-muffled.

Say what? AnnMarie said, frowning.

Niki laughed, then pushed herself off the wall, adjusting her ball cap. I didn't say nothing . . .

AnnMarie tsked. You a muthafucker, you know that . . .

Niki shrugged, falling in step beside her. AnnMarie shoved her and Niki pretended to stumble, laughing.

You stupid, AnnMarie said, glancing away, grateful the moment had passed.

48

That evening, after she sang Star to sleep, they took the dollar van to Latania's mother house in Jamaica. It was still warm where the sun hit your skin. That warm feeling like something good could happen.

Mary J. floated out the stereo as they drank Fresca and looked at *Ebony* and *Jet* on the front steps of Latania's porch. The girl Niki'd been talking about, Paloma, came over and sat with her feet tucked off to the side. She was like a black China doll her skin so smooth, AnnMarie'd never seen skin so smooth, her eyes kinda chinky with long lashes and she smelled good too.

AnnMarie asked her what kind of perfume she was wearing. Paloma told her it was Poison but she didn't look up when she said it and AnnMarie got the feeling she knew she was fine.

Latania was saying, You hear Megan left Shalisha for a boy.

Say *what?*

Um-hm. Shalisha call me last night, she was crying . . .

Damn, Niki said. Who the boy? What Shalisha do.

What can she do. Her heart get broke like that.

Megan a slut.

She ain't a slut.

She was cheating. Shalisha found pictures of them together. Way back since her birthday.

AnnMarie felt tongue-tied, making out with Niki still on her mind, not knowing who Megan or Shalisha was and wondering if Niki'd said something to Latania when they first arrived. She kept quiet, flipping through *Ebony*, looking down at all the glossy pictures, until Paloma's finger came down and stopped her.

That there is Dre. He a designer. Here, look, turn the page . . .

AnnMarie turned the page and saw mad sexy models sitting and standing on fake rocks like boulders with stiletto heels, wearing nothing but Dre's bikinis, their dark skin rubbed with glitter gold.

Niki leaned down and looked over AnnMarie's shoulder. She nudged her with the side of her leg and said, Mm-mm-mm . . .

AnnMarie ignored her.

She said, Look at that silver one. That one's nice, I like how the straps crisscross like that.

Paloma said, That girl? She stuck up. But that one's nice—her name's Candy.

AnnMarie looked at her sideways: You know these girls?

Mm-hm. Some a them.

She felt Niki's leg pressing, felt the heat there where their bodies touched and without meaning to, she sat up and shifted.

Paloma said, You ever model?

AnnMarie hesitated, then said, Nah, but I act. I'm a actress.

Word? You was in the movies?

Niki snickered. Yeah, she a movie star.

Shut up, Niki, I'm just saying . . . Damn. Jealous.

Niki laughed.

Shut up, Niki, Paloma said. She looked at AnnMarie. What movie? Can I see it? How can I see it?

It already played in the movie theater but the director said it's gonna come out on TV soon—BET channel.

Word?

Um-hm.

I give you my number, you can tell me when it's on.

AnnMarie could feel Paloma looking at her and she smiled

inside, wondering if she was a feminine gay girl for real or if Niki just want it that way.

AnnMarie turned and looked up at Niki. You wanna move over, you're pinching me in.

But Niki act like she don't hear, looking up at Latania who'd gone inside and was coming out now with a bottle of Hennessy and some cups.

Where your mother at.

You know what, we fill it back with water, she never know.

Niki nudged AnnMarie again and said, I let you have *one* drink.

AnnMarie just tsked. Niki getting on her last nerve.

Latania suddenly shrieked and grabbed the magazine out of AnnMarie's hand. Look, look . . . There she is. Look what she wearing.

It was Carmen Electra, shining off the page.

That be me! See that, by this summer, that be me!

The girls looked at Latania for a minute 'cause she was plump. More than plump, she was big and *always* on a diet.

No, for real, Latania said. I already lost two pounds. Lose twenty by June.

Problem is you love to eat.

Latania glared at Niki. Shut your mouth you don't got something positive to say.

What? All I said was you love to eat, Niki said laughing.

So what, I can control myself.

No you can't.

Look who's talking. Muff-diver. You like a fucking dog with your tongue hanging out. Can't stop licking.

The girls bust out laughing, even Niki, and AnnMarie thought, *Nasty,* tha's just nasty. But Paloma was reaching her hand up for daps from Latania as Missy Elliott broke from the speakers, her voice whipping rhythmic. The girls screamed all at once, clapping they hands and Niki went after it, saying Come on, AnnMarie as she started up a syncopated beat and AnnMarie couldn't help it—she found the key and let loose a harmony, weaving through Missy's voice, stretching out the notes to counter Niki's beat. Her body swaying, brushing up against Paloma, shoulder to shoulder, all the girls swaying, but her eyes on Niki, and only Niki.

The next two days it rained. Day after that, more rain. Rained hard all day. Three days she stuck inside with Miss Doris who was never happy about nothing. Three months she been the lady's home health aide, not once had she seen her smile, say please or thank you.

AnnMarie slipped out with the garbage. Walked it down the hall to the chute, then stepped inside the stairwell to call her mother.

Last night Star'd been sick with a cough. AnnMarie lay next to her, keeping her head propped up with the pillow but still she barked like a seal. AnnMarie hadn't slept at all.

How she doing, Ma.

She fine. She playing.

Where she playing?

She playing.

I know she playing. But she on the floor or in the Pack 'n Play You got to keep her off the floor. Did Ondine get the dust up?

Huh?

Ma!

What you yelling for, AnnMarie.

I can hear her coughing, Ma. I can hear it.

You know what? You don't like how me doing, get yourself another damn babysitter.

AnnMarie!

She heard Miss Doris shouting so she hung up the phone and

stepped from the stairwell. Miss Doris got her head out the door, wagging a finger: *I'm calling the agency you don't put that phone away!*

AnnMarie walked past her into the apartment.

Sorry, *Miss* Doris. What can I do for you now?

AnnMarie came home from work. Changed the water in the humidifier. Added salt. Got the steam going.

You want to eat, Boo?

Nah . . .

Eat something. Look, I brought you some noodles.

Star climbed into her lap and played with the paper takeout bag, squishing it together and pulling it apart until AnnMarie took it away and told her she got to eat. Star said, No Mama, no . . . Coughing once, twice but she sounded better. AnnMarie lined ten noodles up in a row, told Star to count, one, two, three . . . Got her to eat that way, playing a counting game, 'til the noodles was gone.

She looked out the window. The rain had stopped. She watched the dying sun cut through gray clouds, last light on the building there, bricks glowing red. She pulled the curtain closed, leaned over Star in the crib, rubbed her back, sang a sweet song. It took a while but Star fell asleep, thumb in her mouth. She thought about Darius. Wondered where he was. But she didn't call him.

She called up Niki. Bodie answered. Why you have Niki's phone, she asked. He told her he waiting to hear about a job. He told her Niki gone to Latania house.

She called Latania. Latania's mother said, Hello AnnMarie, how are you, how is Star, Latania is at Paloma's.

She passed into the kitchen and out again, she stood in the

living room, then in the doorway of Blessed's room—her mother on the bed, flopped over like a damn walrus.

Snoring. AnnMarie wondered if she snore like that when she sleeping. Hope not.

She flipped channels for a while then turned the TV off. The sun was down, sky dark, nearly gone to black but there—in a far-off part of the horizon, look at that, a thin strip of clouds gleaming white, the sky a pale, pale blue. She stood for a long time, watching the line cool off to pink, then purple then nothing at all. The stillness so deep it made AnnMarie sigh.

Then Star coughed. AnnMarie turned, listening. She knew she was sitting up in the crib now, coughing.

AnnMarie went to the bathroom, got the baby Robitussin. Ain't but a dribble come out. She checked her pocket. Five dollars. No-name brand cost $3.99. She just make it.

She lifted Star out the crib and carried her into her mother's room, set her on the bed.

Ma!

She shook Blessed 'til she rolled over and cradled Star in the fold of her body.

Out on the street, Thriftway was still open. She went inside, stood on line, flipped through *Essence* magazine, bought Star medicine. She went home, climbed the stairs, and when she turned the corner onto her hallway, who standing there waiting but Darius.

She looked at him.

What up, he said.

What you doing here.

I miss you, why you think.

She went past him, carrying the medicine in the Thrift-way bag.

You knock?

No one answer.

She put the key in, pushed open the door. It was quiet. Star was quiet.

Shhh . . . Go in.

She looked in her mother's room. Star was sleeping. She stood for a moment wondering whether to give her the medicine or let her be.

She went into her room, Darius had already emptied his pockets, set his phone, blade, pocket change up on the dresser like he thought he staying the night.

Stretched out there on the bed.

He said, Come here baby . . .

He said, Why you act like that.

She sat down and looked at him.

Why you carrying your blade.

Ain't nothing. Got a beef to solve.

Who with.

Nobody. Come 'ere and lay with me for a small little minute.

So she laid down and his arm went around her, his fingers brushing skin.

Star sick. I gotta listen for her cough.

Okay.

He rose up on his elbow and leaned in, found her lips, his smell familiar, his taste like the beedie he smoke. And she felt the loneliness expanding, like a balloon stretched tight, making her reach for him.

Then his body was on hers and she could feel him getting hard as he licked and sucked, his hands stroking her body, rubbing between her legs, and it felt good, so she put her tongue in his mouth and felt him grow harder still, then he was pulling her pants down 'til she was free and clear, waiting to be entered but it was Niki she was thinking of, Niki's hands brushing her skin, Niki's lips on hers and her taste, the taste of her and it didn't take long, soon she was there and it was pouring through her and she tried to make it last with every thrust—she met his with her own, not Darius but Niki on her mind.

49

All week, Niki'd been on her—she kept asking, So you and Darius getting back together, what's going on, he been by to see Star. Or she'd drop things here and there like, I saw Darius go by on Bayport. Ain't that over by his other baby mama house.

A whole month since that first kiss and not once had Niki brought up Darius until now. Not a word. The month passing with little play-fights on the bed, tussles turning into kisses, the kisses into full-on make-outs, hands up the shirt, legs entwined, Niki rubbing and pressing and AnnMarie didn't know what was happening exactly, all she knew was that she liked how it felt, all the attention Niki was giving her, the way Niki was putting her first over everybody. Nadette. Latania. Even the black China doll.

AnnMarie'd never been more confused in her life. Niki was her best friend. She was mad cool, funny as hell, and she loved Star like her own but did AnnMarie *like* her like her? Niki, who'd walk in without knocking. Was she in love with this girl?

Something had shifted this past week—her best friend replaced by someone else, Niki hangdogging AnnMarie with questions about Darius, dropping seeds a doubt, putting her on the spot with where she going and who she seeing, and do she still like cock, busting on her and laughing, but underneath AnnMarie felt Niki's neediness like a weight around her neck. Pushing AnnMarie to choose. Hurry the fuck up and choose.

So she finally said, flat out—Yeah, me and Darius back together, even though it wasn't true. She'd said it not knowing what would go down, how they friendship might change, knowing only that this secret with Niki just wasn't working.

They'd been heading over to Nadette's.

Niki said, Oh so you gonna stay with a muthafucker who beats you and fucks with your head and can't be faithful to you.

AnnMarie tsked. She said, Faithful. What about you, you can't even tell nobody we hanging out.

I don't care what you do.

AnnMarie looked at her. You told me don't say nothing to Nadette. She too fragile. It'll break her heart. Like you cheating on her with me.

Niki laughed. You so stupid, AnnMarie, how can I be cheating when we ain't even a thing.

AnnMarie went quiet. Niki's words making her cheeks go hot. Trying to mess with her head. Just like Darius. Well, fuck her, AnnMarie thought. And by the time they walked into Nadette's building, AnnMarie was mad tight, Niki taking the stairs two at a time—each walking in alone, one after the other. Nadette and Teisha was on the sofa, music playing from the stereo, Nadette with a glow on her face, like she'd kissed the sun.

Right away Niki slumped down in a chair and was texting on her phone. AnnMarie said, What up? What y'all doing. Fronting like everything peachy.

Teisha glanced at Niki. What's wrong with her.

Niki didn't bother to look up. Kept her head down, texting. Texting. And AnnMarie felt uneasy as Nadette raised her arm, bending her wrist to show off a mad big diamond on her finger.

Oooh, where'd you get that, that is beautiful, Nadette, AnnMarie said, crossing to look at the ring.

They engaged, Teisha said.

Who engaged, you got engaged? To Dennis?

Mm-hm. Proposed to me yesterday.

I thought y'all broke up.

Where you been AnnMarie . . . He left that skinny-ass clown last week, came back to the one and only true thing, word.

Niki was slumped back in the chair, staring at Nadette. Ann-Marie didn't even have to look, she could feel the hatred pouring out her eyeballs, all of Niki's questions and neediness making sense all of a sudden. Rejected again.

Nadette lifted her eyes and glared. She said, What. You got something to say?

But Niki just got up and walked out the door.

Teisha shook her head. Why you gotta fuck with her like that.

What, you the one who said they engaged.

AnnMarie stood for a moment, her own heart collapsing. Niki's shame left behind, like a shadow.

Where you going, AnnMarie, Nadette said. But she didn't answer, she went out the door, down the stairwell, calling Niki's name.

Finally catching her in the hall leading to the street, she reached out and grabbed her arm, saying Hold up, Niki. Hold up. But Niki swung around and backed AnnMarie up against the wall, pinning her there with both hands.

What the fuck, Niki, let go. And she did, slamming her hard one last time before backing away and disappearing into the bright white light of the afternoon.

For a second, AnnMarie stood dumb. Feeling the stab of pain where her spine had collided with concrete, pulsing now after Niki had released her. She hesitated, then told her feet to move, went out the door and up the block, catching Niki at the intersection. AnnMarie tried to think of what to say as they crossed the street.

Nadette be mad cold sometime, she finally said.

Niki didn't answer. Hands in her pocket, she didn't even shrug.

Did you know they back together?

Niki still didn't answer so AnnMarie got up the nerve to glance at her face, saw her eyes crumple as she fought back tears. She'd never seen Niki cry before. Not once in her life and it scared her.

She reached for Niki's hand but she dodged away, saying, bitch, Don't touch me.

Niki, wait . . . AnnMarie said. You my best friend. You my one true friend.

Fuck that. Don't call me no more, AnnMarie.

AnnMarie stopped walking, her heart pounding, watching Niki cut across the street, calling over her shoulder: *Any a y'all, don't call me no more.* Then she stopped. In the middle of the street, she stood still. Even as a car pulled around the corner, horn blasting, she don't move, the car swerving as she tapped a cigarette out her pack, tilted her head and lit up.

50

When AnnMarie and Niki stopped talking she didn't have nobody. Four, five months, she was alone—it was Star and work and her mother. She stayed away from Nadette and Teisha, steered clear of their building on her way home from work. Sometimes Star would say, Niki. I want Niki. But AnnMarie didn't answer. She didn't know how to explain what had happened. All that drama and heartache. A whole mess a shit.

Sometimes she'd call up Dean and say, What's going on. Any little parts for me? He'd say, Not now AnnMarie, I call you if I hear something And weeks went by like that, phone calls to Dean, leaving messages on his answering machine, trying to hide the loneliness in her voice. Wondering where her life was going and when something good would happen.

Then one Saturday late in May, they met for lunch. AnnMarie took her time getting dressed, choosing a outfit for herself, then for Star. They hopped the A train, took it to Jay Street where Dean had told her to make the transfer. They rode the F line all the way to Second Avenue, and by the time they arrived Star had fallen asleep. AnnMarie lugged her up the three flights of stairs 'til they was out on the bright, crowded intersection of Houston and First Avenue.

Dean was waiting. He smiled and gave her a hug but he looked different somehow, maybe 'cause it'd been so long since they'd last met. He led them through the East Village, the streets lined with

255

brick tenement buildings, little shops selling trinkets and wedding gowns, used-clothing stores, bookstores and bars, tattoo parlors. You grow up here? AnnMarie asked, looking into the shopwindows, glancing at all the different type people passing.

Dean laughed. No, I grew up in New Jersey. In the suburbs.

How'd you end up living here?

Beats me, he said. I really couldn't tell you. I've lived all over the place. San Francisco. Boston for college. Atlanta. Washington DC.

Word, you lived in all those places? I want to live someplace.

Get yourself a mohawk. You'd fit right in.

AnnMarie laughed. She said, No, for real, Dean . . .

But they'd arrived at a corner restaurant where people was chilling at café-style tables right there on the sidewalk. Dean said, You want Mexican? We can eat outside.

AnnMarie blinked. We gonna eat out here?

In or out is fine with me . . .

Nah, nah . . . Outside is good. But AnnMarie thought it was strange, sitting out by the trash cans, an ambulance idling at the curb, somebody walk by, they could reach out and grab your food. The waiter took a chair away to make room for the stroller and they sat down at a corner table with Star who was still napping. Next door, a old grizzled dude sat on a milk crate in front of the deli, a newspaper open in his lap. His eyes drifted from Dean to AnnMarie, studying them for a moment, before going back to his paper.

AnnMarie stared at the menu. She didn't feel hungry. Dean asked how she doing, how her mother was, if her job going good and AnnMarie tried, but couldn't seem to find her voice, so deep had her loneliness been. All she could do was sit up and say, Yeah, yeah. It's all good. Everything fine, how you doing? You got a new movie? Tell me what's going on with you.

You don't want to know. Family stuff. Dean hung his head,

shaking it back and forth for a second. My father crashed his car last week. Pressed the gas instead of the brake pedal. Car sprang forward, jumped the curb, ran right into the window of a bank. AnnMarie's eyes went wide. Word? He'd said it halfway smiling, like he was picturing something funny so she laughed, then swallowed it as he went quiet.

Makes you think about what we take for granted, you know . . . ?

Word, that is sad, Dean, I'm sorry for your father. So he don't know how to drive a car no more?

It's complicated, AnnMarie. My mother says he got confused but we think she's in denial. My sister says it's Alzheimer's, early onset, you know, 'cause he's only sixty-two . . .

AnnMarie'd learned about Alzheimer's at Caring, something to do with old age, a old-person disease but couldn't remember what it meant. So she said, You got a sister, Dean?

I've told you about her. She lives in Chicago. A brother too.

Oh, AnnMarie said, that's right, I remember now.

He glanced at her, then away, his face unreadable but she'd heard the irritation in his voice and didn't quite understand it. AnnMarie studied him for a moment.

I guess it's 'cause I always think of you as Dean. You know, like you popped outta thin air or something. Just Dean. No family. Got your own thing going. Making your movies, living your life and alla that.

And as soon as the words spilled out, partways resentful, it welled up all at once, the divide between them.

Yeah, I've got my own thing going . . . *now*. But I had to work for it, AnnMarie.

She shrugged. I didn't mean nothing by it, 'cept I forgot. About your sister.

Dean looked away, glancing at Star in the stroller, her head tipped off to the side. AnnMarie reached over and righted her.

But she couldn't look up, couldn't look anywhere 'cause if she did she'd start to cry. She felt it brewing, an unmistakable sadness, as if the sidewalk had pulled apart, Dean on one side, receding into his own life, leaving her sitting at the edge of a vast and impassable hole. She kept her eyes on Star, pretending to straighten her pant leg when he said, You know why I like this place?

He waited for AnnMarie to look up, then leaned forward and said, You can spy on people and they don't know it. Like eavesdropping. AnnMarie let her eyes go to the street, seeing all the different styles walking: yuppie-type moms pushing strollers, mad punk rockers, a hobo bumming change. Across the street a Chinese dude and dark-skinned girl wearing a African wrap around her head stood together by a wall. Chinese dude got his shirt off, looking like Bruce Lee over there with his six-pack stomach.

He your type, AnnMarie?

AnnMarie smiled. Word. He is fine. I could go for Asian.

How about one a them?

AnnMarie turned, looking over her shoulder to where Dean had gestured. Two white dudes coming up the block, dressed in tattered jeans, chains dangling, one a them mohawked, metal rods poking out both cheeks, the other with a tattoo covering his entire face like a stamp.

AnnMarie bust out laughing. Hell no. That is nasty.

Dean laughed and their eyes met for a moment as the punks went past, stinking of patchouli and sweat. AnnMarie's gaze drifted back then, watching one passerby after another step to the side, parting for the boys as they moved up the block. *Spying,* AnnMarie thought and she laughed out loud.

After Star woke, AnnMarie put her in the toddler seat and they ate the enchiladas and beans the waiter brought over, Dean telling them they got a playground across the way. So when their meal was done he paid the bill and they walked into Tompkins Square Park, entered the playground through the gate, Star running straight for the slides, passing tire swings and spinny seats and a fountain spraying water. Kids running around, a whole playground full of kids, getting sloppy wet, stomping through puddles, rolling on the ground, mothers and fathers hanging close by, soaking up the late afternoon sun.

Star had a nice time. After a dozen times down the slide, and a turn on the swing, her feet flying up to kick the sky, AnnMarie let her take her shoes off, go in the sandbox. Dean sat down next to AnnMarie on the ledge and they watched her play. A white mother with a crew cut and baggie jeans sat in the sand. She gave Star a bucket to play with and a shovel to dig. Talking to her softly, holding up her own daughter who was light-skinned, with baby dreads. The two children playing, patting at the sand with the shovels. Dean took off his glasses and rubbed his eyes. He said, I know I've been busy.

She shrugged. I know you got your problems, Dean . . . She glanced at him then, saw the wrinkle lines by his eyes. He'd trimmed off his goatee, that's what it was. That's why he looked different.

I'm still here for you, AnnMarie. 'Cause I'm so *together*. She laughed, bumping him with her shoulder and she took the opening, finally telling him all the things she'd kept bottled up—Miss Beatrice with her teeth holes getting taken by the police, and about the new one, Miss Doris with her mad stupid glares and sharp mouth, how she ain't seen CeeCee, not once around the way, even though she knew her child almost two years old. And Niki, she finally got to Niki and how much she missed her.

On the long subway ride home, AnnMarie held Star in her lap. Glimpsing her reflection there in the train window. She thought about Dean. How he'd pushed a fold of bills into her hand when they said good-bye, and made her take it. She smiled for a moment, picturing that tattoo-face muthafucker coming up the block. How all the people had stepped out his way.

The train picked up speed, must be going under the river, the car rumbling mad loud, 'cause she felt the pressure build in her eardrum as Star squirmed out of her lap.

She let her go to climb onto her own seat. Sit right, AnnMarie said. So Star straightened her legs, folded her hands in her lap and started up a staring game with the lady across the way. This person like a older version a Niki. Same type skin, wash a freckles and a curly 'fro. Niki's prettier though, AnnMarie thought. Ain't-give-a-shit attitude. Switching up her style, cutting off all those curls. AnnMarie always thought it'd been about trying to find a look—Female Rapper Extraordinaire. But now she knew it was about trying to own something. Define herself in a world a straights.

AnnMarie turned her face to the window, staring past her reflection as the lights in the tunnel blurred and ran. Always going after the wrong girl, AnnMarie thought. She cringed, picturing it—Nadette showing off her ring. *You got something to say?* Slapping Niki with the reality that she ain't wanted. Trying to find love in Far Rockaway.

Maybe that's why she started going out to Jamaica where Latania live. To be with a group of lesbian girls, where she had a fighting chance. All those times Niki'd taken her along—hop the dollar van, spend the day outta Far Rock. Hanging out, gossiping. Listening to music. One time they went all the way to Kings Plaza, walking through the mall, sipping ice coffees, cracking jokes and talking.

She missed alla that since they stopped talking. Yeah, she missed it.

there she go

51

One Sunday afternoon, the month before her eighteenth birthday, she went by to Nadette's, asked if she could get her a fake ID. Turn eighteen, ain't no way she sitting around, everybody else in the world out there clubbing, having fun. Nadette said, I get you one but what you been up to, AnnMarie? Where you been?

Ever since the fallout with Niki, AnnMarie had stayed away. She knew Nadette was still working nights, engaged to Dennis and settled.

AnnMarie said, You know, same ol' thing. Working for that cranky lady on Beach 96th.

Oh, you goin' all the way out there, how you get out there?

Take the 22, then the 17. It be mad slow, take a hour-fifteen each way. She got something wrong upstairs. I gotta tell her everything. Brush your teeth, do this, do that, help her with her potty.

That's nasty, AnnMarie, why you do it. You know I introduce you to my boss. You still got a figure on you. Get your *chicas* done, you make mad money.

AnnMarie looked down at her chest. What, my breasts too small?

Girl, I hook you up.

AnnMarie thought about it. Do she want to dance like Nadette? She'd seen her one time up on stage. All that attention. Grown men clapping, whistling. Do your thing.

Monday morning, AnnMarie knocked, then leaned into the door. She said, It's me, Miss Doris. It's AnnMarie. Then she used the key she'd been given by Miss Doris's daughter. The daughter telling her she don't trust her mother to open the door.

It was mad stuffy in there, no air moving, first thing AnnMarie did was open the window.

You ready to take a walk?

Where we going.

Outside. Let's get some air.

I'm hungry.

You ain't eat breakfast yet?

There's nothing good in there.

What you want.

Miss Doris said, They got that mushroom pizza down on the corner.

Let's get pizza then.

She used to hate Miss Doris. She'd have AnnMarie on her hands and knees cleaning behind the toilet, behind the radiator, mopping the kitchen floor even if it still clean from yesterday. But something had happened. Old age. Dementia, the daughter had called it. AnnMarie wasn't sure what that meant. All she knew was now the lady don't ask her to do nothing.

She helped Miss Doris out of her pajama top, her breasts sagging like two flaps a brown leather. Put her in her tracksuit, only thing she liked to wear.

What we doing.

We going for a walk, AnnMarie said.

I have to go to the bathroom.

You want me to come with you?

Hell no. I can do it myself.

She checked her phone for messages. Paloma had called. Outta the blue. Black China doll with her mule shoes and sweet perfume, hadn't seen her in six months. Ever since AnnMarie and Niki stop talking.

Miss Doris was still in the bathroom.

You okay, Miss Doris?

AnnMarie poked her head in.

What? What do you want?

Let's go. We going for a walk.

It's too hot outside.

Nah, come on. You see, it feel nice. We go around the block, then get some pizza.

AnnMarie picked up the twenty dollars and shopping list Miss Doris's daughter had left on the counter.

They sat on the bench in the shade, a breeze blowing warm on AnnMarie's face.

See, isn't this nice?

What we doing out here.

Just sitting.

I know we're sitting. What are we doing, AnnMarie.

Taking the air, Miss Doris. What, you forgot already?

I didn't forget.

Okay. 'Cause you know I have to write it down on your forehead you start forgetting.

Miss Doris glanced at her.

You think I'm losing my mind too.

No, I know you losing your mind. How old you now, like a hundred fifty?

Miss Doris tipped her head and laughed.

AnnMarie smiled.

Come on now, jus' feel that breeze.

When she got home that evening, she called Paloma. Paloma said the designer Dre, he looking to do a fashion show and do she want to meet him. AnnMarie said, Hell yeah, I meet him.

She laid in bed long after Star had crawled in next to her, two o'clock in the morning. She'd outgrown the crib, had her own bed that AnnMarie had made for her out of a foam mattress and blankets she got on sale at Marshalls. But do she sleep on it? Hell, no. Star sleepwalking to the place she knew be safe.

AnnMarie shifted, moving Star's hot little body off to her own side. Pushed the sheet off, the room stiflin', even with the fan blowing she felt sweat beading on her skin. She knew you could make money modeling. She didn't know how much but it had to be more than $8.50 an hour, that's for sure. She closed her eyes. She pictured herself up on the catwalk, strutting in some designer clothes. Then it became a stage with poles and dancers and a light, a single beam of light falling, girls grinding, their skin brown and glistening like oil been rubbed there, then it was her dancing, back arched, leg around the pole, her nipples pierced by tiny points of light. She woke up sweatin'. Sat up, carried Star back to her own bed, covered her with the sheet.

Got into bed but didn't go back to sleep. Instead she pulled her notebook off the sill and flipped it open. She pulled the curtain back for some light and wrote:

AUGUST GOAL—

make more money

She listened to Star breathing, could tell by the sound her thumb in her mouth, saliva dripping on the sheet. Sheets need changing. Gas bill, electric, phone, MetroCard, she bring lunch to work tomorrow, peanut butter and jelly and a orange—couldn't think how much she had in her pocketbook, trying to picture what food there was in the fridge, turkey, American, mayo . . . No, mayo finished off. Buy some tomorrow, clip coupon tomorrow—spread it on thick.

52

She met Paloma outside the Jay Street station and walked two blocks to the building where Dre had his studio. Took the stairs to the third floor and walked into a big room with racks of clothes lining the wall, rolls of cloth stacked on shelves, big black work-tables and a sewing machine. Dre took both of AnnMarie's hands in his and said, Hello, beautiful. Why don't you walk for me.

He put music on and she worked it right there in the room, the whole while Dre hollering Yeah! Yeah, girl! Go on. That's it. And out the corner of her eye she caught Paloma laughing into her hand.

They went to Dunkin' Donuts after.

Paloma got a Vanilla Bean Coolatta.

She said, He a fem but he got mad talent. He likes you, he gonna put you top a the show, I can tell.

Cool. Cool. Cool. I forgot to ask him. How much he pay.

Oh, he don't pay nothing. It's for the exposure.

Oh.

Oh, AnnMarie thought.

Paloma sipped her drink and they sat in silence, Niki being what they got in common.

AnnMarie said, So how's Niki, what she up to.

She good. She fine. You know, me and hers together now.

Word?

Paloma shook out her wrist and showed AnnMarie a gold bracelet with gold charms dangling off the side.

She got me that for my birthday.

You had a birthday? When's your birthday.

July 30th.

Okay. Happy birthday—mines is coming up.

How old you gonna be, Paloma asked.

Eighteen. Tha's nice though. Tha's real nice a Niki to get you that.

Yeah, Niki's very sweet to me.

Paloma smiled, still looking like a black China doll.

That night, AnnMarie practiced walking in the hallway outside the apartment. Put on the pair of four-inch heels she borrowed from Nadette and started in front of 4F. Hands on her hips, shoulders back, chin up, her ankles wobbling a couple times but she kept going.

Star sat on the stairs watching.

Whatchu doing, Mama?

AnnMarie got to the end of the hall, struck a pose, giving her daughter a little cat-eye look, like the magazine girls do.

Ma, whatchu doing!

How I look, Boo? Do I look good?

Yeah, you look good. But why you walking like that?

I'm practicing. I'ma get up on stage and model some fashion. Like those girls you see in the magazine.

Hands on hips, shoulders back, chin up, AnnMarie strutted. And out the corner of her eye she saw Star watching. Hands folded in her lap, eyes bright, breathing her mother in.

53

The fashion show was Saturday night at Splash Bar, in a neighborhood Paloma said was called the Chelsea.

She liked the feeling of all those eyes on her, Dre's clothes hanging like silk, working it at the end of the ramp—the model Misu there next to her, they'd only practiced a couple times, leaning back into each other, letting the people see the dresses drape down their backs.

In the backroom, there was powder in the air, a rush of movement, clothes flying, the scent of girl all around her. Girls getting naked, stripped to G-strings no bra, AnnMarie didn't have no G-string, wearing regular old cotton but that was okay 'cause no one was looking, everybody busy getting in and out of outfits without smearing makeup on Dre's clothes.

Line up!

Line up!

She got in line next to Misu again, Misu who was a true professional, the way she moved her hips, gliding down the runway. Two and two they moved together, AnnMarie keeping stride with the fashionista pretty girl.

After the show there was laughter, girls laughing and talking, Dre walking through the racks saying, You all beautiful. Thank you thank you thank you. And they could hear the dirty house music start up, some of the girls dancing right there while they dressing—putting on they thigh-high boots, little miniskirts.

Niki came into the room, walked right past the curtain, laughing 'cause a couple girls shrieked, throwing clothes at her telling her get the fuck out, no free peeps.

AnnMarie was done dressing and had turned when she heard Niki say, What up girl, long time no see. Frontin' like there ain't been nothing wrong between them. Nothing at all.

Hey Niki, AnnMarie said. How you, you look good.

Thank you, thank you I try to keep myself in the fashion way. AnnMarie laughed.

Paloma was leaning into the mirror, touching up her makeup. She said, What'd you think, baby? You like the clothes?

Y'all worked it. Y'all tore it down.

Niki came up behind Paloma then, put her arms around her waist, spooning her right in front of everybody.

Dang. AnnMarie glanced around. No one was looking. Huh-uh, that ain't right. No one cared. Niki kissing Paloma right in front of everybody. Now that was something.

AnnMarie peeked her head past the curtain and saw the club spilling people, crystal ball turning, the stage broken apart now but dancers up on raised levels, podium-type things, all the bodies grooving, having fun.

Niki and Paloma climbed onto one of the raised levels and people made room, room for her too, Niki reaching for her hand, pulling her up and by the time AnnMarie made her way off the dance floor she was pouring sweat and needing water. She slid her way up to the bar to get herself something to drink and saw a fella standing over there—leather do-rag, white tank, black leather pants, one foot hooked up on the bar stool. Nice face. Body, long and lean.

AnnMarie turned away, sipping her water. She hadn't been with nobody for a long time. Only hands on her these days was Star's. She watched the mirror ball spin crystals of light across the floor, across all the bodies moving in the dark.

Then Busta slammed out the box and she felt the crowd swell all at once, the model Misu appearing suddenly behind her, saying, Come on AnnMarie, let's dance, pulling her back out onto the floor as AnnMarie let her gaze slide back to the fella at the end of the bar just as those pretty eyes turned and met hers.

Next thing she knew he'd danced his way into their circle, was dancing right up next to her and AnnMarie kept her rhythm, looking now into those eyes and saw that the boy was a girl, no two ways about it. Busta's beat locking them in, the two of them almost touching, dancing so close AnnMarie could see the pearls of sweat on her bare shoulder, saw the brown nipples poking through her tank and AnnMarie didn't back away 'cause she felt it, the sudden pull of attraction. Like a magnet, this girl was. When the song ended, a slow jam came on. AnnMarie glanced at the girl just as she hitched up her pants, neither of them talking but no one moving neither. Awkward. Just plain awkward. Couples paired up to dance, but the girl just leaned in and touched her arm. She said, Thanks. And AnnMarie didn't know why she did it, but she followed her through the crowd and out the door where the bouncer sat on his stool. AnnMarie glanced at him, said, Can I get back in? He said, Yeah, you get back in.

The girl was leaning against the wall. Had her phone out, texting somebody so AnnMarie waited digging around in her purse until she looked up.

She said, That Busta song was dope.

Word.

AnnMarie dug around some more until she pulled out a pack of Pall Malls.

You want one.

Nah, I don't smoke. Then the girl said, I saw you up there before.

You was at the fashion show?

Yeah, you was walking with Misu.

Oh, you know Misu?

Yeah, yeah. We cool.

Oh, okay.

The door pushed open and a group of people spilled out, laughing. A fella spinning around with thin arms, then walking like a runway queen, his friends laughing. They high on something. She saw it was Bodie and that Niki was with them, lighting up a blunt.

Niki!

Niki turned, then walked over with her swag on. Ignored the girl altogether as she moved in on AnnMarie, holding her hips and leaning in for a kiss.

Hey baby . . .

AnnMarie pushed her away, laughing. Stop bugging, Niki. You soused.

But Niki slid her hands around AnnMarie's waist and wouldn't let go. Nuzzling in, it was embarrasing, the girl standing there watching, Niki's weed breath on her face.

Stop, Niki, AnnMarie said, pushing until she finally broke free. Niki stumbled, then regained her balance.

Stupid, AnnMarie said.

I'm playing with you.

Playing, Niki said as she raised her hands and backed away.

Ain't she with Paloma, the girl asked.

AnnMarie tsked. Supposed to be.

She got the grabby-hand disease.

AnnMarie laughed, and their eyes met briefly before Ann-Marie looked away.

They stood for a moment without speaking. Then AnnMarie asked, So you a lesbian too?

The girl shrugged. Kinda sorta maybe.

What you mean, kinda sorta, you either is or you ain't.

Why you gotta define it.

What I mean is, is you with somebody?

Oh. Nah, nah . . . Not at the moment.

AnnMarie didn't know why she was acting this way, frontin' like she knew what she doing, flirtin' with this girl.

She was happy, what it was. The air warm at midnight, summertime in the city. Forget about the little things. Dre'd said she'd done good, he liked her style. Didn't matter about the money, sometimes exposure is enough. The door opened again, music pouring out, Destiny's Child harmonizing, AnnMarie start to dance right there in the street. The girl laughed.

So you gonna tell me your name?

AnnMarie.

AnnMarie put out her hand and the girl took it, held on and said, I'm Lu.

Lu . . . Lu like Lu-lu or Lu like LuAnn, AnnMarie asked.

There you go again.

What?

Trying to define me.

AnnMarie laughed and Lu smiled.

Nah, I play for Brooklyn College—women's basketball. They got L-U on the back a my jersey. Number 18. Short for Lucinda.

Oh, okay, AnnMarie said.

So you a ball playa.

Lucinda laughed, shaking her head and AnnMarie thought right then she was just about the prettiest girl she ever seen.

54

Darius called, Blessed said.

AnnMarie was getting Star dressed.

Daddy, Star said.

What the fuck he want, AnnMarie thought.

Last time they'd seen him was two weeks after Star's third birthday, musta been July, around then. He popped up with a Plush Puppy, took the two a them to Burger King where Star got a Happy Meal and a gold paper crown. AnnMarie couldn't help it—tight the whole time, not even able to fake she happy for her own daughter. Muthafucker had promised to get balloons and a cake with HAPPY BIRTHDAY, STAR spelled out in purple icing. Her birthday had come and gone—AnnMarie'd had to run to J&B, get a box cake from the bakery, put the candles on herself.

Did he say anything?

No.

Momma you gonna call him? Star asked.

I call him.

But she went to work, got Miss Doris into her tracksuit, even though the weather was way too warm for that. Lady gotta whole closet full a clothes. Beginning of June, Miss Doris' daughter had bought her some sleeveless button-ups, cotton dresses but Miss Doris refuse. It was tracksuit or nothing. Food stains down the front, won't let AnnMarie wash it. The day she brought over the clothes, the daughter tried to strip her mother naked, but Miss

Doris strong for a old lady—gripped her daughter by the wrist and twisted. Her daughter said, I'm done, AnnMarie. Her face screwed up in anger. *I am done.* What you mean you done, AnnMarie thought.

On the bench now, Miss Doris got her eyes closed. AnnMarie glanced at her, couldn't tell if she sleeping or not. She tipped her own head back, felt the sun kiss her face and thought about calling Nadette. She'd seen her dance, seen the floor managers come up on stage and pour buckets of money on top of her when she got done. Buckets. Nadette had tossed the bills up in the air like confetti.

She opened her eyes, turned and looked at Miss Doris. She wondered how old she was for real. Bony hands curled in her lap. AnnMarie thought, I could just get up, walk away—you never even know. Miss Doris. Sitting there breathing.

Outside Splash that night, Lucinda had said, Y'all want a ride? I drive you.

She'd dropped Niki and Paloma first. Then she turned to AnnMarie. AnnMarie said, You got to turn around, go back to New Haven then up Gateway. It's a one-way. Lucinda backed up the car, the streetlight hitting her face, and for a second AnnMarie thought, What the fuck'm I doing. The girl telling AnnMarie how she'd been in a serious relationship for a while but how they ain't together no more. She living at her mother's house in Lefferts.

Oh, okay. Lefferts Boulevard? AnnMarie asked.

It's over there by the Park. Prospect Park. You ever been there? Nah.

They got horses over there.

Word? Horses, in the city?

Lucinda laughed. Near the park. There's a stable over there. Word, I never knew that.

Lucinda pulled up outside the building. This it?

Yeah. Thanks for the ride. AnnMarie unlatched the door and pushed it open.

Lucinda said, What's your rush. Sit for a minute and let's talk.

So that's what they did. The two of them in the front seat, windows rolled down, the predawn air mild and balmy. Lucinda put the radio on low, some late-night mixtape jam, and they listened for a while, then talked some more and when AnnMarie finally got upstairs, Star was still asleep in her mother's bed but the sun had risen, bleaching the world over.

no shame in love

55

The first time they hung out, Lucinda picked her up and they drove out to Kings Plaza where they roamed around, going in and out of stores, laughing and talking about Brooklyn College and basketball and music and the new album out by Missy, talent agents and talent scouts and how it's important to have representation if you want to make it in this world—they mouths going a mile a minute, talking about everything under the sun. The second time, Lucinda brought her ball and they played in the courts behind Far Rock High School, Lucinda spinning around AnnMarie with the grace of a dancer. AnnMarie laughed, grabbing on to her waist until they both fell over in a heap and Lucinda stood up wincing, faking her ankle got broke, limping away crying Foul, foul, foul. Then they wandered down to the boardwalk and sat on the benches eating ice cream and talking some more, not noticing the people walking by and how the sun was sinking into the horizon, swatting flies away, not noticing nothing but each other until AnnMarie said, Let's go to my house.

In the apartment, AnnMarie sat Lucinda down on the floor of her bedroom and combed out her hair. She said, What kinda braid you want. I can do geometric, diamond or crisscross, I can do swirl, I can make it curvy, like go off to one side, what you want.

Lucinda said, I trust you, just make it look nice. And don't pull too hard—I got a tender head.

AnnMarie teased, yanking her head back and Lucinda swatted her leg. She said stop and AnnMarie did. She got her hands to settle down and stop shaking and they eased into it, first time in AnnMarie's bedroom, Star asleep on Blessed's bed, AnnMarie wondering what it be like to kiss this girl but too shy to make the first move.

My mother used to braid my hair but now she got arthritis, Lucinda said.

Word? She can't do it no more?

Nope. She comes to all my games though—brings my sisters. They sit up in the bleachers cheering.

Sisters. I thought you had one sister.

Nah. I got two half sisters too. They young, five and seven. They with their mother most a the time but my mother takes care a them on weekends.

AnnMarie shook her head. I don't understand that.

Yeah, she get walked on by my father. He say jump, she jump.

I told you about CeeCee, right?

Yeah . . . You ever see that girl?

Huh-uh. She had a boy. But you know what? I don't care. For all I know Darius living with her right now. Could be he got bored, he with some other chick.

You got a dog for a baby father.

Word.

They was quiet for a minute, then Lucinda said, Yeah . . . don't matter they ain't hers. My mother, I guess she loves those girls anyway.

AnnMarie felt the breeze pass through the window. She combed out another piece of hair, liking the feel of Lucinda leaning back against her leg, easy, no worries, like they got all the time in the world.

———

After that, Lucinda just started showing up. AnnMarie'd come up the block, 6:15 from work, her face would light up, seeing the car there, looking in the driver-side window and finding it empty—her heart would start to pound knowing that girl already upstairs. She'd get inside, see her playing on the floor with Star or helping Blessed with the dishes. You don't got to do that Lu, Ma why you got her doing that. Lucinda'd shake her head and say, Chill, Ann-Marie. Chill.

One evening she came home, opened the door, looked around and said, Where Lucinda at?

She down at the check-cash.

Why.

She paying the phone bill, Blessed said.

What you talking about she paying the phone bill, why she paying our phone bill?

Blessed shrugged. Ask her.

No, Ma, I'm asking you, why the hell you giving her our bills to pay, what she gonna think.

Blessed stared at the TV.

When Lucinda got out the elevator, AnnMarie was waiting in the hallway. She said, You don't gotta pay my mother's phone bill.

Lucinda shrugged.

Why you do that, you don't gotta do that.

Ain't no thing.

AnnMarie heard the soft way she said it, thought of the quiet way Lucinda had a talking, and felt her heart flip over.

Lucinda said, Why you looking at me like that—we going inside or we gonna tell the neighbors about it?

But AnnMarie wasn't listening, she was thinking, *what the fuck am I waiting for*. She knew what she wanted to do and just as

Lucinda opened her mouth to speak, AnnMarie took a step and kissed her. Her lips parting, pressing against Lucinda's, kissing her the way she'd been dreaming of. She felt her heart melting, her whole body go slack as Lucinda's hand rose, pulling AnnMarie into an embrace. A month of waiting and wanting, a whole month and when Lucinda drew away, AnnMarie whispered, I think I'm in love.

What your mother gonna say? Lucinda asked, softly.

Fuck my mother, what she know about love.

One evening, not long after, they was coming from the J&B where they'd gone to buy toilet paper and groceries and a toothbrush for Lucinda since she'd started sleeping over. Lu was talking about the game she played on Tuesday, how she'd tried to get in front of the girl but had slipped, the girl landing a three-point jumper.

AnnMarie was saying *uh-huh, uh-huh, uh-oh,* but was only halfways listening 'cause she saw the fellas standing on the corner and felt a stab of apprehension. She slowed down some, falling out a step with Lucinda who didn't seem to notice, tossing the ball up in the air, still talking her ball-talk when AnnMarie realized one a them was Raymel.

Hadn't seen him for a long time, heard he'd gone upstate for burglary. She wondered how this gonna go down, one fella pacing, gold flashing on his teeth, his voice loud like he some type a cock-a-the-block. So she kept her eye on Raymel and when she saw the look of recognition pass across his face, she let herself breathe.

What, you gonna walk by, not say hello, Raymel said smiling.

AnnMarie stepped up and hugged him. How you doing, Ray, where you been?

I've been good, you know. Keeping it real.

Other fella said, Fuck that. He been on vacation, word, what up.

Raymel laughed, Tha's right—I been on vacation. Reaching over, taking daps from Gold Mouth, then sipping from the 40 he got tucked in a brown paper bag.

Gold Mouth eyes glassy, pacing, high on something. Ann-Marie could feel him moving behind her, his eyes moving from her shoulder to her ass, and all she wanted was to be the fuck outta there.

But Raymel was saying, Where Darius at?

His mother got a place in Redfern. He over there with her in 12-70.

Y'all still together . . . ?

He my baby daddy, let's put it that way.

Introduce, Raymel. Introduce us to these fine young things, Gold Mouth said, and do they want to party wit' us?

Raymel looked at her now, like he drinking her up. Something he never woulda done if Darius been around.

Who your friend, AnnMarie, y'all wanna party wit' us?

But before she could answer, Lucinda said, No. We don't wanna party wit' y'all. Come on, AnnMarie, let's go.

Raymel's gaze drifting to Lu, checking her like *Who this bitch*, and in that moment, AnnMarie felt herself do it—shift, just a inch, but enough to put space between her and Lu, then it was done.

They walked the rest of the way home in silence. A wall between them. Finally, Lu said, How you know he over in Redfern. I thought you said you hadn't seen him.

That fool popped up a couple a days ago, wanting to see Star.

So you let him in.

Yeah, I let him in. He Star's father, ain't he.

Oh, okay.

Why you questioning me?

I ain't questioning you.

Truth was they'd played on the floor for a while, the three of them—he'd brought Star a doll and when she pulled the string, the doll cried *Mama* or *Baba* or *Feed me*. They'd laughed, listening to that fake child sound and when he leaned over and kissed her, she'd kissed him back. She didn't know why. He'd given her money for Star, peeled off five twenties from a wad so thick she could see the bulge after he'd tucked it back in his front pocket.

When they got back to AnnMarie's building, Lu held out the bag of groceries and said, I'm out.

AnnMarie frowned. Why?

Lu glanced away.

Then she said, I don't like how you acting.

Fine. Leave then.

Upstairs, she put the groceries on the counter, went into her bedroom and closed the door.

Star walked in and said, Ma, can you—but AnnMarie cut her off, saying, Leave me alone. I play with you in a minute. Star threw herself on the bed next to AnnMarie's face and started whining so AnnMarie stood up, lifted her daughter and carried her out the room. She said, Sit down, watch TV. Star burst out crying but AnnMarie just turned and went back into her room, closed the door. She didn't care Star was wailing, her mother's voice hollering through the door. She laid down on the bed, unable to move, a heavy feeling pressing on her chest like a brick.

When AnnMarie finally rose, she went into the living room and sat Star on her lap, hugged her close. She said, You wanna help me put the groceries away? Star perked up, scrambling from her mother's lap, excited over this simple chore and ran to the kitchen where the bag still sat untouched. AnnMarie followed, and the two of them put the cold cuts in the fridge and the bread up on the counter. Star reaching in the bag, pulling out first a roll of toilet paper, then Lucinda's toothbrush. AnnMarie looked at it in her daughter's hand. She pictured herself on the street. Shifting, leaning away. Knowing she'd cheated Lucinda outta something and hating herself for it.

She thought, What the fuck you got to be afraid of. You is you. Fuck everybody and they opinion. If you love her, then love her.

You is you.

Be you. Be happy.

She called up Lu's house. Lu's mother said, No AnnMarie she's not here but I'll tell her you called.

Don't she got a ball game this weekend, AnnMarie asked.

On Saturday, she got Star dressed in a child-size basketball jersey she'd found at Payless and a mad cute pair of high-tops. Got on the subway and they rode all the way out to St. Francis College in downtown Brooklyn.

AnnMarie and Star found a seat up near the top of the bleachers, clusters of families sitting together, everyone waiting for the game to get started. Feeling flutterflies in her stomach, she watched the girls break from the huddle, black and green jerseys filtering onto the floor, Lucinda taking her position at the circle, ready to pounce for the tip-off.

Look Ma, there she is. There's Lu, Star said.

That's right, Boo. Number 18.

And then it started, ref tossed the ball in the air, two centers springing, green team got the tip but all of a sudden there was Lu, reaching in, lightning quick, stealing the ball away from the big girl who was startled, then angry and a step behind. Ann-

Marie was on her feet as Lucinda headed for the basket, her stride long and graceful, making the two-point layup, easy, no problem. Couldn't hear the swish 'cause somebody was shouting, *That's my girl! That's my baby!* AnnMarie looked down and saw a woman standing—Lucinda's mother with two little girls, five and seven, clapping and pounding their feet.

Dang, AnnMarie thought. She don't lie.

56

One night after they made love, Lucinda showing AnnMarie what felt good, how to use two fingers and a palm to make her come—they lay side by side, Lu's head nestled next to hers, the curtain pulled back to let a breeze in. AnnMarie was drifting into an easy sleep when a image appeared out the blue—her mother standing on Gateway Boulevard, raising up her hand, waving all those food stamps around. *Who want ice cream. Who want ice cream*, her mother had shouted, not caring two cents who saw or what it meant. Thinking of AnnMarie and only AnnMarie. No shame in love or how you claim it.

AnnMarie opened her eyes, listening to Lu breathing next to her. She said, I used to look down on my mother. You know, I blamed her for how she is, like she stupid, she lazy, acting like a invalid—never trying to get better, get a job, nothing.

AnnMarie heard Lucinda laugh softly in the dark. She said, You a harsh critic.

AnnMarie nudged her. I'm serious . . . All those disability checks coming in, it was like why bother, you know . . .

Lucinda was quiet, then said, Once you in the system, it hard to get out.

AnnMarie lay still, listening for a long time to the night sounds coming up from the street below. Garbage truck making the *bweep bweep bweep* as it idled somewhere out there. She said, I ever tell you about Blessed coming to New York?

Lu said, Hm-mm . . .

So AnnMarie told her the story all the way from the beginning, of Blessed leaving the man who abused her, coming over with a bag a clothes and AnnMarie just a seed in her belly, not knowing what hurdles there was to jump but jumping blind anyway. How she stole back her life.

And when she got to the end she knew Lu'd fallen alseep somewhere along the way, her breath coming soft and low. AnnMarie started to reach for her arm, to set it across her waist but stopped herself.

She thought about how she'd made Darius *it*, the number one be-all, end-all. Even with making the movie and getting out in the world, she'd tethered herself to him, first for love, then for Star, then simply for the sameness of it. There'd been a comfort in the sameness. She'd never had the guts to tell him down. Five years, coming and going. He could punch her. Fuck her. Kick her in the head. She'd get up . . . Yeah, she'd get up but she'd say, Come on in.

She didn't speak these words aloud. But she understood them suddenly and in a deep way. Maybe it was 'cause of Lu laying next to her, the quiet way she spoke, the way she'd spin the ball on her finger, saying, Yeah, I'm listening . . . Maybe it was 'cause of Niki or the movie, of having known Dean and Albert and Maya, having gone out into the world and come back again, seeing her life as a map with lines and markings . . . all the boundaries to cross and the ones she'd accepted. All the markings scratched out by petty beefs and throw-downs, the want of attention and money, by having a baby too young. The weight of an arm confused with a promise.

It came to her just before sleep, an idea crystallizing in the dark—how maybe the size of your world ain't what matter, whether it expand or shrink up or expand again. Hurdles to jump. You jump. Erase the lines, draw new ones. Chart a course and follow.

57

Right around Star's fourth birthday Darius came by knocking on the door.

He said, I need to talk to you for a small little minute. Can you step outside?

AnnMarie leaned against the doorjamb considering . . .

What you want, Darius?

Nah, nothing. I came by to see you. My homeboy Marco, he says he saw you over there at Splash—what, you modeling these days?

A little here and there, yeah . . .

Well, I wanted to say congratulations and whatnot.

Acting mad nice. Ducking his head like he got admiration and shit. Saying, Yeah . . . I been over by to Splash, that place sick. You know the DJ, he go by Master XBomb, he work all over the city . . .

But she stopped paying attention, knowing where this was leading, any second now, he gonna say, How you feel and can I come in . . .

So she said, Hold up, Darius. I be right back.

She left him in the hall, closed the door, Blessed calling from the bathroom, Who that, AnnMarie. Who knocking . . .

But AnnMarie didn't answer, she went past Star playing on the couch, opened the door to her bedroom and said, Darius out there.

Lucinda looked up, her expression blank.

That piece a shit coming to bother you? What he want.

AnnMarie shrugged, crossing to the window where she peeled the curtain back and stared down at the street. Her heart strumming, trying to collect herself. What the fuck she gonna do. He ask to come inside and Lucinda in her bedroom. What she gonna do. It ain't been a secret but she hadn't told nobody neither. At least not in Far Rock, the two of them spending most a their time in the West Village of Manhattan, hitting the clubs on All Girl Night, making out in the corner, on the dance floor, in the bathroom stall, acting wild and crazy, dancing up a storm, talking, laughing, meeting other girls, new girls from all over the city. She'd been having the time of her life.

She could feel Lucinda's eyes on her, waiting.

You want me to leave?

AnnMarie shook her head. Stay here. I'ma go talk to him.

Out in the hallway, Darius had taken a seat at the top of the stairwell.

He sighed.

Word, he started . . . I just wanted to tell you congratulations, you know . . . All these muthafuckers posing, like they doing something—I need people in my life who got motivation, you feel me. That's what I like about you, doing the fashion thing, I need that AnnMarie, respect, word up.

She leaned against the wall. She said, Thank you. That's nice of you. I appreciate it. But her mind was lifting off, thinking, how she gonna do it. Is she gonna do it?

He kept on rambling, talking about how he doing a R. Kelly remix, and do she want to sing the female part, he gathering some beats, getting his studio together . . . hit it at the clubs with a new mixtape . . .

Sounds good, Darius. Let me know when you get the studio set up . . . I be there.

Darius sighed, pulled out his phone, read a text.

He looked up at her. Where Star at? You gonna let me in?

She let her eyes fall on his face, studying him for a moment. Then she pushed herself away from the wall. She said, Come on then.

Star looked up when they entered. Darius said, Hey baby what you doing . . . She was standing at a TV tray, putting the pieces of a puzzle together—picture of Dora and that monkey Boots. Star said, It's a puzzle.

And before Darius could take a seat on the couch, AnnMarie motioned with her head to follow.

He came up behind her as she opened the bedroom door, revealing Lucinda stretched across the bed with her tight jeans and leather do-rag, flipping through a magazine, looking beautiful as ever.

AnnMarie watched his eyelids fly up and hit the ceiling. He stood there dumb.

She said, Darius, this is my girlfriend, Lucinda.

She said, Lu, this is Darius, my baby father.

Lu sat up, and by way of hello lifted her chin but didn't speak, gazing at him in that quiet way, and waited.

AnnMarie could feel his body go stiff and she held her breath, sensing the confusion rise up and fill his mouth, his words coming out jumbled, *Okay, word, how you doing* . . . and AnnMarie didn't try to fill the silence, the two of them waiting him out until he finally took a step and backed out the room, saying, Yeah, yeah . . . okay, well, hold it down then . . .

Yeah . . . I've been holding it down.

Lu said it straight, matter-of-fact. And Darius cut her a look, filled with a sudden suspicion but AnnMarie was already calling to Star. She said, Star show your father the puzzle you playing with. Star looked up at Darius, expectantly. He took a seat on the couch, glancing up at AnnMarie, waiting for her to join them, to hang the way they'd always done. But she didn't, she stayed where she was, watching his face scrunch up, like *What the fuck you doing*, as she swung the door closed.

Inside the bedroom, AnnMarie leaned forward, halfway crouching, hands on her knees, trembling with excitement or fear, she didn't know which, but giddy as hell—she start to laugh, mad quiet, but she was laughing and Lucinda reached down and picked up her ball, spinning it on her finger, a smile playing on her lips. AnnMarie raised her eyes and they looked at each other across the room. They didn't have to speak. Ain't nothing to say that wasn't already understood.

Next thing she knew, the door flung open and Star was standing there. She said, Ma, Daddy says he wants to speak to you. Ann-Marie glanced past her and saw the living room empty.

She said, Where he at?

He waiting for you out there.

AnnMarie turned and looked at Lu.

He try anything, Lu said, holler and I be there.

Darius was leaning up against the wall in the hallway.

So that your girlfriend-girlfriend or that your friend.

She's my girlfriend.

He pushed himself away from the wall, shaking his head. I can't believe it. What made you go that way . . .

Her heart pounding in her chest, she said, It ain't no thing, I'm just taking a break from men for a while.

He kept looking at her, his eyes narrowing in disbelief.

So you a muff-diver now. That is disgusting.

She said, It ain't no thing, Darius. I'm just having fun with my life.

Well, what about me and you—we still gonna get up with each other . . . ?

She wanted to laugh, thinking, You beat me, you rape me, you punch me in front of Star, hell no, I ain't interested in fucking you.

But she shook her head, watching the anger and impotence brewing right below the surface, his eyebrows scrunched, mouth tight until finally he stepped past her and jabbed the elevator button to go down.

So you ain't gonna hang with Star, she asked.

Nah, nah . . . I come back later.

AnnMarie didn't wait. She left him standing by the elevator as she turned the doorknob and went in.

exposure

58

Dean called.

He said, AnnMarie, I got a part for you.

He said, It's not a big part like last time. You'd play a waitress. You have to sing "Happy Birthday" to a customer.

She said, Dean, you know I do it.

He put the script in the mail.

When it came, she flipped through it and found her scenes.

She had three scenes, Waitress #2 highlighted in yellow where she suppose to learn her lines.

The day of rehearsal she got up early, showered, pressed her jeans, put on a blouse she knew she looked good in. She practiced her lines in the mirror.

You decide yet?

What can I get you.

Have you decided yet?

What can I get for you.

She asked Blessed to watch Star.

Star said, Where you going, Ma?

She bent down and hugged her daughter. She said, I'm goin' to the city, Boo. I'm gonna act in a movie. How I look?

You look good, Ma, but I wanna go.

Why don't you wave to me. Go on, get up there and look for me.

AnnMarie waited as Star ran to their bedroom, heading for the window. Then she turned, walked out the door, went down the stairs and out the building. Across the street, AnnMarie looked up, shielding her eyes from the sun. She saw Star's head bouncing up and down, two palms to the window, shouting now 'cause she'd spotted her.

Ma! Ma! Look here! Ma! Ma! Up here! Maaaaaa . . . ! Like a refrain from a song, AnnMarie thought as she waved both arms high over her head, laughing, not caring who saw, not caring one bit about being loud and crazy because this was the view from the window, this is what Star saw:

AnnMarie turning north, going the rest of the way up Gateway until she reached Mott Avenue. Star lost sight of her there as she crossed the street, heading west, passing first Cornaga Avenue, then Central, finally arriving at the stairs of the subway where she followed them down into the station.

59

It wasn't no big thing, no big romantic thing with Cupid shooting arrows and hearts and alla that. It was just a regular day. Lu came into the bedroom, ball in hand, tossing it back and forth. She said, How much money you got saved.

AnnMarie said, Why. What's the matter.

How much?

About sixty dollars, maybe a little more.

How much your next paycheck gonna be.

What's going on, Lucinda? You in trouble? What you need.

She said, Nah . . . nah, you know my uncle that manages the building over by the park. There's a apartment that just went empty.

AnnMarie looked at her, like *What you mean, an apartment.*

She'd been sleeping over a lot lately, since school was out for the summer. Blessed'd been like, What's Lucinda doing here all the time, don't she got her own house to live at? What you girls doing in there?

Sometime AnnMarie wonder if Blessed blind outta her good eye. Like, *Duh. This girl eating my pussy, I'm walking around with a smile on my face—can't you tell we in love?*

But AnnMarie knew Blessed liked Lu. Sometimes Lu'd show up with little things from back home—things like the tamarind fruit still in the shell, ginger beer and sugar cakes. Blessed would marvel. She'd say, Lucinda, where you find this? Lucinda'd laugh. I got my ways, Blessed, you know I do . . .

The rent's eight hundred fifty a month, Lucinda said. We split it down the middle fify-fifty. We don't need a reference, no first last and damage 'cause it's my uncle . . . AnnMarie's mind start going a mile a minute, thinking, Move in with Lu? Is she serious?

Well, who gonna watch Star when I go to work?

They got a Head Start over there on Empire Boulevard. My sisters went there. It's a good program.

AnnMarie thinking, She's serious, she *is* serious. She wants to live with me. Like for real, not just squashed in here at my mother's house, but paying rent together. Lu still talking, saying something about her student loan and a stipend, how she got some kinda scholarship to play ball, not a lot but she'd done the math and it could work if they's careful.

AnnMarie sat down next to her, took the ball outta her hand. She said, Hell yeah, I move in with you.

Next paycheck came in, they down at check-cash, pulling money out the metal drawer, adding the three hundred fifty to the sixty dollars AnnMarie took outta her sock drawer, counting out the cash on the bed, pooling their money together. Going in and out of the apartment, bringing back empty boxes, packing up all her things, Star's clothes, loading them into the car. Blessed said, What y'all doing? Where you going?

She said, I'm moving out, Ma, and you welcome to come visit.

60

The apartment building was on Flatbush Avenue, above Biggs Barber Shop, two blocks from Prospect Park. You could stand in the living room and see the tops of trees, green leaves rustling out there through the window, a real window in the living room, separate from the kitchen. They'd already been to the park four, five times—saw the different playgrounds, a drumming circle, a lake with ducks and paddle boats. On the far side, one day walking, Lucinda showed them the horse corral nestled in a grove of trees.

AnnMarie'd been busy, getting settled, making lists of things they need—couch, kitchen table, chairs, curtains to hang. Dishes she found at a stoop sale right around the corner, cups and glasses Blessed had gave them, and from Lucinda's mother, they got some mix matched forks and knives and spoons. Still she had work to get to every day, traveling a hour and a half each way. There was Head Start forms to fill—she'd been mad slow with it, dragging her feet even though the deadline was right around the corner. Two copies of the birth certificate, copies a health forms, pages and pages of information to fill in—where you live, what you make, your income, who the mother is, who the father is, if there a doctor, if there insurance and she'd stare at all those pieces a paper, her eyes swimming, thinking, Why they got to know all this shit about my life.

Star ain't got no doctor, just the clinic back in Far Rockaway. They gonna take her, she ain't got no doctor? Do she put Darius' name down or do she leave it blank? Do she write Lucinda instead a Darius?

Another form said, Describe your child. What her personality like? Does she have trouble separating? Any major changes in the household? She thought, *Separating*. What they mean, separating. Star stubborn as hell. Do she put down *stubborn*? The whole process making her feel uneasy, deep-down inadequate, so the last day, the very last day of the deadline, she found an excuse. She said, Star you wanna go pet the horses? Star said, Yeah! Mama, let's go. But Lu came outta the kitchen right then and said, Where you going? Did you fill out the forms?

I'ma do it later.

Lu said, There is no later, you better do it now.

AnnMarie didn't answer, kneeling down to strap on Star's sandals.

Lu said, You don't get Star into the program, then what you gonna do, who gonna watch her when you working and I'm at school.

AnnMarie tsked, an impulse, old and familiar, rising. She stood up, glaring.

I know that already, stupid, why don't you stay out my business.

Lu said, Who you calling stupid. You need to take care a this shit.

Why you acting like my mother.

Why you acting like a child.

And that was it. AnnMarie said, Fuck this shit. I'm out. Grabbed hold of Star's hand and yanked her out the door.

Outside on the street, Star had to hustle to keep up, AnnMarie walking fast up the block. At the corner, she waited for Star, took her hand, then entered the deli.

She said to the deli man, What do horses like to eat.

He thought about it, then said, Apples?

Yeah, yeah, let me get a couple of apples. Star grab a couple a those right there.

Star turned, reached up onto the shelf where the produce at, took a couple of apples in her hands.

She said, I'm hungry. AnnMarie glanced at her, said, Go on, eat one then, we save the other for the horse.

At Ocean Avenue, they left the sidewalk and cut into the park, walking along a narrow path through a grove of trees. Up ahead, a two-way bike lane snaked through the trees and grassy patches—people out jogging, cyclists zipping by, fast walkers moving their hips like they on a dance floor. AnnMarie stood at the curb, waiting for a break in the flow and Star reached up and took her hand. They stood for a moment longer, then darted through the foot traffic to the other side.

They wandered down another path, pausing at a bridge to watch the ducks gliding on the pond below. The sun beat down and she felt her neck damp with sweat. She squinted in the brightness. Up ahead she could see the path split off in two directions. Dang, she thought, which way do I go. Off to the side, some Rastas was playing soccer, their dreads flipping as they dodged and darted, kicking the ball up and down the field. She felt Star's hand moist in hers and glanced at her. That girl still chewing on the apple, eating the seeds and all. AnnMarie felt a breeze brush past, saw the leaves swaying against a cloudless sky. Who the fuck cares, she thought. It's a beautiful day.

So they made the ascent up the grassy hill, cut across the path running parallel to the baseball fields and dugouts and some black dudes playing cricket, Star trailing behind as AnnMarie moved them through the field of green and up another hill, and as they rose to the top, she saw it.

The horse was mad tall, with a shiny black coat, its mane braided, two dozen narrow braids laying flat against its flank. And on its back sat a girl, maybe nine, ten years old, holding the reins with both hands—the girl and the horse inside the corral made of narrow slats of wood.

AnnMarie said, Star look, look at that. Star's eyes went wide as the girl snapped the reins and the horse began to trot, the girl's behind bouncing up outta the saddle. She looked scared but she was doing it, leading the horse around the oval path, jumping over a log set across the dirt.

AnnMarie scooped Star up into her arms, carried her the rest of the way to the fence. She could see the riding teacher now, must be the teacher—calling out words AnnMarie ain't never heard before, *post . . . posting . . . she's above the bit, bring her down, down, go to cant . . .* Her hair long and gray, wearing the pants that poof out at the sides and tall black boots. The horse and girl coming around in a trot, round and round the path, inside the fence.

AnnMarie set Star on the top rail as the riding girl came toward them and Star reached out her hand, holding up the apple, she said, Apple? but the riding girl didn't seem to notice, her eyes straight ahead, and AnnMarie's heart kinda shrunk up right then. What the hell she thinking, bringing Star all the way out here.

This ain't no petting zoo. Lucinda'd been right. She had forms to fill but she'd froze. It came at her sharp and sudden, a stab of panic, wondering why she'd done it. Moved in with Lu. Trying to make it on her own, living outside her mother's house. The horse was trotting fast now, braids bouncing, then it began to gallop, the girl's face fixed in concentration, body crouched, her boot toes wedged tight in the stirrups.

Fuck it, AnnMarie thought. Come on, Star, we going. And as she turned to lift Star off the rail she saw it. A figure, far off in the distance, cutting across the field. AnnMarie did a double take, her heart skipping a beat as she realized who it was. Lu, tossing that damn ball back and forth. She watched her climb the grassy slope, and it was as if their eyes had met in that instant, 'cause Lu cocked her head off to the side, like she do when she embarrassed. Trying to act all nonchalant. Trying to bounce the ball in the grass. And AnnMarie had to laugh. The ball sitting there like a hunk a cement. She couldn't help it. She laughed, reaching for Star just as the girl rider went past, heard the gallop like the thrum of a baby heartbeat, knowing Lu was there, coming to see where they at.

Acknowledgments

This book is a work of fiction inspired by the life and oral accountings of my dear friend and sister traveler, Anna Simpson. Singular, beautiful, and sanguine, without her, these pages would be blank.

Huge credit goes to the Film Club kids from the Brooklyn School for Collaborative Studies, including but not limited to my young friends Faustino, Maya, Monica, Rahmel, Woody, Raheem, Achim, Jason, Tati, and Millie, whose voices, musings, and unbridled energy pushed through the walls of an auditorium and alighted as muses to influence the spirit and character of this book.

Also, I thank Messiah Rhodes, who taught me resilience, time and again, by defying his own circumstance and leaping the great divide.

To my early readers, friends and heroes, I thank you: Alyce Barr, Shari Carpenter, Adele Parez, Bruce Weyer, Daisy Wright, Kate Griggs, Mikha Grumet, Lenny Bass, Joseph Entin, Sophie Entin-Bell, and Alexandra Aron.

For their support, encouragement, and kindness along the way, I deeply thank Donna McKay, Kerry Washington, George Pelecanos, Rosie Dastgir, Nelson George, Ted Hope, Vanessa Hope, Anya Epstein, Jacqueline Woodson, my publisher Nan Talese, and my agent Alice Tasman.

Acknowledgments

And finally, to a group of collaborators whose remarkable talents, generosity, and patience I leaned on during the creation of this book, I thank you Ellis Avery, Jennifer Pooley, Ronit Feldman, and mostly and forever, Jim McKay.

A Note About the Author

Hannah Weyer is a filmmaker whose narrative and documentary films have screened at the Human Rights Watch and the New York Film Festivals and have won awards at the Sundance, Locarno, Melbourne, Doubletake, and South by Southwest Film Festivals. Her screenwriting credits include *Life Support* (2007), directed by Nelson George, which earned a Golden Globe Award for its lead actress, Queen Latifah. Weyer has worked with teens in the media arts for the past fifteen years and, along with her husband, the filmmaker Jim McKay, started an after-school film club at a public high school in Brooklyn. *On the Come Up* is her first novel.

A Note About the Type

The text of this book is set in Goudy, a typeface based on Goudy Old Style, which was designed by the American type designer Frederic W. Goudy in 1915 for American Type Founders.